Copyright© 20

    This is a wo

Author's Note

This is a new edition of my first novel, **Misguided**. In this version, I re-formatted the entire work, and I had this one edited by Catherine at Quill Pen Editorial. The front cover is also different because I changed the title for each novel in the Knox Mission trilogy; this book's title features the Jesus Assassin, so I created an image that portrays the anti-hero and gives him the spotlight – whereas the first edition featured a close-up shot with half the assassin's face sharing the cover with a murdered imam.

Although this edition does not change the story, I wanted to include a different note to my readers to describe a reason for a new edition, as well as the different title. First of all, I have to confess, the first edition of this book was self-published in haste – and impatience. Although I felt like I read the first version more times than I can count, it still had mistakes and problems that would take more than just my eyes, or even a friend's eyes to catch. I went ahead and put my own version out there because I just wanted to share this story with the world, and I didn't want to wait around for publishers, agents, and even editors – to do it! So the first **Misguided** came about, and even though the novel earned many fans from the internet that are way outside my friend circles, I still received enough feedback to know that the book could be sharpened and fixed…professionally edited. So that is what I have done with this new version of the work.

However, I even mentioned in my author's note in the previous edition that I considered the title, *The Jesus Assassin*, so with this new edition, I thought it would be a good time for an experiment with the title. We will see if I get more attention. I have noticed in today's world, people become fixated with dark names and titles; even the most straight-laced individuals are drawn to twisted terms and controversial items; the term Jesus Assassin is a controversial oxymoron, to say the least.

So there you have it – some of the reasoning behind a new edition of my very first work. This is still an intriguing story that introduces readers to characters who have become my favorite fictional people of all time. Since I have now written two novels about Agents John Knox, and Malik Sharif, and I am about to finish the third installment in the trilogy – I have become fully invested in the lives of these fictional good guys. This book is just the beginning, but if you stick with me, Knox and Malik will continue to entertain you, enlighten you, thrill you, and touch you in more series to come. If this is your first time reading my work – I hope you enjoy, and please read the next book in *The Knox Mission*, **Mistaken**.

MISGUIDED

By Jason E. Fort

To: the West Family
Thank you for
your support.
God Bless,
Jason E. Fort

PROLOGUE

Edwards Air Force Base
California
September 11, 2001

Chief Petty Officer Robert C. Brady stood at the foot of the ramp of a Globe Master III C-17, waiting for the rest of his SEAL team to board for a routine HALO (High Altitude Low Opening) training jump; their Master Chief had decided it was the perfect day to go up and get some wind in their faces. Before he was ready to board, he had to borrow the satellite phone to make some important calls to his family; his parents were going to be tourists in New York City for the week, and his wife just started her school day in Blacksburg, Virginia. First he dialed up the number and called his wife while she was at school. He knew she didn't have kids yet. They were three hours ahead in Virginia; she was an art teacher and she had a planning period first thing in the morning. It was still very dark in California, although he could see a small red line over the horizon at the end of the tarmac.

She gladly picked up on her cell phone at the first ring and said, "Hello?" She couldn't help but notice a heck of a lot of background noise as her husband said, "Hey honey!" on the other end. His wife's name was Rebecca, but he just called her honey. She had to ask, "Baby, what is all that racket? I can hardly hear you." Brady replied, "Oh, that's just the Globe Master, honey. They're cranking her up so we can take her for a spin. You talk to my folks yet?" Rebecca shook her head back in Virginia as she answered him on the phone, "Not yet. But you better give them a call early this morning. Last night, your mom sounded excited about the busy day of site-seeing they had planned. And you know your father; once he starts, he'll want no interruptions." Brady couldn't help but agree with her on that point, "Good point; I'll hang up with you and give them a shout before we go jump – I mean flying...Crap! You weren't supposed to hear that, Rebecca." He always thought that his wife worried too much about him, but she laughed it off.

"It's fine babe; I may not know the details - especially the classified ones. But I know what you do for a living. I love you baby, but I gotta go; I have a conference with a parent in a couple of minutes." Brady always hated this part, but knew he had to let her go; "Bye sweetie. I love you – see you when we get back to the East Coast." Then he ended the connection.

****

The ramp had been lowered; super cold air filled the inside of the body of the plane as SEAL team 3 prepared to exit the plane at 30,000 feet. All the SEALs wore heavy fatigues and flight suits to keep them safe from the temperatures, and everyone wore special oxygen masks that sealed to their faces, but still allowed them to communicate with each other through special intercoms and invisible earpieces they tucked into their ear canals like hearing aids. They all stood in formation, and the Master Chief was in front of everyone holding his right hand up in a fist to keep anyone from initiating the jump too early. Brady watched the Master Chief's hand in anticipation, ready to run to the edge and jump off into nothingness. A bright red light shone to the right side of the exit. It turned green. The Chief flattened his right hand out and made an overt chopping motion forward, and the team moved in unison – a group of seemingly small bodies, jumping out the back of a perfectly good airplane, and catching the wind. Chief Petty Officer Brady fanned out his arms and legs to increase his wind resistance. His teammates did the same; each member assuming a different spot in relation to the others. At first they were all at different planes, but with adjustments of their bodies – small movements of their arms and legs – they all made a circle and grasped hands. The Master Chief then released the hand of the SEAL to his right, motioned a three count, and gave a static filled command over the SEAL team's earpieces that everyone would release on a three count - watching his hand. Then he started counting, and signed an emphatic one finger – two fingers – three fingers…and they all let go.

Chief Petty Officer Brady could see the small square below him that was the tarmac at Edwards Air Force Base. He had a feeling he could beat everyone back to the hangar; on the way up the team placed bets, and the Master Chief had the money. The catch was that they had to beat the Master Chief, too. Brady could see all six of his other team members; everyone was still on a similar plane in the sky. He looked down with his head and shaped his body like a pencil. Whatever wind resistance he had was lost, and he took off past the other SEALS. The rest of the team followed, and pretty soon everyone was shooting toward the earth like missiles.

Suddenly a static-filled transmission came over their earpieces; "SEAL TEAM 3, SEAL TEAM 3! PREPARE TO MOBILIZE AS SOON AS YOU LAND! COUNTRY IS UNDER NATIONAL EMERGENCY! REPEAT – COUNTRY IS UNDER NATIONAL EMERGENCY!" As far as each SEAL team member was concerned, all bets were still on. The faster they got down, the better…so they continued to come closer to the ground at break-neck speed.

Soon after that, from the ground they would have looked like small flowers blossoming in the sky, but the chutes began opening. Each SEAL felt like they were hurled back up to the sky as their parachutes opened, and their almost terminal velocity slowed to a mere thirty miles per hour and falling as the parachutes slowed their descent. But the Master Chief and Chief Petty Officer were still in the competition. They dove downward past their teammates, and it was going to be a close one; finally both stubborn SEALs looked at each other and fanned out their arms and legs, and as soon as they came out of their dive, they pulled their cords. It was going to come down to boots on the ground. Both men came down at a long, shallow angle headed towards the hangar, and they both came into the tarmac running. They dropped their chutes and tore off their straps. The other guys were just falling onto the tarmac, but they had fallen too far behind to catch their senior officers. Master Chief and Brady finished climbing out of their harnesses and busted it to the hangar. Chief Petty Officer Brady crossed the line of the hangar door first, followed closely by his leader. They came up to the ramp of the Globe Master that had landed earlier, breathing hard and gasping for air, like Olympic sprinters right after the 100 meter dash.

Finally, as they were both bent over at the waist, with their arms resting on their thighs, Master Chief leaned heavily on Brady with one hand, and dug out a wad full of cash with the other. "Guess I owe you this, big boy." An officer who had been checking more equipment into the large plane came down the ramp, out of the belly of the plane. "Master Chief, America has been attacked, Sir! We've been told to get you guys back in the air ASAP; we are your ride to Shaw Air Force Base." Chief Petty Officer Brady chimed in, "The East Coast? We're preparing to stage something from there? Where were we attacked?" The officer – the same one who had loaned the satellite phone to Brady before takeoff and who knew he had to talk to family in New York-looked at Brady with a long face. "New York City, sir. Someone flew two jet-liners into the World Trade Center."

****

The doorbell rang at the front door on the inside of the screen porch. The small cabin was on the shore of a hidden pond, nestled in some woods in the beautiful Shenandoah Valley. Rebecca answered the door, and a large, red headed Irish American Navy SEAL was standing there. All she had to do was take one look in his brilliant green eyes to know her husband had received confirmation of the fate of his parents. He then bowed his head and sank to his knees, and his little lady knew exactly what was wrong. He began sobbing into her waist as she stood there, her arms wrapped around his large shoulders and neck. She didn't say anything. There was nothing she could say to calm the storm of pain and loss that Brady felt. She helped him up, and they both walked over to the sofa in the living room. They held hands and held each other for an hour. Rebecca finally noticed it getting darker outside. She got up slowly and told her husband she was going to bed. She beckoned him to follow. He told her to go on ahead, and that he would catch up soon. She went to their bedroom and closed the door, and he slowly made his way into his study. He sat behind the large wooden desk and pulled out a small journal. Chief Petty Officer Brady opened the journal, grabbed a pen from a coffee cup nearby, and began to write.

Entry #1, September 29, 2001

Dear God,

Guide me, I pray. We have enemies at our gates...and I need to rally the troops. Lord, help me have courage to bring these merciless killers to justice. Father, I don't just pray for justice for my mom and dad. I pray for justice to the enemy behind all such mindless and pointless acts of violence. I want to be part of the flames that lick the feet of these sinners as they descend into Hell. Lord, help me learn my enemy; help me learn about all his ways and all his weaknesses. Use me as your tool, and not just to

bring these people to justice, but to prevent this kind of thing from happening to more of your followers. I would not pray this pain I feel on anyone; the pain of losing those who matter most. But justice must be served Lord. Not just for the Americans who lost loved ones in New York, or Washington, D.C., or the field in Pennsylvania – but Christians everywhere who are scorned by this enemy. Let me be your champion, and let my race start today. I pray all these things in Jesus' name.
Amen

He closed the journal and placed it back in the desk drawer. He wanted the woman he loved, and he had wanted her for over two weeks; but sudden circumstances had kept them apart until now. His family had just gotten smaller by two. He couldn't stand that thought. Perhaps he and Rebecca could get started on a remedy for that…so he went into the bedroom. He and his wife would finally spend quality time catching up, and reminiscing his parents and their crazy antics, and discussing funeral plans. But all of that really didn't matter as much as the results of that night. When it was all said and done, he and his wife made love. They made love like they had never made love before. And then time passed by, and they discovered the family was going to get bigger again. Nine months later, he was fighting the battle that he prayed for; only it was on a slightly different battlefield. He began working for the CIA, and his wife was taking a year off for a child. That same nine months later they had that child; a beautiful bouncing baby girl. He had a second little lady now, and she had the most beautiful, brilliant green eyes.

Blacksburg, Virginia
2015

Jessie's mom had told her to wait in the car for just a moment; she had to run back in to the grocery store because she had forgotten to pick up some mouthwash for her husband when he got back home. Jessie and her mom Rebecca had decided to run to the store to buy some things for a surprise welcome home dinner for her dad. Robert Brady was away on a certain job for the CIA, and was scheduled to be back home in the next couple of days. Jessie sat in the front seat of their minivan in one of the closer parking spaces to the entrance of the store. She was stroking the head of her pet black rat snake, Stanley, as she played a quick video game on her smart phone. The long, slender black snake was acting a little restless and began slithering up her arm to her shoulder.

She reached up and gently grabbed him near his head and brought his little head down in front of her face. "Don't worry, Stan…Mom will be back in a jiffy. Calm down and maybe I can feed you a frozen mouse when we get home," the vibrant young red head told her pet snake.

Jessie didn't notice the large black van parked nearby, its occupants watching her small movements in the van as they waited for the mother to re-appear.

Inside the cargo area of the van, Sayeed Mussaad told the other two large Syrians that they needed to wait until the American spy's wife walked back and got inside or behind the minivan. That way, they could capture her and the daughter without giving them a chance to run. Sayeed was following orders from the leader of his cell; Barack Al-Hussein had acquired inside information on the location of some family members of one of the intelligence agents who had been making life for ISIS quite miserable for the past three weeks. As the Syrian terrorists looked through to the front windshield, they could see the very attractive figure of Rebecca Brady pushing yet another grocery cart back to the minivan. They quickly pulled on black ski masks to conceal their Middle Eastern identities.

Jessie looked in the side mirror, and noticed her mom approaching with another buggy.

"Stan, can you believe she got even more food?"

She laughed as she climbed out and walked around to the trunk. Her mom had hit the remote key fob to open the trunk. Both of the loves in Brady's life stood there behind the minivan, taking turns loading the last minute items Rebecca decided to pick up for her husband. She couldn't wait for her husband to come home; he had been gone for three weeks now.

She spoke up to her daughter, "Jess, Sorry it took so long. I had to get mouthwash for your dad...and frozen pizzas, and yogurt...and you know how he gets if he doesn't have his coffee."

Sayeed grabbed the small-framed teen-aged girl from behind and scooped her up off her feet. At the same time, his two Syrian friends grabbed the mother. They quickly rushed the girl and her mom back just a few feet to the large sliding panel door of the black van. They had moved it closer as the two females had been loading the groceries. Once Sayeed slung the sliding door open as he held the little teen in a tight head lock with his hand over her mouth, he lashed out with a scream of his own as the black rat snake surprised him with a bite to his hand. He didn't see the snake wrapped around the girl's shoulders under her long red hair as he snuck up behind her. He forcefully shoved the girl inside. The two large Syrians threw the mother into the van, in the waiting clutches of two more thugs dressed in dark clothes, who immediately held the females down and bound them with duct tape. The large black van peeled out of the parking lot, with Sayeed cursing because of the large lacerations caused by his rush in yanking the snake off his hand, tossing it to the ground. The only things left behind were black skid marks, an empty grocery cart, and the trunk to the minivan, standing wide-open.

PART ONE

Cairo, Egypt
2016

His chambers were quite elegant, for someone who claimed that there was no need for material wealth in this world. The room was large, octagonal, with golden tapestries hanging from what seemed like innumerous anchors around the walls. The opulent quarters also included several prayer rugs in the center of the room, as well as a small finely-polished wooden water basin. That is where the sole occupant of the room stood now, washing his hands and face. The quarters belonged to a very important man of the Muslim Faith. Muhammad Ibn Abdullah Mahmud was the Imam of the Cairo branch of the Muslim Brotherhood. He was well respected by most world leaders; especially those in the Middle East. He was also known as one of the more peace-loving Muslims of his time, in comparison to several of his Muslim brothers. It was because of his outspoken thoughts of peace that he normally did not have high security inside his most sacred place; he understood most threats to his kinsmen to come to the ones who were more known for their violent habits and tendencies. Although he did have guards set up outside his palatial hallway, he saw no need to have security watch over him in his inner-most sanctum: his personal quarters where he meditated on his words with Allah and said his prayers religiously at all the customary times of day, always facing Mecca.

It was at this time that if he had known he was not alone in the room, he would have definitely felt the need for a security guard, or two…or three. A black form hid among the tapestries, with nothing but lethal plans for the religious leader. Ibn Abdullah Mahmud was bent over the wash basin, rubbing water thoroughly through his thick black beard, and around his dark bushy eye brows. He had to make sure he was cleansed, for one did not kneel down before Allah in ritual prayer until they were clean. The black form slowly materialized out from behind one of the tapestries directly behind the holy man. Silently, slowly, he crept over carpeted floors and even over a prayer rug or two. The silent intruder was clad from head to toe in all black: a black hood; small night vision shades covering the eyes that could adjust to any amount of light; a black BDU top covering a black bulletproof vest; a coil of 500 pound-test climbing rope wrapped around like a miniature sash on a holy man's robes; black pants with several pockets full of extra ammunition as well as smoke bombs, knives, etc.; a black Glock pistol in a thigh holster strapped to his right leg; and black gloves and boots solely meant for stealth.

The black form was an assassin; an agent of destruction that would stop at nothing to cause injury and annihilation to representatives of Islam. He crept up to Muhammad Ibn Abdullah Mahmud so close...so close. The Egyptian cleric finished washing his hands and reached to the side of the basin for a towel and began drying his face. Just as the holy man had let the towel cover his face, the assassin struck. First he used his large frame to envelop the man in a tight embrace; the killer placing one large gloved hand over the man's mouth so that no screams could be heard. While the assassin hugged the man's head in tight close to his neck, he used his other hand to inject a small, silver hypodermic needle into the man's carotid artery on the left side of his exposed neck. The Muslim leader struggled but to no avail; a strong toxin, engineered using snake venom, raced to his brain and immediately caused his body to asphyxiate. The man dressed in black was appropriately dressed, for he had brought death quietly and quickly, like a haunting wraith. Just before Ibn Abdullah Mahmud died, his eyes opened wide one last time. The stranger in the room took his hand off his victim's mouth, and the bearded man tried to take one last breath. That was the last thing he ever attempted – then he fell motionless to the floor. The man in black moved the dead imam's arms and crossed them over each other. He placed the body perpendicular to the direction of Mecca, in which all the prayer rugs had been deliberately placed. In the right hand he placed a small gold cross, and laid the right hand back over the left. He pushed the Imam's eyelids closed, to give him a more rested appearance. Then the man in black, who brought death to the chambers, slowly crept out of the room with as much stealth as he had when he came. His mission was accomplished. The Jesus Assassin had taken his first victim.

Langley, Virginia
Two days later

It was a rather simple office for a government agent with an important position. At least it was a corner office, located on the fourth floor, with a decent view of some of the landscape around the building that housed the Central Intelligence Agency. There was a very basic office desk made of oak in the center of the office. There was a large glass set of shelves along the front wall in front of the desk, containing several photographs that were of sentimental value to the killer. If a stranger unfamiliar with the man's line of work were to walk in and see the pictures on the shelves and the office desk, as well as the certificates on the wall behind the desk, he would have thought he walked in to the office of your All-American boy who'd made it to the top. On the corner of the desk, set aside for anyone to see as they entered, was a large leather bound edition of the King James Version of the Holy Bible. Large windows lined the entire far wall of the office across from the main door to the hallway. Behind the desk was a door to a small storage closet.

It was around 11:30 p.m., and most of the agents and administrators had left for the night. The killer opened the door to his office and walked immediately into his storage closet. He punched in the digital code on the door of his gun safe, opened the thick metal door after hearing the bolts move out of the way, and placed his 'Little Black Bag' in the far right side of the top shelf. His bag contained the essentials for his every day job: black outfit, climbing rope, Glock 21 pistol, .45 caliber hollow point ammunition, night vision glasses – you know; the kind of things every man requires when in the clandestine line of work of a field agent. Before the man closed his safe, he couldn't help but glance over in the far left-hand side of the top shelf. There was an open-top box, lined with felt like your typical jewelry box. Inside was a large stack of palm-sized golden crosses collected over a lifetime. Recent events had stirred the owner of the collection to start putting those crosses to use for something important; something that the man felt passionate enough about that he had no choice but to send the loudest message he could, yet as undercover as he could. He closed the safe, punched in his code and followed it by pressing the 'star' button. He listened for confirmation that it was locked as the bolts clicked back into place and then closed the closet door. He had a long, tiring few days; both doing work for his job, as well as doing the Lord's work. Although he was ready for a good night's rest, he still had one more thing to do before driving home to his quaint family cabin. The killer could tell no one his secret; there was too much at stake. He had already made his pact with God. He told God every night before he slept that no matter what, he would hold up his end of the bargain. He was on a mission to bring about what this corrupt, evil world needed the most. He could talk to nobody about the work he did for the Lord, because he knew it might jeopardize the success of the mission. His whole life had been about carrying out missions; meeting objectives. This was no different. But since he could not talk to anyone but himself and God about the matter – he kept a journal. It was that journal that he had to write in now; for he had accomplished his first mission objective. He took a small key out of his front right pocket of the tan slacks he was wearing. He sat down and opened the bottom right-hand drawer next to the hard drive under his desk. There was a lid containing a lock, slid in place over the top of the drawer as you pulled the drawer out. He unlocked the lid, slid it open, and pulled out his journal. He flipped several pages in, and placed the journal on the desk. He took out a common Bic ball point pen and began to write:

Entry #26, March 28, 2016

God, My Father, Which Art in Heaven- I did it! I used my cover with which you have so blessed me by performing my normal duties in my worldly job. I was able to infiltrate the Imam's palace. I was able to sneak past the guards without detection, and get into his private quarters where he plans his words of blasphemy. I was able to attack him and steal his human life the way his religion and its followers had stolen the lives of countless Christians. I was able to make him feel the poison in his veins so that he would understand the consequences of the poison he puts out to the rest of the world. Lord, I placed the cross in his hand so that whoever found him would know that Jesus is coming. Lord, I know that if I continue your work, you will come back to us soon. I know that if I can strike twelve of the Evil One's servants, it will put forces in motion that will give you no alternative but to intervene. Lord, bless me on my mission. Help me force Your Great Hand. These monsters who have taken so much from so many are only getting hungrier. Help me give them the violence that they seek. They believe the twelfth Imam will be their savior. I will make them realize who the savior is, and I will give them their twelfth Imam. I pray Lord God – continue to give me courage to grab their attention. Amen

He closed his journal and locked it back in its secret hideaway. He rubbed his eyes and got up and headed over to his glass shelves. He reached up and grabbed the picture frame on the top shelf. He brought it down to eye level and gently touched the two faces in the photograph. The figure in the photo on the left was a beautiful blonde-haired, blue eyed California girl he had met when he was a young sailor. The cute, red-headed, green-eyed girl on the other side was none other than his daughter. They had been his little ladies. They had been his ultimate blessing from God. The work he did now would mean he would get to see them again, just as Job received blessed loved ones after his suffering. It had been a year and three days since they were taken from him. The classified video that he and his counter-terrorist team had uncovered played over and over in his head. The graphic images of both the people he loved most in this world, captured in low quality, low budget video made for You Tube – showed their lives taken from them in a most gruesome, horrifying manner.

The video started with the executioner, wearing the typical cowardly kafiyah wrapped around the head, nose, and mouth to aid in hiding their true identity – who spoke in clear but heavily accented English. "You Americans think you can kill who you want. You think you can come into our lands and murder our women and children with your missiles? Here are a woman and a child. We came and took them, from one of your capitalist spies! We will now show you who it is okay to kill – if it is in the name of Allah!"

Then the camera zoomed out and showed his two girls, sitting in chairs with their legs tied together and their arms tied behind their backs. His two little ladies let out shrill screams; the terrorists hadn't even blind-folded them! The terrorist executioner stood between the two female victims, raised two large scimitars over his head, and –NO! He shook his head and tried to block out the image. Even though the horrible scene of violence is what kept him focused on his mission, it was too much for even the likes of him – a former SEAL, a top level field agent, a government hit-man – to be able to take. A new force to fight against evil was born that day. That force, a year later, would begin a quest of redemption not only for the father and husband of a beautiful family, but the redemption for all Christians that would soon come that had been prophesied by John of Patmos millennia before.

Brussels, Belgium

General Secretariat for Interpol; European Union

Malik leaned back in his office chair. He was exhausted - he had just closed a case of human trafficking that had taken him all around Europe, and lasted 6 months of his life and consumed all his days, including his weekends. Malik Sharif was a police officer for Interpol; the international police force that enables police agencies around the world to work together to bring down the crime that effects more than 190 countries. Malik had just finished tying up loose ends with the case, finalizing reports on his computer. He let out a big sigh of relief, thankful that his hard work had paid off, and that his experience in law enforcement in the United States had helped him track down a group of sadistic, greedy old men, who profited off the sale of sex and young girls. Malik had been so involved with his work that he hadn't even talked to his family in at least three months. He was just about to dial up his mother back home in Kuwait, when his supervisor came out of his office and walked directly to Malik's desk. Malik put the phone down; he could tell by Chief Inspector Holcroft's intense expression that his family would have to wait a little longer.

Marcus Holcroft was the Chief Inspector of the General Secretariat of Interpol; a tall man of German descent that did not mince words or fool around. He had gotten to where he was because of his intense nature and his ambitious drive to get things done.

'The Chief', as his underlings referred to him, started in, "Inspector Sharif – I have another assignment for you, and I'm afraid it cannot wait." He continued in his German accent, "It appears we are going to be needed in Egypt; we have a possible terrorist situation on hand in Cairo. The Egyptian authorities told me they want a counter-terrorism expert. They also said they could not accept any investigator who was not Muslim."

Malik sat back in his office chair again and replied, "Chief, I am not a counter-terrorism expert. You know I have been working on Human Trafficking and Organized Crime for the past two years."

The serious Belgian shook his head. "They did not seem too concerned with the terrorism expertise; but they demanded a Muslim investigator. So I am sending you. I will have your travel plans arranged. You probably want to contact your family; I can make additional arrangements for you to travel to Kuwait – but only once you are finished in Cairo," the Chief finished. Malik nodded in understanding, but had to know more. "What exactly is so important in Cairo, Chief? Why are we involved? Doesn't the Muslim Brotherhood usually take care of their domestic terrorism 'in-house' down there?" he asked.

The Chief answered, "It turns out to be a little more delicate situation than that, I'm afraid. The Egyptian police are not sure where to begin because of the nature of the crime. One of their most beloved Imams, Muhammad Ibn Abdullah Mahmud, was killed in his royal palace. But the killer left a calling card – a gold cross placed in the Imam's right hand. As you probably know, there is not exactly a very open population of Christians in that territory."

Malik thought out loud, "Wow! That is a pretty strong affront to the Muslim faith. So I guess that means they really think this could only be done by an outside foe?" The Chief responded, "That is usually why they call us in, although I thought it was an early request. I would have thought the Egyptian authorities would want to try to discover a little more for themselves; maybe rule out any possibility of a suspect being a little more local."

"Well, Chief Inspector – I was kind of looking forward to some rest and relaxation. But, if you say I'm your man – then, I guess I'm your man," Malik said as he stood up and took his jacket off the coat rack next to his desk. "I knew I could count on you Sharif. You be careful over there; I hear those Egyptians can be pretty rough," his boss stated. Malik gave him a small grin as he started heading away from his desk; "Rough? You forget sir – I grew up in the Bronx. Egypt seen as rough…forget about it." Malik started walking away, and his Chief Inspector stopped him one more time. "Inspector, where are you going right now? I haven't had our secretary make your travel arrangements yet," the Chief finished. Malik quickly replied, "Well, I just got back from traveling all over Europe. It just occurred to me – I have some major laundry to catch up on before I go on any more trips." With that, he threw on his sports jacket and walked out of the building through the main lobby. So much for his well-earned vacation.

Dearborn, Michigan
Islamic Center of America

Imam Ibrahim Ibn Mustafa was leaving with a contingent of loyal Islamic followers who served as his body guards. The American Islamic leader had on a long, heavy white robe, and a standard black and white checked kafia held in place on his head by a thin black head band. Mustafa was a large man; a bearded, barrel-chested, dark skinned man with dark hair visible on his wrists as they were exposed at the end of his thick sleeves. He also wore a pair of black sunglasses to block out the afternoon sun. The Imam's closest followers led him out to the large parking lot in front of the mosque. A crowd of seven large Arab American men surrounded the Imam as he climbed into the back seat of a white Mercedes sedan with heavily tinted windows. A Salat (large prayer meeting for many Muslims to gather) had just ended, and Ibrahim's closest advisor, La'iq Hussein, had climbed in the back seat with the Imam. The driver had been instructed to take the Imam to his personal quarters on the outskirts of the city.

As soon as the car was in motion, La'iq looked over at his leader as if waiting to be acknowledged. Ibrahim nodded at him and said, "Well young friend – how goes our plans behind-the-scenes of our beloved Michigan town?" La'iq smiled a devilish grin and replied, "Everything is in place, your Holiness. When the mayor addresses the city tomorrow night at the City Council meeting, we will have a large host of opinionated protesters planted around the room to voice their thoughts. There will be no way for the council to responsibly cast a vote to further increase the Christians' stronghold in this city. It will at least buy us more time until we can plan a more permanent solution to the problem, Imam."

The Imam took off his sunglasses and glared seriously at La'iq. He spoke up, "And these plants in the crowd...are they obvious Muslims? I want them to blend in. I do not want City Council to think I put these protesters up to the task. They must appear secular; they must not claim any loyalty to Allah in their outbursts." La'iq nodded, "Fear not your Holiness...it will be as you have said. It has been arranged."

The Imam sat silently for the rest of the ride. He put his shades back on and stared out the window as they drove down the interstate, billboards and business exits zooming by. The Mercedes pulled off one of the exits and made its way to a gated subdivision of high class duplex condominiums. The Mercedes turned into the gate and the driver punched in a number code for the gate to open. The driver then pulled into the subdivision and drove down to the last two units at the end of a cul-de-sac. The condos were two stories, and the two adjacent units (#501 and #502) both belonged to Imam Mustafa. His driver got out and opened the door for the Imam, and La'iq got out on the other side. The Imam's adviser got back in the front passenger seat; the driver would take him to his own house a couple of miles away. As La'iq sat in the front seat, Ibrahim turned to say goodbye. "*Asa lama lakum,* my friend. Keep me abreast of the dealings with the City Council," and with that, he turned to head in to his condominium home. The Mercedes drove away as an escort of two large Arab men came out from the front door of the unit to the left, Unit #501. The unit next door was specifically for housing a harem of women that had been hand-picked by Ibrahim himself, to serve him in all sorts of ways. #501 was the Imam's personal quarters, and that is where he headed now, escorted by his two body guards.

One of the guards opened the door to the condo, walked in and gave the place a walk-through to check all the rooms and entry points. He came back shortly and informed the other guard that the condo was safe, and the Imam came in and told his guards he would be getting some sleep. He dismissed them to the condo next door; he told them to go have a good time, and make sure that he was awakened in six hours. The guards acknowledged him, then looked at each other with conniving smiles and headed out the door. Ibrahim watched as the two deadbolts turned, one guard using his keys to lock the Imam in his home. His two trusted body guards, Akeem and A-sim, had been at the condo all day. They were twins, and they guarded his humble abode(s) every day like two human guard dogs. Ibrahim felt safe when they were around – even when they were lost in forbidden erotic fantasy next door, pleasuring themselves with very lovely Mediterranean ladies. He knew that if any danger were nearby, his two 'guard dogs' would have sniffed it out before his arrival. He turned and walked upstairs to his bedroom. As he entered, he walked straight to his prayer rug in the large empty space in front of his bed. He had already prayed the required five times in one day. However, he knelt down to make supplications to his God, Allah, every evening before he went to bed.

After his prayers, he disrobed and went into his bathroom to prepare for bed. As he returned to his bed, he turned down the covers and climbed in to get comfortable. He reached over to his nightstand and pulled the cord on the lamp to turn out the light. As he rolled over on his side, he couldn't help but think of the City Council meeting that La'iq had made the plans for interrupting. The council was meeting to take a vote on whether or not the city would allow public displays of nativity scenes in any public places besides churches. There had been a recent in-flux of Christians moving into Dearborn over the last year and a half, and several of the local businesses had littered their display windows and front patios with small nativity scenes over the last Christmas Holiday season. Since there was a high population of Muslims in the city, this was quite offensive to the city residents. Although the city was not under Sharia Law, some of the local residents stated that these festive displays showing off the Christ child should be kept only at Christian churches, and not in public businesses. The City Council treaded lightly on the subject because of the First Amendment. The Imam felt that if he could convince the council through so-called non-biased citizens of the city, they could put some pressure on the council to not allow these idols of blasphemy to be shown. Ibrahim trusted La'iq, and took him at his word when he told him that there would be plenty of opposition at the meeting. He started getting sleepy, and finally drifted off to dream land, hoping to wake up to good news in the morning.

Cairo, Egypt
Police District Headquarters, Downtown Cairo

Malik studied the photos in his hand. He had just been handed some high quality pictures of the crime scene by the local police commandant for the central downtown district of Cairo. Commandant Sacur al Akbar spoke to the investigator from Interpol, rambling on about something to do with being glad Malik was taking over the investigation because of the delicate situation with the Christians and the Muslims in the area. Malik was only half listening because the first photo in the pack was so captivating. Whoever the crime scene investigator had been, he or she had taken some pride in their work in portraying the crime scene in clear and colorful detail. The first photograph was a close-up of the murdered Imam; an older man in his 70's with amazingly clear wrinkles and scars on an old gray and dark tanned face. The man's eyes were closed, but not tightly. The man's true facial features were disguised by his thick black beard, with the occasional silver hair sporadically growing in the rest of the holy man's mane. But the man's loosely closed eyes still made him almost look at peace. The picture had also captured the top part of the man's upper body, with the hands crossed over the chest. Malik noticed that in the right hand, which had been laid over the left hand, was a small but distinct gold cross. There was no mistake that the killer wanted the cross to be the center of his work. The assassin wanted the Muslims to know who was behind this, almost calling them out for their beliefs. The Imam's killer had intentionally placed that cross close to his heart – as if that is where it belonged.

The other photos were images of the Imam's body taken from further away. As far as Malik could tell, the rest of the room surrounding the victim's body had been left undisturbed; no sign of foot prints; no sign of forced entry; no objects of interest accidentally left behind. Yet it was obvious that someone had come in and committed the act of murder. One did not die and naturally assume a funeral-ready pose. Someone had taken a very calculated risk. Not only did they have to get past the twenty guards the Imam had placed around the palace; they would also have to get past the guard dogs out in the thin line of grass around the perimeter of the palace inside the wall. There was also an electric fence around the outside of the perimeter along the top of the wall surrounding the palace– signs warning of the 180,000 volts awaiting anyone to come in contact who was bold enough to try to climb over. Malik left his thoughts of puzzlement and focused back on the photos. Then he realized the position of the victim's body – angled perpendicular across the prayer mat, or sajadah. The killer had left yet another cross. Malik reached up with one hand, scratching his head and asking himself why one person would want to kill to prove a religious point.

He spoke up to the police commandant, "Commandant, did your forensics team determine the exact cause of death?"

Sacur quickly answered, "Yes, sir. We wanted to help you as much as we could by being fully prepared for your arrival. An autopsy was performed, and we know the Imam died of acute asphyxiation. I even had the labs run a toxicology test. The killer used some kind of toxin, very similar to the venom of a snake known as the Black Mamba."

Malik shook his head, becoming more perplexed by this killer by the moment. "So you're saying our assassin slipped in to this veritable fortress undetected, just to poison our guy. Were any puncture marks left on the body?"

Commandant Sacur nodded.

"There are some photos of the autopsy as well. In a photo of the neck in particular, there was bruising left from a large needle that was pushed into his carotid artery," the police leader added.

Malik thought out loud, "So our killer poisoned our victim with a neurotoxin almost directly to the brain, causing almost instant organ failure. Then he intentionally placed the victim's body in such a way as to declare war on Islam. Commandant – I think we need to keep a lid on this. Right now you might want to suggest to the media that the cause of death is still unknown." Commandant Sacur nodded. "Yes sir, I came to the same conclusion. That is why we were glad to have you come, Inspector. Now you see why I called it a delicate situation," he replied.

Malik did not know how religious the commandant was, but he thought it was safe to assume he was a Muslim. Even a Muslim who was not a devout follower would realize that the killer had it out for Islam. Malik knew he would have to tread carefully. If too much information regarding this case got out to the wrong people, it could start a religious war. Malik knew two things: one – the killer was a Christian (a misguided one at that), and two – the killer was a very secretive, well connected individual. Malik had spent part of his life when he was younger in New York. Although not exactly the Bible belt that Malik had been told about that took up the southern U.S., he had his share of Christian friends in New York; mostly Catholic. He also knew a lot about Christians from talking to his father. His father was an American soldier, who had fallen in love with his mother while stationed in Kuwait. His father was not a Christian, but had told him about several of his friends who served in the army with him. Between the friends that his dad had talked about, and his own friends back in the Bronx – this assassin did not seem to be like those Christians. Malik was not offended by the killer's message; he was not one to be easily offended anyway. But he wondered if there was something more behind the driving force and motivation of this murderer. Malik didn't know exactly what to do next, but he did know one thing. He had a feeling that this was just this killer's first victim. There would be more death to come – and right now, Malik didn't have a shred of evidence or clues that could tell him where the assassin might strike next.

Dearborn, Michigan
Unit #501

The assassin clad in black had a new plan in store for this Imam. Not only did he plan on taking out the Imam in his humble abode; he had plans for his body guards and their harem as well. He waited in the closet with the slatted doors. First, the plan required that he take out the Imam. He had been waiting for almost half a day, sneaking in through the back patio door earlier in the day so he had plenty of time to prepare for the Muslim leader to come home. He had scaled the wall by using a large fire blanket and flinging it over the top of the razor wire on top of the concrete wall. He was surprised the Imam was foolish enough not to have watch dogs or guard dogs inside the back patio and courtyard, considering his two body guards only patrolled the outer perimeter of the house most of the day – not even bothering to have anyone watching the neighborhood that bordered the back yard wall. Although it took him some time and effort, the assassin had managed to not make any noise as he finally scaled the flimsy wall made of a thick fire blanket weighing down the sharp razor wire. The assassin was a natural at picking locks; apparently there was so much faith placed in Allah and his two body guards, the Imam felt no need for a burglar alarm either. He had broken into the house and crept upstairs, and then he found the Imam's master bedroom and waited patiently in the walk-in closet. He stood in the dark closet now, controlling his breathing and being perfectly still just like back in his sniper days with the Navy. He didn't even need to be so cautious; the Imam was snoring so loud that redwoods being cut down in California made less noise. He had primed the syringe just before he heard the Imam come in to prepare for bed, while he still had time to use his flashlight. The black hooded killer slowly opened the closet door, unable to hear whether it was squeaking or not due to the snoring Muslim in the room.

He walked slowly towards the bed; some moonlight shined through the blinds, but the room was very dark, and the killer stayed in the shadows. He withdrew the hypodermic needle in his chest pocket on his vest with his right hand, being very careful not to step on any objects on the floor hidden in the dark. The Imam rolled toward the assassin just as he went in for the kill. His snores were suddenly interrupted by muffled attempts to cry for help; the killer's left hand placed firmly over the mouth as the venom was pushed through the syringe into his artery. Within seconds, the deadly man in black removed his left hand, and all that could be heard were short gasps. The victim's diaphragm had stopped working – he could not draw a breath, and all his brain could do was force his eyes wide open and flex his muscles all over his body. The assassin backed away from the bed and waited for the last few death spasms to pass. He then dragged the body of the Imam off the bed and into the middle of the room where the prayer rug was pointed towards Mecca. He placed the body directly across the sajadah, and then fumbled around in his other chest pocket for the small gold cross. He folded the dead man's hands over his chest, and placed the cross in the right hand. He didn't have time to sit around and admire his handy work; he still had more death to deal that night.

He went downstairs quickly, and headed out the back sliding glass door through the kitchen out onto the patio. He still used the shadows to hide, and he went to a small clearing in the mulch and bushes. He picked up the large black canvas bag that was twisted several times; he couldn't help but notice how the bag moved on its own before he scooped it up. That was because there were several living, breathing things inside the large bag. The killer's daughter's favorite thing in the whole wide world of science was snakes. Her fondness for the reptiles always came to the father as strange, but when he lost his little girl, he planned to use something she loved against the devils that took her from him. His daughter's favorite snake was one of the deadliest of them all – the Black Mamba. He had three of them in the bag now. Each one measured somewhere between eight to ten feet long. Although there was a substantial amount of weight to the serpents, the assassin had no trouble carrying them around due to his large arms. He used his typical stealth as he moved across the courtyard shared by the two condos.

He hid behind a large hedge on Unit #502's side, trying to detect any light or movement inside the dwelling. The other unit's kitchen was dark, so he snuck up to the back door. He put the bag down again to pick the lock on the door. This door was hinged…not like the sliding glass door on the Imam's condo. That would make his job easier; he was a master at cracking deadbolt locks. After he popped out the lock and opened the door, he and his bag silently moved on through the kitchen. He made sure there was no movement downstairs. He had done a quick walkthrough of the other condo, assuming its twin had a similar floor plan. He had been lucky; they were laid out the exact same way except everything was on opposite sides from the other unit. He knew that after getting to the top of the stairs, the master bedroom was down the hall to the right. Although he knew he was taking some big chances, he felt like he could adapt and adjust if for some reason he was detected by Akeem and A-sim. He knew they would be naked – how else does one spend time enthralled in sexual desire with your very own harem? Fighting a fully armed trained killer while naked always tipped the favor towards the guy with more than his underwear on. Nevertheless, the hooded figure was able to make it all the way to the bedroom door.

The agent stooped down to the floor and tried to listen for any noise in the next room. It was dark, and it sounded like everyone was asleep. He slowly twisted the door knob and pushed the door open, inch by inch. He unraveled his black snake bag and carefully nudged the creatures from the bottom of the bag towards the opening that he had placed through the space he had revealed with the door. Black Mambas were notorious for their speed and aggression. They did not need much coaxing to find the opening at the top of the bag and slither into the next room. Once he knew the bag was empty, he closed the door, and snuck down the stairs. The assassin knew that unarmed naked men stood about as much of a chance against those deadly snakes as they would against him. It was only a matter of time before someone moved in their sleep. Black Mambas in particular react to movement. Once the biting began, death would not come quite so quick as it had for the Imam. The killer hoped that there was a chance some of the women in the room might not get bitten. He was okay with that. Damage would be done, and yet another message would be sent. If anyone were to survive long enough to call 9-1-1, they still might be dead by the time medical staff got there. He knew the bodyguards would die. It was in their nature to fight – whether they were fighting to protect the Imam, or the women. But naked, they wouldn't stand a chance. The local law enforcement was going to have a field day with this. He knew because of the status of the Imam, the big dogs would be put on the case. He was also okay with this. All he had to do was stay ahead in the count. After that, nothing else would matter. Two down – ten to go.

Detroit, Michigan
FBI Field Office

Agent Knox would seem out of place to most people who visit the Detroit office. He was your typical W.A.S.P. (White Anglo-Saxon Protestant), with very conservative political and religious views. But the thing that made him stand out the most was his southern accent. His 6 foot 3 inch frame with his linebacker build looked a little awkward in a suit, but he still pulled it off pretty well. He was sitting in the break room, sitting in a chair with its back facing his small audience of co-workers, telling one of his token "Back in Alabama" stories. However, Agent Knox was a lot deeper person than most people gave him credit for – except those that were closest to him. Special Agent John Knox was from Thornbush, Alabama. He had gone to University of Alabama and graduated with a degree in Exercise Science. He had also been a walk-on for the varsity defense of the Crimson Tide – but unfortunately never saw a single snap during TV coverage.

After figuring out early that fitness was not going to be steady enough money for him, he got into law enforcement and patrolled a beat; first in Birmingham, then Detroit. Knox decided that uniform patrol wasn't going to be his cup of tea, either. After working his way up through the ranks to be an investigator, he left Detroit PD and decided he would go federal. He had been with the FBI now for eight years, and was getting close to forty years old. But the agents in the Detroit Field Office liked Agent Knox because he was always younger than his actual age, full of energy, and always had a story to tell. Everybody in the room was laughing at his story about getting his 4x4 stuck one night in the Alabama mud, when the SAC (Special Agent in Charge) walked in to get a cup of coffee. Special Agent Jones McCoy was a very serious man, and when he entered a room, there would be no more laughing. It's not that he didn't allow it; it's just that no matter how hard anybody tried, you couldn't make the man laugh – so everyone stopped trying.

Although he wasn't a funny man, he was a reasonable and fair supervisor, and was well respected by the other agents at the office. "Good morning everyone. Knox…White…in my office," was all he said as he finished pouring his cup from the fresh pot.

Agent Knox was one half of a dynamic duo who had a knack for solving hate crimes. Not just any hate crimes, but the kind where people ended up dead. Not only were they good at finding out who did it, but they were good at putting together solid evidence to back their cases up. The better half of the pair was Special Agent Beth White. Agent White was everything Knox wasn't; that's why they complemented each other so well. Beth was the quiet, analytical and mathematical type. Agent White had graduated magna cum laude with a degree in Mathematics from M.I.T. After a tragedy in her family that took the life of her older brother who was a police officer, Agent White had decided she wanted to put criminals away. She had been working at the federal level longer than Knox, but was the same age. She was also only about 5 feet 5 inches tall, but had a body to die for. She always wore her strawberry blond hair in a short pony tail. Knox was the brawn, and he always looked at the big picture; White was the brain and always looked for the details. The two agents had worked together for two years now, and the most recent development between the two was that they were dating – a little known fact that they really hoped SAC McCoy did not know. They both went into McCoy's office and closed his door. They took their seats in front of his desk as he stood behind his desk, coffee mug in hand. McCoy waited until they looked comfortable.

"Got something pretty local for you guys…just down the road in Dearborn. Eight bodies…one witness…and snakes," McCoy began. "Snakes?" questioned a puzzled Agent Knox. McCoy continued, "The reason I am putting you two on this is because some Christian out there didn't like the Imam at the Islamic Center of America. The Imam was found dead in his condo this morning. Cause of death is unknown for him as of yet, but it appears similar to the victims found next door in the adjoining condo. That's where the snakes come in – the one witness saw the snakes in the room and froze, while everyone else in the room panicked and died from the bites. When the witness realized that the snakes had found a crack in the closet door and a place to hide under the bed nearby, she made a run for it out the bedroom door and ran to a neighbor's house with nothing but a couple of pillows. When hearing about the snakes, Animal Control was brought out to wrangle them before investigating the deaths any further. The Animal Control officer captured and identified three black mambas. All seven of the victims – two males, five females – died from snake bites. The young Arab girl who escaped was very lucky."

Agent White spoke up, "Sir, where does the scene fit the bill for a hate crime?" The SAC replied, "Well, the seven who died from the snake bites don't. But the Imam was found, lying down with his hands over his chest – with a gold cross in his right hand. But that is not the only reason we are picking this up. Although it hasn't been publicized, our sources say that a similar incident occurred in Egypt. An Imam was found dead in his palace, dead and holding a cross. We might have some strange religious serial killer on our hands." Knox nodded in understanding and interjected, "The Egyptian media is probably being controlled by law enforcement and not letting the story leak out. But you know over here, it's only a matter of time. I guess we better get over there quick, before some over-zealous reporter gets wind of the murders."

SAC McCoy finished, "I texted both of you the address. It turns out that because of the snakes, and the time Animal Control officers had trying to catch them, you can probably still get over to the crime scene before everyone clears out and leaves the property all taped off."

Knox and White got up from their seats and headed out McCoy's office, when the SAC did something nobody would have thought was possible; he said something witty. He smiled on their way out and calmly said, "I am counting on you two lovebirds – just don't make me regret keeping you two together on this."

He winked at both of them as his door closed behind them. Agents Knox and White glanced at each other worriedly for a moment, but then Knox just shrugged it off and went to fetch his sports jacket off the back of his chair in his cubicle. Agent White was a little more concerned, but knew time was of the essence, and took off down the hall after her partner.

Dearborn, Michigan
Unit #501

Agent Knox knelt over the Imam's body. The body still lay in the same position, holding the cross close to his heart. Knox looked up at his partner; "This is crazy. Whoever did this was very deliberate. This was personal. Look at the look of peace the killer left on the victim's face. If you know anything about Islam, you would know how offensive this would be to their religion – and yet our murderer left the Imam looking as if he were at peace with the situation," he finished. Agent White replied, "You're right about that. But what I want to know is how he pulled this off. Did you see the razor wire on top of the wall in the back? Also, the sheer size of the bodyguards next door – they'd be enough of a deterrent for anybody, unless we're talking about a real professional."

Agent Knox stood up and watched where he stepped as he walked around the room. Nothing looked out of the ordinary to Knox. But the careful eye of his partner glanced at the walk-in closet. The doors on the closet were fold-away doors on a track in the top of the doorway; White noticed one was closed all the way, while the other door was pushed open.

She walked over to the closet. "I think our murderer waited to strike from here."

She took out a small flashlight from her inside jacket pocket and shined it around the inside of the closet. It looked like several of the clothes hanging in the closet had been disturbed.

"From the looks of it, I'd say our killer is of a large frame. I could hide in this closet without messing up those clothes too much, but someone about your size would make a mess of the place – you see how the rest of the closet is in perfect order? Let's get the forensic boys to come and scrounge around for any hairs on the clothing that doesn't match with the Imam," Agent White said.

Knox looked at the closet and shook his head.

"See, Beth, that's why it's good to have you around. Guy like me is sure to miss the details from the closet. I just took a brief look; you caught the disturbed clothes out of place. He probably got in here hours before the Muslim. If I were a betting man, I'd say our guy came in over the fence somehow. The two behemoths from next door would have been too watchful of the front of the house for him to just stroll in from there."

Agent White responded, "Excuse me, what makes you think our killer is a guy? And speaking of our two behemoths, any word on how to tell where the snakes that were used came from?"

Knox shook his head.

"Come on Beth, you just said a person my size. I'd hate to meet a woman my size; especially one willing to covertly kill religious leaders. I spoke to one of the Animal Control officers. He said that one of the black mambas had a belly scale with a small burn mark located in the typical spot zoos and conservatories mark their serpents. He thinks whatever number was there was intentionally burned off. As for the other snakes, he thinks they were acquired on the black market. Snakes that exotic – and dangerous - would not be easy to get hands on without some major cash and connections."

The federal agents both looked over the victim's body. Agent Knox tried to see part of the body's legs and arms, pushing up the legs of the robes as well as the sleeves. He saw no signs of injury. He gently rolled the Imam's head over to one side and pushed the thick beard out of the way as he ran his gloved fingers over his neck. Seeing no injuries, he turned the body's head the other way. There on the left side of the Imam's neck was a deep bluish-black bruise all radiating out from a single point.

"Whatcha wanna bet that the same stuff that killed the people next door was injected directly into this guy's artery?" Agent Knox added.

White nodded her head and added, "Definitely not a snake bite like the ones found on the victims next door. So we've got a collection of crime victims, but no real criminal evidence pointing at anybody! What do we do now?"

Agent Knox shrugged his shoulders and answered, "Well, the one witness from the next unit was worthless because she said there was nothing but panic in the room once everyone was awake. She said that she just happened to wake up in a position difficult for the snakes to reach her. She remembers nothing about any strange persons sneaking into the house. That leaves us back to square one. I think all we can do is wait."

"Do you think this guy is just getting started?" asked Beth.

"Not only do I think this guy is just getting started,"- continued Knox, "but I think if he is as good as I think he is, he might be a few steps ahead of us for a while."

Virginia
Somewhere in the Shenandoah Valley

The agent lifted the large plastic lid and slid it to the side, giving him enough room to slide in the long snake hook towards the black mamba's head. It was part of the tricky and arduous task of obtaining snake venom for his new trade. The mamba had been in the cooler, shadier corner of his terrarium, so he was more docile than he had been the last time he was handled. The man's hands had gotten used to being gentle with the snakes while still using just the right moves to detain the dangerous head and lightning-quick strike. With his left hand he placed the flat end of the snake hook down at the back of the snake's head and held him down just firm enough so that it could not rise up and lash out at him. With the right hand he firmly grasped the snake just behind the bottom jaw and squeezed the neck and head just hard enough to immobilize it. He let the snake hook fall down to the outside of the tank as he then reached over to the shelf nearby and grabbed a small glass beaker with a thin membrane of latex stretched over the top of it. He put the lip of the beaker up near the snake's mouth as its jaws were open, trying desperately to bite any part of its handler but unable to move its head. He finally got the top of the latex membrane parallel with the top jaw of the snake as its fangs penetrated the thin layer and it tried to put its potent venom into the animal whose thin skin it thought it had just pierced through. A small thin line of a viscous yellowish orange liquid began to trickle down the side of the beaker.

At the same time, sweat began to trickle down the man's forehead as he tried to get every bit of venom he could out of the snake. "Sweating bullets" was the term that came to mind, as he remembered a scene from the re-runs of his daughter's favorite show, The Crocodile Hunter. Steve Irwin had been her hero, and he couldn't help but think of the old episode when Irwin wrangled a black mamba with his bare hands – the very scene that inspired him to use the deadly serpent in his new mission. Irwin had used the phrase "sweating bullets" as he held the snake out at maximum arm's length, the snake trying to strike him on the inner thigh. The agent couldn't imagine trying to mess with one of these things with bare hands – he was sweating enough just trying to get poison from the creature in a somewhat controlled setting while using tools. But then that was a good thing; he knew that if this ever started to 'get easy', that would open the door to complacency. That was something he could not tolerate. He focused back on the task at hand. He got every last drop of venom into the beaker, then carefully popped the snake's fangs out of the latex. He slowly placed the snake back in his terrarium, and held him there as he grabbed the snake hook with his left hand. He planted the hook down on the back of the snake's neck, and with speed and agility like the snake in the tank, he quickly let go of the snake's head with his right hand and withdrew the hook from the tank. He put the plastic lid back on the box and secured it into place. There were several small holes cut into the top of the lid so the snake could get plenty of air, but it was of sound enough strength that the large snake couldn't bust out. He left the beaker of venom on the shelf; he would deal with it later. He had other important tasks to tend to, such as writing in his journal.

He left the warm, tropical air of the small building he used to house his snake collection, and went to cool off on the screen porch that encircled the quaint yellow house overlooking the wide open valley pond. He had brought his journal with him after returning from his last mission; he had decided it was time to get out to his family home to clear his mind and reflect on what he had accomplished, as well as focus on his plans for the future. He took out his journal from the small shelf underneath the coffee table in the center of the porch. He grabbed a pen from a coffee mug sitting on the mantle over near the wall and sat down in an old hickory rocking chair and began to write. The words came easy to him because of the relaxing breeze drifting in through the screen, and the sound of the rustling leaves and branches surrounding the cottage.

Entry #29, April 14, 2016

Lord God Almighty, I am continuing your work. I killed another Imam; another holy leader of the blasphemous religion they call Islam. Shortly before acquiring my target(s), through my worldly job I learned of the ties between the target and a widely known terrorist group out of Egypt. In my last assignment I learned several names of supposedly peaceful Muslims who have ties to the same group. Of course after learning what I needed to know, I gave all the information pertaining to the evil terrorists to the appropriate authorities in the Army like I am supposed to. Hopefully they will deal with those agents of evil accordingly, while I deal with mine. I want to thank you for the success you've given me thus far, Lord. But I also request that you continue to bless the mission. Please give me courage and wisdom to stay ahead of the Enemy. Thank you again Lord for the connections and means to pull off everything I've done. I pray you only forgive me for the possibly innocent lives lost at the other condo on the last mission, Lord. In my worldly job, the lives of the women lost would be called collateral damage, but Father I know that there is a chance the women could have been forced in the position they were in. For that I am sorry – but I had to kill the bodyguards. I had the means, and they were warriors for the

Enemy that could cause harm to other Christians in the future. Lord I pray you give me the fortitude to accomplish the next mission; it will take me into dangerous lands, and I can only make it through You who gives me strength. I pray all of this in Jesus' name –
Amen.

Just as he closed the journal, his pager went off. He didn't have any one supervisor he reported to; he just took calls as they came. This one came from an encrypted number, but the message on the pager was short and sweet. It gave him geographical coordinates for a rendezvous point and a time to be on board a plane – it was up to him to get there. Of course, with the resources his country had so aptly given to him - that was only a matter of flight time. He was off on his next worldly mission; to help prepare him for his next objective for God.

Detroit, Michigan
FBI Agent Jon Knox's Apartment

He laid there with his eyes open and stared up at the ceiling in his dark bedroom. It was 6:00 a.m. and his alarm had gone off exactly five minutes earlier. Agent Knox was about to get up and face the day, when his cell phone rang on the night stand by his head. He turned over groggily and picked up the phone.

He hit the green box on the touch screen and answered, "Hello." The voice on the other end of the line replied, "Agent Knox, you don't know me, but I am sure we were bound to meet eventually. I am sure you've started working on the case of the Imam that was assassinated near you." Knox piped in, "You've got my attention – not too many people know about the case just yet. It hasn't been revealed to the media. Who the heck are you?" The international police officer on the line answered, "The name is Malik…Malik Sharif. I work for Interpol, and I have been investigating an eerily similar case over in Cairo. I was wondering if we could meet."

After hearing a rundown of what happened in Egypt, Knox told the Interpol agent that he would meet him. He was curious as to how this guy from Interpol got to the states so fast; he mentioned that the murder in Cairo had only occurred a week ago. He got up out of bed and headed to the bathroom. On his way to the shower, he dialed up his partner, Beth.

She picked up on the third ring, "Agent White – go ahead."

Knox chuckled and asked, "Why so serious? Hope you didn't have any big breakfast plans – we have a meeting."

Beth was smiling on the other end; she always needed Knox to bring her back down to Earth.

"A meeting? With whom?" she asked.

Knox couldn't believe how alert she was at this time of morning; she sounded like she had been awake for a while.

"A guy from Interpol – Malik Sharif. Sounds like Interpol is dealing with the same guy we are; a killer left the same trademarks with a victim of similar social status over there in Cairo…you know – Egypt," Knox answered blandly.

He kept going, "I don't know if I like the possibility of having to work with Interpol on this, but after such a lack of evidence with the Imam in Dearborn, I told him we'd give it a shot."

White replied, "John, you know it might just be a smart move. This Malik might have some insight that we don't."

Agent Knox sighed; "I suppose you're right. It's just – his name bothers me. I think he might be a Muslim. I mean don't get me wrong; that might not be a big deal, but obviously our killer has it out for

Muslims. What if this Agent Sharif can't be objective about the case?"

Beth responded kindly, "Sweetheart – must I remind you that you are a Christian. At least, that's what you have been preaching to me. He might wonder if you can be objective, if he finds out what you believe."

Knox spoke back to her defensively, "Honey – I thought we talked about this. You sounded like you had no issues with my faith"-she cut him off.

"John, relax. I am not saying anything is wrong with being a Christian, but you are going to have to open your mind and be objective about this, too," she finished.

Agent Knox was lost in thought for a few moments. His partner was right; he was a Christian. He knew in his mind that the man they were after was a Christian. How could he look objectively at this case? He and his partner Beth had been dating for about two months now, and one of the things she said attracted her to him the most was his faith. She said that although she grew up in a Catholic family, they were not devout attenders at Mass. She had told him one night at dinner that she didn't know what it was like not to worry about things; that's why she analyzed everything. But she knew Knox was different. She said that the way he just rolled with the punches, and never acted worried, was confusing to her. So she had asked him how he did it that night, and that's when he started opening up to her about his faith. Knox told Beth that night by a candle light dinner that he was at peace about his future because his life was in the hands of something – someone – much greater than himself. He told her that although he had grown up in a Christian home, he had grown up in a life of struggling with the burden of a bad temper; real anger issues that he knew he inherited from his father. He told her that losing his temper had more than once gotten him in serious trouble, and it started eating away at his soul. He had started to feel like he wasn't worth anything; that his temper was going to scare all the people he loved away. Then one day in high school he happened to be sitting in the back of a little church in a small town, and a young minister had said the words that he needed to hear. But he had gone on to explain to her that he didn't feel like the minister was saying the words.

He had looked deep into Beth's eyes and said, "God told me that if the good Lord Jesus could save the criminal hanging on the cross next to him, then he could save me, too." He went on to tell Beth that that's why he didn't worry; because he had given his life to Christ that day. He said that now, through good times and bad, he knew that Jesus was going to pull him through.

"John…Hello? John!" Beth was calling him on the other end of the cell.

Knox snapped back to reality.

"Sorry, Beth. I got distracted there for a minute. You're right – I need to be objective, too. We'll figure it out. See you in about thirty-five minutes, at the Starbucks around the corner from the Field Office building," John answered.

"There's the optimist I know. Okay, I will be there in thirty; I have been ready for the past hour," Agent White replied.

John disconnected the call and headed for the shower. He knew Beth had been right about the challenge of objectivity; he would just have to keep praying about it and leave it in bigger hands, and as usual, it would work out one way or the other.

Detroit, Michigan
Starbucks near FBI Field Office

They sized each other up the moment Agent John Knox walked through the swinging glass door at Starbucks. Malik and his slender, agile build and dark brown skin, looking relaxed yet confident as he leaned against a counter top; was already holding a coffee cup in one hand, with his elbow propped up on top of a newspaper spread out over the same counter. He and Knox locked eyes on each other as all 6 feet 3 inches, 240 pounds of the blond-headed FBI man walked directly towards Malik, followed closely behind by a much shorter, unexpected, attractive young woman with strawberry blond hair- wearing a sharply pressed gray suit.

They extended hands simultaneously as Agent Knox was the first to speak, "Agent Sharif...I'm Agent Knox, and this is my partner Agent Beth White." Malik stood taller as he straightened up to shake hands with both FBI agents, only standing an inch shorter than Knox. When they shook hands, it wasn't a test of manhood or anything like that; just a firm, professional handshake that made all parties realize the confidence of one another.

Malik was the first to speak about the business at hand, "Agent Knox, I was told that you were lead investigator on this case. I was not aware you had a partner – you didn't mention her on the phone. At any rate, Agent White... very nice to meet you." Knox responded, "Oh I didn't mention her by name; I do remember telling you WE would see you here. I am just in the habit of people knowing that wherever I go, my partner White here is close behind."

Agent White blushed slightly, but joined in, "So Agent Sharif – or do you prefer Inspector? What exactly happened in Egypt?" Malik smiled and replied, "Please, just Malik. I am not very formal, and never will be. But I will be glad to call you by your last names if that is what you're used to." Agent Knox answered abruptly, "Last names are good for now – we just met. But go on." Malik nodded but continued, "Anyway, I was assigned the case in Cairo from our office in Brussels. They initially sent me as a Counter-terrorism expert. So at first that is what I thought I was going to – a terrorist attack of some sort. What I discovered in Cairo was the body of a dead Imam, lying perpendicular to his prayer rug... holding a golden cross in his right hand."

Malik took a manila envelope out from under the newspaper and handed it over to Agent Knox. Knox took out the first of several photographs, perused it with a heavy brow, and handed it over to his partner. She glanced at it and nodded, "That is exactly what our victim looked like; only a little bit younger."

"So what is your first impression of the killer, Knox?" asked Malik as the FBI agent studied the other photographs in the packet. Knox looked back at Malik after glancing over the photos a little longer while Agent White studied them with her eye for detail. "Well, one thing is for sure – it is a person with a grudge against the religion of Islam. I am guessing someone with Christian influence judging by the intentional placement of a crucifix at both crime scenes. Other than the age of our victims, and perhaps the price of the surroundings at each location, I'd say the crime scenes are virtually identical," he finished.

Malik nodded in agreement. "I personally think our killer is sending a message, or even a warning, to the Muslim world. It is seen in the deliberate placement of the bodies and crosses; the use of poison; the identity of the victims. Although I am not easily offended, I know that the use of a religious idol such as the cross is an 'in your face' mockery of Muslims if placed in the hands of a murdered leader of a mosque."

Agent Knox jumped in, "Hold on – the cross is no more an idol than the crescent moon used on so many Muslim countries' flags and at the top of mosques. It is a symbol of Christians' belief in what Jesus did for them. I think there is a message here, but I don't think it is an attack. I think the killer is trying to tell the Muslims where they've gone wrong."

Malik leaned back against the counter again and gave a smile.

"So glad to know I get to work with someone who thinks like our killer," Inspector Sharif said. "If you're referring to the fact that I am a Christian, you're right. But that's where the similarities stop. I aim to catch this guy just as much as you, for killing your Muslim comrades. I am assuming you are a Muslim," Agent Knox rebutted. Malik nodded, "I am, and so are both my parents. I can assure you, Agent Knox, that it will not hinder my working with you and Agent White. I actually think it will be quite helpful, because I agree that our assassin is at least familiar with Christianity. I admit I am not very familiar with Christian teachings and practices, but although I am not what you would call a devout Muslim, my mother and father have taught me much of the Koran since I was a child. Perhaps that knowledge can help you as well. Agent White – you've been quiet; busy studying those photographs quite closely I see."

She looked up and said, "No – I've been thinking more than looking. The photos just triggered the thoughts. Whoever our killer is, it is a person who avoids confrontation. Forget the religious implications for a minute here, guys. Our guy, or even girl, is someone who not only avoids confrontation and fighting, but they have it down to an art. Now what kind of people are masters of stealth; so much so that they can become virtually invisible?"

Knox and Malik looked at each other. Malik half joked, "A cat-burglar?"

Knox immediately added, "A special forces soldier?"

Agent White sat there for a moment, then piped in, "Perhaps somewhere in between."

The Congo
Outside the city of Kinshasa

He had arrived by an old cargo plane arranged by his American government; he had boarded the older plane after taking a chartered flight into Tunisia under an alias – one of the many perks, and necessities, of his line of work. His unofficial job title, known only by the highest authorities in the military and CIA, was an *activist*. He unofficially worked for a very clandestine branch of the US government simply referred to as The Activity. There were two main positions in The Activity; one was either an activist, or an operative. The operatives were basically what the media and the world knew as Delta Force – highly trained elite soldiers who were sent in to perform the most dangerous secret military missions; knowing that if they were ever captured or killed, their government would neither confirm nor deny their knowledge of The Activity. The activists were different; although just as highly trained as the operatives, their job was not military in nature. Their training had a much narrower focus; they specialized in the most covert operations ever carried out. They were not to be combatants; they were to be invisible. Their jobs were to infiltrate enemy territory and learn, observe, and record anything and everything about the enemy. That is what the assassin did for a living –

the ultimate spy. Once completely into a mission, his job was to blend in with general populations, and then vanish.

This was his current mission in Africa. He was to find and track a known terrorist leader in Kinshasa, Mbeki Thimbosa, and follow him to a secret terrorist training camp deep in the Congo. Once inside the camp, he was to send the geographical coordinates through encrypted messages using his GPS on a new high tech satellite phone. Although the Democratic Republic of Congo was primarily a Christian nation, the terrain and isolation of much of the country would provide the perfect hiding place for Muslim terrorists to train and perfect their fighting and survival skills. Informants had already leaked information to The Activity that such a place existed within the Congo; it was up to the activist to pin down its exact location.

He was wearing several loose fitting robes and layers of clothes to hide the fact that he was a white American. The head dress and coverings were not all that unusual; the bright colors reflected much of the heat and sunlight, and prevented sunburn from the intense African sun. The humidity would be unbearable, but the activist only had to play the part of a chameleon among the crowds of people for so long. Once he was in the jungle, he could don the black outfit he was so accustomed to. To leave the airport, he boarded a crowded old bus that picked up locals outside the airport and took them to the nearest small town. It was this small town, Rumbi, that Thimbosa was said to have been staying. The activist surveyed the village and the surroundings as his rickety ride came close to an end. He noticed several ebony-skinned men standing around the street corners holding AK-47s. He saw a similar bus, coming from a different direction, stop at the next street across from where his would stop. This would be his chance to get lost in the crowds.

The streets were already bustling with activity, but it wouldn't be too difficult to pick the activist out of a few people, especially since he was a large man. He had to time his movements just right and make his way out into the town to find his quarry. When the bus came to a full stop and the air brakes made the loud whoosh one always hears when a large vehicle comes to a halt, the activist seemed to drift out with the wave of locals, and ride the wave of a crowd past armed men until he reached a small bench around the corner. He sat down next to a blind beggar who was seated on the ground next to the bench, holding his head down, with his hands held high, beckoning for some passerby to drop some coins or food in them. As the activist bent over while sitting on the bench, he flipped a gold coin into the beggar's hands just before resting his elbows on his knees with his head bent down to hide his face. He couldn't help but smile to himself as he saw the look of surprise and satisfaction on the face of the blind man as he realized what had fallen into his hands. Now the activist sat and waited. He was in surveillance mode, and the hard part of his mission had begun. First he would have to observe the movement of patrols through the street. He would watch who was talking to whom. He would take in every detail, and the image of Thimbosa was burned into his mind. He would only move when he was sure nobody would notice. He would become a walking piece of camouflage, using every skill he had honed in training. He sat, and he waited.

An hour passed, and the activist had been waiting patiently, but no sign of Thimbosa. The beggar that had been sitting close by had inched his way further down the wall of the building that was against their backs, but no one else had given him anymore money. The activist's inner black outfit he wore under the robes was keeping him cool because of the high-tech Kevlar and fabric that made up the advanced clothing. To passersby he appeared to be a poor derelict wasting away in his very own bench, just lucky enough to scrounge robes together to protect him from the sun. He listened to conversations in several dialects that he could not understand; some between soldiers patrolling the streets, others between random street urchins and locals. But the activist was trained to be patient. After what seemed only minutes to him, a large, green military truck came barreling up to the street corner one block away - not too far from the activist.

He lifted his head high enough to be able to see each of the occupants of the vehicle disembark from the old truck. First several soldiers took turns jumping out the back of the truck. Then the activist saw him; he had been sitting in the front passenger seat (which in this country was on the left side like in England – the activist always found countries that did this quite odd) and walked around to join the men at the back. He spoke in an African-accented dialect of French – very rapidly, but assertive. He shouted out orders; what the activist knew in English could be interpreted as commands to round up the current soldiers on foot patrol and switch places. Following some organized chaos, the activist observed the soldiers getting off duty climb into the back of the truck. He couldn't help but see that three of the soldiers each dragged boys of adolescent age behind them. As each of them pulled their young prisoners to the back of the truck, they gave them hard shoves towards the back bumper and practically threw them up into the passenger hold. He noticed Thimbosa shouting at the last stragglers to hurry up and climb up into the back of the truck. Then the dark-skinned imposing figure, carrying his AK-47, ran around to the passenger side and jumped into the cab of the truck. He pounded on the outside of the door, making two loud metallic thuds to give the driver the signal to drive, and the military truck that had probably been commandeered by the terrorists from another nearby town – roared its diesel engines back to life. As the truck idled for a few moments, probably letting the engine remember how to move the behemoth truck, the activist studied the undercarriage of the cargo/passenger hold. There were several inches of ground clearance, and there appeared to be several places or parts to hold onto if a skilled stunt man happened to hitch a ride from underneath the vehicle. He continued to watch as the truck performed a wide three point turn and head back in the other direction. He watched the truck rattle down the road until it faded from sight. He turned his head slowly in both directions, watching out for any patrols who could be observing his moves. Seeing no interference nearby, he casually got up off the bench and proceeded down the same path that the truck took. He walked into crowds, careful not to bump into any foot soldiers or draw attention to himself. Along the way, he looked for a convenient spot to possibly 'hitch' a ride on the military truck during the next shift change.

He perused the surrounding streets, and imagined what they would look like once late night darkness had set in. There were several dilapidated stop signs for intersections along the road, and the activist was looking for the perfect corner block that might keep him concealed in shadows, in order to sneak under the truck while it would pull to a stop. If he waited until it was dark, and kept out of the light given off from street lamps (he noticed there were very few of these), he might be able to catch his ride on the next truck. He knew there were not too many signs of civilization in the direction the truck headed because it was in the opposite direction of Kinshasa. He could only assume the soldiers were heading back to the terrorist training camp. Finally he came across a corner on the same side of the road that the truck would be going down when it left town again that had several large crates piled up in front of a market place. In the black of night, in his favorite black suit, the activist found where he would punch his ticket. Now all he had to do was stay invisible for a few more hours – and during the next shift change, he would hopefully take a little trip to his final destination; at least for this mission objective.

Detroit, Michigan
FBI Field Office

Special Agent in Charge (SAC), Jones McCoy, was sitting at the end of the conference table. The other two people in the room were Agent Knox, and Interpol Agent (or Inspector; he never had a preference) Malik Sharif. The two agents each had small stacks of manila envelopes and file folders – Agent Knox had rounded up as much information as he could on Imam Mustafa out of Dearborn, Michigan; Agent Sharif had brought files on Imam Mahmud. Everyone in the room was waiting for Special Agent White; she had called McCoy and told him she was running a little late. Agent Knox was drumming his fingers on the table, and Malik was drawing the beginnings of some kind of chart or timeline on a dry erase marker board. The SAC was looking at his watch, when Beth stumbled in carrying stacks of pages and file folders. She let the pile of information smack hard on the table, and then she took her seat next to Agent Knox.

Malik and Knox looked at each other, and then back at White. "What? I had a hunch, and I got my buddy at the Farm to give me some goods, that's all." The guys just shrugged, and then Malik cleared his throat and glanced over at the SAC, waiting for him to acknowledge him to go ahead and begin.

McCoy gave him more of a 'Go ahead' gesture with his eye brows, and Malik turned toward the marker board.

"What we have here…is not much. But it will give us a good starting point," Malik began. He reached over and took a photo and put a small ball of tape in the center of the back, and slapped it on the far left side of the board. He continued, "First of all, our first victim was an important man in the city of Cairo, Egypt. Imam Muhammad Ibn Abdullah Mahmud was the Imam of one of the largest mosques in the Middle East. He was a staunch supporter of the Muslim Brotherhood, and he was generally known as a peaceful man. From the data we have access to, the Imam was a very religious man who publicly abhorred terrorism and denounced all the big players – Hamas, Hezbollah, Al Qaeda, etc." Malik kept going, "Our assassin came in past a heavily fortified perimeter in a location with plenty of deterrence and means of detection. He was able to sneak up on the victim, considering there were no signs of a struggle or resistance. The killer obviously knew something about Islam, because he mocked the Imam by placing him exactly perpendicular to the direction of Mecca, in which the sajadahs were facing as if to say Mecca, the most sacred of Muslim cities, is not the right city. He also left an iconic image (glancing at Agent Knox's reaction as he said this) in the victim's right hand and purposefully set the Christian icon directly next to his heart. So we know the assassin is either prejudiced against Muslims, or wants to send a message. But the gold cross is his only calling card. He leaves no other messages, or signals to let anyone know his purpose."

Agent White briefly interjected, "Well I have some information that might help, pertaining to the assassin's skills, but I will wait until John has gone over the Dearborn case." Malik nodded, but had more to add, "The assassin's method of execution is poison. Not just any poison, but a very concentrated venom from a poisonous snake native to various parts of Africa, the Black Mamba. He seems to have an obsession with both religions – Christianity and Islam. As you know, in both religions, the serpent, or snake- has a significant reputation. Agent Knox – I think you're right about the assassin trying to tell Muslims where they've gone wrong. I think the killer is trying to illustrate that Islam is like the poison. I think he is sending a message that says the spread of Islam throughout the world is like the spread of poison throughout the body. In other words, he is letting whoever discovers these murders know that if Islam continues to spread, the human race will die."

Agent Knox was impressed. He couldn't put his finger on it; but he was captivated by the confidence in the sincerity of Malik as he spoke about the killer, who obviously had the upper hand at the moment, and who was an arch enemy of Inspector

Sharif's own religion. Knox had an actual longing to like the guy – this investigator from a different agency; a different culture. He knew they had their differences of opinion and beliefs, but as he watched the Interpol man deliver with confidence what he thought the un-sub was thinking, he felt like he was watching a kindred spirit in action. Malik had finished, and he looked at Knox. Agent Knox took the glance as his signal to go up to the board. He got up with his own photo. He placed some rolled up tape in four corners of his picture, and posted a photo of Imam Mustafa immediately to the right of the first Imam.

He began, "This is the Imam of the largest mosque in the United States. Imam Mustafa is seen – I mean was seen - and recognized by Muslims around the world as one of the great hopes for the spread of Islam. As we all know, the US is not exactly known for its Muslim history. However, whether other countries like us or not, our country has more influence on the rest of the world than any other. What better way to get Islam to become the world's religion than by infiltrating the most powerful country in the world? Although a rich and powerful man, the Imam has avoided any bad publicity regarding the use of violence or force in any of the influence his mosque, the Islamic Center for America, has on the surrounding community of Dearborn. Mustafa was killed by the same means as his counterpart in Egypt.

The venom killed him quickly, but caused extreme pain for a brief moment before he died."

Then Knox went on to describe in full detail what happened to the body guards and the harem next door. He talked about the lone witness in the entire case so far…and how all she could tell them was how she escaped the black mambas. By the time he had finished, he almost sounded discouraged.

However, Agent Knox took a deep breath and then looked right at his SAC. "Sir" – he began. "I know it sounds like we don't have much…but I think I can think like our un-sub. I think I know why he is doing this." Malik perked up and was ready to hear further explanation.

Knox continued, "Our subject is angry about something. He is mad at Islam, just as most of America was back in 2001. I think he is associating these imams with something he knows about Islamic jihadists. That doesn't make him right," – he looked right at the inspector from Interpol when he finished, "But in his mind I believe he thinks he is right. I think our assassin is an American Christian, who in his own misguided mind, thinks he is doing the right thing."

McCoy was tapping his temple with the eraser on his pencil as he sat there looking at Agent Knox. Then he sighed and said in response, "So what both you men are telling me is we have bupkis… except that maybe our killer is one of 120 million suspects, give or take a few – who hates terrorists that claim to worship Allah. Is that about right?" Malik cleared his throat. "Special Agent McCoy, we will get more. But we need more time... and we need the killer to attempt to attack again." McCoy chuckled, "Son, don't let the press get wind of you saying that. Anyway, I am glad to know what I had pretty much already read in each of your reports. Ms. White...you said you had something to add. Surely that stack of paper and thin cardboard holds something of interest for us." Agent Knox took his seat, and Beth got up with the folder that was on top of her pile.

She jumped right into explaining, "Well, I was busy yesterday and the day before when I had some time away from the boys, and I started thinking about our un-sub's ability to get around everywhere, totally unseen. I mean it is like he is invisible. I knew that the CIA actually trains its most elite field agents at the Farm with just the tactics to pull this kind of thing off. I mean they teach them to pick several types of locks; how to blend in to crowds; how to use the shadows on a sunny day to remain in hiding – you name it. *SO* I contacted a friend of mine who happens to train CIA field officers at the Farm. Since mistrust of Muslims hit an all-time high on September 11, 2001, I had him run down a list for me of the numbers of recruits they have had graduate from their tradecraft and paramilitary training since 2001. That at least cuts down our list of possible suspects of 120 million." She paused with a smile at her boss. The SAC just motioned with his hand to continue.

"I also figured our guy, who we have estimated to be about the size of Agent Knox there, was probably ex-special forces. So I had my guy narrow the list down for me even more to all the recruits who made it through who were former Special Forces soldiers. That got us down to a pool of less than 400 people, sir. Unfortunately, he didn't have a search engine with enough specific capability to narrow it down to recruits who were over 6 feet, 2 inches tall. So that's why I was late this morning. I just flew in from Virginia. I left early yesterday morning to pick up anything he found. Even though he wasn't supposed to, he made copies of the recruits whose files are still active (they're still agents), and he let me have the archived files that were more than 5 years old. So here they are. I think our guy is in there."

Jones McCoy's eyes got real big for a split second, and then he smiled at Agent White. Then he looked at Agent Knox and laughed, "That's our girl." Malik couldn't help but be impressed, but Knox wasn't surprised in the least. He just wished she had let him in on her little get away plans. He and Malik had been going over photographs and running over scenarios or possibilities for how the killer operated so smoothly, without ever being detected. Both agents also needed their rest, but of course Agent White the energizer bunny kept right on working. No wonder they hadn't seen her.

McCoy straightened up and went back to serious mode. "Here's what I want you guys to do. Run down the lead with these files. Hell, start by looking at how short or tall everyone is. That should narrow it down. Any possible suspects who have a particular conservative background – we need to know about them. If we need to look up certain military personnel who have had interaction with any of those leads, let's make that happen. You guys aren't doing too bad, after all. Just keep me posted on what you find out. Now get moving on those files," he finished and abruptly turned to leave the conference room.

Knox and White immediately started gathering their things and left for their office carols. Before McCoy made it out of the room, Malik gently tugged at his shirt from behind. "Sir, may I have a moment with you in your office?" he asked. The SAC simply motioned Malik past him and let him lead the way back to the big boss's desk.

****

McCoy showed a welcome gesture to one of the chairs in front of his large oak desk. Malik pulled the door closed behind him as he entered and sat down in front of McCoy. He began, "Sir, I came in to the office today, fully expecting to have to complain to you afterwards of my suspicions of Agent Knox being unable to work on this case with an open mind. But the more I am around those two, the more I appreciate the opportunity to work with your agency. So I guess I just wanted to say thank you. I thought at first, after learning that Agent Knox was a Christian from the South, that he might have a problem with me working the case alongside him and Agent White. But after getting to know the two agents a little better, and seeing their ability to convey their thoughts and see how they work together, I am more optimistic. Hearing Knox tell us today that he could think like our assassin – that gives us a big advantage I think. So I also wanted to apologize if I caused any tension with my initial arrival to the case," he finished.

McCoy just sat there and took it in stride. He replied, "Look, don't get me wrong; everybody around here knows what a God-fearing boys' scout Knox can be. But trust me – he wants to catch our bad guy just as much as you. Think about this for a second…that guy out there is making Christians everywhere look bad. Oh sure, the world may not know about him yet – but they will. It's only a matter of time. In the meantime, tolerate the boys' scout. Also listen to that partner of his. Beth is a rare gem around here. She'll keep both of you in line. Pleasure to have you working with us on this one, Inspector Sharif." He stood up, and Malik followed suit. They shook hands firmly, and the man from Interpol just grinned. "Please sir – it's just Malik."

****

Malik had finished up in the SAC's office and left the office for a while, presumably to check in with his home office in Brussels. Knox and White had begun working on the list of capable suspects. Agent Knox had decided he would look at all the heights and weights of the people in the pool of names; Agent White decided to try to focus on any commonality found in the trainings listed in each soldier's files. While Knox whittled away at the names, using the basic description on each soldier's profile – he was blown away by how efficiently Beth just opened file folder after file folder, making quick notes in her notepad, then moving on to the next file.

He was just finishing up recording the last soldier's name on his list and writing his height and weight, when Agent White closed the last folder and looked up. "I think I am done for now….let's grab a late lunch." Knox finished scratching something down, and smiled. "It's a date then…let's go down the street to Burrito Joe's." Burrito Joe's was a relatively popular Southwestern place that served burritos down the street from their office building.

Once inside the restaurant, Agent Knox ordered a "Joey's Burrito of Goodness", and Agent White got a "Home Maker". The couple picked a quiet corner booth at the back of the restaurant. They sat down to eat, and Knox bowed his head and said a short blessing before eating his meal. When he looked back up, he noticed Beth hold her head up at the last split second.

She gave him a knowing smile. "Can we talk about something other than work?" Beth asked her law man. Knox nodded and replied with his mouthful, already taking a huge bite of his burrito, "Sure, babe – anything you want to talk about." She laughed at him, and then got somewhat serious again.

"You want to know what I did last night before I caught my red-eye flight back to Detroit?" Knox nodded as he continued to chew. She answered calmly, "I read the Bible...one of those Gideon Bibles that you find in the night stands in motels." Knox immediately put his burrito down and stopped chewing.

He gave a big swallow, and chased it down with a swig of sweet tea. "That's great, Beth! What brought that on?" he asked. She breathed in deeply, and continued, "Well, I got to thinking that it would be awesome to have the comfort level you have – you know; about the future and stuff – and what comes after all this. I also thought that maybe if I knew more about the Bible and what's in it, I could better relate to you." Knox smiled and took hold of her hand. "Wow…that means a lot to me. But I want you to know that any questions you have along the way – don't be afraid to ask. And if I don't know the answer, we'll find it together."

They sat there quietly for a while, finishing their meals and smiling at each other. Neither was in any hurry to get back to the office. Finally Knox chimed in, "So – heck of a surprise you threw on Malik and me back there. I know McCoy was impressed. You got any more hunches under your belt?"

She nodded, and started cleaning up her mess on the table.

"You know all the training each person has logged in those files? Well, several trainings for different purposes were held at this base or that base, but several of the bases don't make the list for everyone. But there is one location that jumped out to me that I noticed was on every single person's file," Agent White finished with a smile.

Knox asked, "Well, where is it?"

White continued with her knowing smile, "Fort Benning, Georgia."

The Congo
Rumbi – after sunset

The dusty streets were dark; the sun had gone down, and a lot of the people became scarce at nightfall because of the poor infrastructure. Poor lighting and nocturnal predators on the outskirts of town did not make for a good night for anyone. Although far enough away from any savannahs to worry about animals such as lions or hyenas, the town was known for leopard attacks in the middle of the night. The bustling activity at the market in the small town during the day kept the jungle cats away while the sun was up; but because electricity was hard to come by on several of the streets, the leopards became bolder at night, in relation to the brightness of the area in which a person was walking. The activist figured the patrols in the town at night would be minimal for this reason, and he was right. He moved like a leopard through the shadows, donning his customary black attire for his trade. The activist had remained anonymous throughout the day, never making conversation with locals, and never drawing attention to himself. As it got darker, he found a small storage shack near the market, and quickly ran in through a curtain that had been hung over the front of the doorway. While inside, he stripped off all the baggy robes and extra garments. He had his normal equipment that had joined him for all his missions in the last several years. He also placed his new hi-tech night vision shades over his eyes. They made his field of vision appear as if it were still daylight. Now dressed for the occasion, he made his way through the dark, abandoned market place, darting past tables and around empty standing cabinets.

The market was under a large sheltered area that resembled a giant picnic shelter, the size of a city block. Several bamboo posts held up a thatch roof overhead, and the roof was approximately ten feet high. He had to slow down every now and then to hide from some of the soldiers still patrolling the streets. The activist finally reached his destination when he saw the large stack of crates placed near the side of the road at the intersection he remembered. He ran up and knelt down behind the largest crate, and waited to hear the sound of the old military truck. After 20 minutes of sitting with his back against the wall of the crate, waiting silently, the loud rattle of the old truck could be heard meandering its way into town. He got up to a squatting position leaning against the crate, and peeked around the corner to see how far away the truck was. It was slowly approaching the make-shift stop sign of his intersection. He quickly shot his head back behind the crate before the headlights came bearing down on him. Then he heard the sound he was listening for – the squeaky brakes and the hiss of the air that old air brakes make when a truck of its size comes to a stop. Ironic how that sound would mark his exit from the town, just as it marked his arrival. He waited to see that the beam of light from the headlights had come to a stand-still. He sat still as he heard troops of the terrorist guards jumping out the back of the truck and rambling on in their African-French gibberish. He slowly stuck his head out again, and saw that his window of opportunity was closing. He could see a tall figure he guessed to be none other than Mbeki Thimbosa, shouting out orders out behind the truck; but he was sure he could make it under the truck before they were fully loaded up. The driver had gotten out and marched off. The activist figured someone else would be doing the driving back to the terrorist outpost. Seeing nobody watching the driver's side, the activist made his break for it. He crouched and ran in one fluid motion, and then dropped into a roll, controlling his body so as to not make more than a muffled thump on the ground; the sound drowned out by the heavy diesel of the truck. Once he rolled onto his back under the passenger hold, he immediately looked up and saw two small places to use as inverted foot holds. He avoided any moving parts of the undercarriage and axles, and reached up and grabbed hold to some metal overhangs. He stayed on the ground staring up and back at the same time, his hands ready to hoist up his weight once the truck was ready to roll. The truck shook each time a new passenger jumped into the back, but this didn't deter the activist.

Finally, he heard the familiar sounds of young kids screaming their protests to larger, brutal bullies who were obviously forcing the youngsters to come along. He heard the bullies toss the boy recruits into the back, and he heard Mbeki yell at the others some final commands as he actually went to the driver's seat. He slammed his door, and the activist heard the transmission of the truck being put into its first gear as the truck lurched forward. The activist quickly lifted his back off the ground and hung on for dear life. The activist had no way of knowing how long the drive was to the camp, but he was sure this was his only way. Years of serving his country had given him the mettle to deal with such odds. Any normal person might be thinking at the back of their mind that this was a bad plan, but not the activist. He just adapted and adjusted as usual. He would hang on to the undercarriage, and he would make it to the camp and infiltrate the training outpost. He would search for his personal objective, and once he found what he was looking for, he would then signal the operatives via his satellite phone...so the operatives of Delta Force could come in and make the camp appear to be a ghost camp. He knew he couldn't afford to fail the operatives on this mission; their post-mission L-Z (landing zone) would be his only ticket out of the heart of the African jungle.

****

The activist had been able to find a way to hang on to some unidentified rod that connected to some other unknown auto part with one hand - all while keeping his feet in place. He would save his energy by holding on with one hand at a time, switching hands and shifting his weight, but it was quite tedious. The truck bounced and shook, and he even felt his grip slipping on a few occasions, as the massive truck would hit deep grooves intersecting the road it was traveling. He adjusted his grip to hang on with both hands whenever the truck slowed down and went around sharp turns. But fortunately it was only a twenty-five minute ride; it turned out that the outpost was deep into the heavy jungle. The activist could tell it was dark; the brighter his field of vision was through the shades, the darker it was in reality without them. From his inverted position underneath the truck, the activist could make out a clearing. He then felt the truck slowing down, and watched upside down as the truck slowly moved between two large gates that were propped open. He could only assume the gates were part of a large fence or wall around the camp. He was getting anxious for his uncomfortable ride to be over, when the behemoth finally came to a stop after pulling into a large, flat clearing. Nearby there was a small, run-down building with a flat roof. The activist waited while the passengers got out; he could feel the truck get lighter on its leaf springs as each person jumped off the back. Finally the engine to the truck was cut off, and the driver got out and once again shouted orders at people. The driver was definitely Mbeki; the activist could hear his voice more clearly since the truck's engine wasn't running. He remembered the annoying raspy sound of a high-pitched voice, and he thought that was so odd for a terrorist who was supposed to stand at 6 feet, 6 inches tall.

Once all the noise from voices leaving the vicinity of the truck had faded away, the activist scanned his surroundings from his awkward inverted view. He slowly lowered himself all the way to the ground. Then he flipped himself over quietly, so his brain could interpret what he was seeing a little easier. The activist noticed that there were lights around the perimeter of a large wall made of giant sheets of tin, held in place in front of wooden stakes. He could also see small huts scattered around in the distance - closer to the wall. However, the dilapidated small building with the flat roof next to him had very poor lighting. He glanced around all sides of the truck that he could see, and rolled out from underneath the truck into a prone position on the ground – ready to react to anyone who might see him. Seeing no patrols nearby, he jumped up into a crouch and ran over to the flat top building. He had a feeling that the small building was where someone in the terrorist camp slept, but he would check out the lay of the land first. He peered around the corner of the building, and could see that the huts were in small, neat little rows of 10 huts per row. The activist was sure that several of the thugs who had caught the ride over from town had gone straight to their little shanties to catch some shut-eye before having to get up in the morning and go back to guard duty, or training, or whatever it was that they were supposed to do.

He didn't have to inhale too deeply to notice the stink of nearby latrines. Guess there was no money for plumbing in the jungle. So the activist knew where the terrorists and recruits slept; now where did they train? When he crept to the other corner and peeked around, he had his answer. The complex spread out before him, and this side revealed to him that it was much bigger than he thought. He saw a complicated maze of obstacles laid out in an obvious challenge course for the terrorist recruits. He could also see other small buildings that he assumed to be some sort of barracks for some of the leaders of the camp. He also saw a small covered shelter with lights plugged into a small generator. In the center of the shelter was a small card table with three Africans sitting around it. The activist couldn't quite see far enough to tell what they were doing, but from their mannerisms and movements, he thought they might be playing card games. He was going to be busy for the next little while. He was going to have to be slow and deliberate; he had to find the information or evidence he was looking for before he sent the signal to the Delta Force team. He knew once he sent the signal, he probably had an hour at the most before silent hell broke loose, and the Delta Force operatives would come in like angels of death and erase the camp from existence. Since he could see several buildings in the distance across the camp, he figured he might as well start with the one right next to him. He was surprised at the slack security; he guessed the terrorists thought the concealed location was enough security for the place.

As he rounded the corner, he realized that there were several make-shift guard towers that had been constructed of bamboo. He couldn't make out how many guards were posted at the top of the towers – they were too far way. But as far as he could tell, he was in the clear as far as anyone seeing him in the immediate vicinity. He finally came around to the front side of the small flat top building, and saw a doorway. He knew the entrance was dark because it was nice and bright through his glasses. He quickly ran in through the entrance. As soon as he entered, he saw a small wooden table in the center of the building's only room. There was also a small single bed against the back wall with the covers pulled down. There were notebooks with various things scratched out on the covers, scattered about the table; some drawings, some writing – mostly in a language the activist did not know. Then he noticed some brochures; travel brochures – from the United States. The activist thought at first that this was odd, but then he realized what they were.

They were colorful pictures of targets. These men were training to wreak havoc on American landmarks! The activist thought to himself that it was a good thing he was about to send for reinforcements and take care of this little terrorist threat. Each brochure was advertising famous American landmarks throughout the U.S., such as Mount Rushmore, The Grand Canyon, the Space Needle in Seattle, the Washington Monument in D.C. – just to name a few. They were American icons, and this terrorist group had them in their sites for a plan of some kind. All of this was of course speculation on the activist's part, but he had come to know the enemy well. He brushed aside the brochures for American destinations, and stumbled upon a map spread out underneath. It was a map of the Atlantic Ocean, and key ports along the Eastern United States, and the West African coast. There were curved arrows tracing between the port cities across the map, with the names of various cruise lines written in red. The activist figured the terrorists planned on using piracy to reach the mainland United States. Of course this plan was dead in the water, unless the terrorists had some way to stow away undetected before reaching port. The US Coast Guard was good at what they did; if there were any sign of a terrorist threat to the mainland, they would be onto it ten times out of ten if the terrorists thought they could hijack cruise ships. Nevertheless, it was obvious that this group had been running this training operation for a while.

The sound of footsteps in the dirt could be heard approaching the one room building. The activist glanced over in the direction of the doorway, and then over to the bed that belonged to whichever terrorist was lucky enough not to have to stay with the others in the small huts he had seen earlier. He was about to try to hide under the bed, when a large profile filled the doorway in the activist's night shade field of vision; the man who cast it had his back turned and was about to turn into the room, but stopped and shouted loudly to someone in the camp far away. Immediately the activist recognized that the voice belonged to none other than Mbeki Thimbosa. The activist knew he was about to have a fight on his hands, and thought he would go ahead and summon the Delta Force raiding party. He pulled out his hi-tech satellite phone and hit send on the small key pad to activate his homing beacon for their stealth helicopter to home in on, and rush to his location. Just as the activist was ready to take on Thimbosa head-on, the camp leader abruptly walked away from the doorway in the direction that he had been shouting. The activist imagined wiping sweat off his brow as the large threat walked away. He was running out of time. Since he had activated his beacon through his phone, he knew he had approximately sixty minutes before the operatives invaded the camp and did what they do best. So that gave him about an hour to get what he came for. Sure, the apparent plot to somehow get their trainees overseas and give them important things to shoot at was important. But the activist knew that these bad guys were only able to come up with these schemes, and provide this training, and obtain AK-47s with one key ingredient – Money.

Money makes the world go round, and he knew that the money would come from a very secret place - or person - in particular. In all his operations, he had found that all the illegal operations for Muslim terrorist organizations had come through a religious leader. He knew his next target would be whoever was funding this second-rate operation. Unfortunately he had not seen any evidence of a trail that would lead to that financial source. The activist was about to do something drastic. He quickly decided his next course of action would be to confront Thimbosa, and force the truth out of him. If he could wait until the arrival of the Delta team, he could use their attack as a distraction long enough to beat the truth out of Thimbosa. But he would have to know immediately when the first Delta member was in the camp. He needed a high point of view…one of the bamboo towers. He slowly peeked out Thimbosa's doorway, and saw that the camp leader was down the main road of the camp, fussing at some underling who was jerking one of the little boy recruits around. There was nobody else out and about, so he made his break from the doorway and ran in the direction of the huts. The bamboo towers didn't have spotlights; just sentries doing a poor job watching out for secret agents, dressed in black, running around their camp. The activist came to the base of a ladder to one of the towers. He tested the integrity of the structure. Once finding that it was pretty strong and sound, he began to slowly climb. He was careful as he neared the top of the ladder. He peered through the small gaps between the boards that made the platform for the observation deck of the tower. He was only able to pick out movement from one guard.

The guard was standing over on the far side of the tower from where the activist would have to make his landing. He was hoping the guard would be looking anywhere but towards him as he slowed his ascent. Unfortunately, as soon as he crested the top of the ladder, the guard turned and saw the activist. Before he could shout for an alarm, the assassin sprung up from the top rung of the ladder and elbowed the guard under the jaw, knocking him up and backwards. The guard fell back and hit the back of his skull on the make-shift railing made of a few bamboo poles that went around three sides of the top of the structure. He was out cold. The activist had to make sure the guard didn't awaken to warn anyone of his presence, so he reached down and grabbed the man's head with both hands. With a fast twist, the popping and grinding sound the activist made with one quick motion indicated that the man's neck was broken. The activist then sat on the edge of the platform, Indian-style.

He scanned the skies, and then looked out over the entire camp. He searched for any signs that the Delta Force guys were already there. He didn't see anyone, so he watched and waited. After ten more minutes of waiting, he heard a very low moaning sound fly overhead. He could see the Stealth Blackhawk flying over with his night shades. It flew a little further past the far side of the camp wall, and the activist could see it fly down and hover close to the jungle canopy. He saw thin squiggly lines hang out of the chopper, and from his point of view, it looked like ants coming out of the helicopter and sliding down the lines, as soldiers were repelling down ropes to the ground. He kept watching – he didn't want to make his move on Thimbosa until he saw the Delta team enter the camp. Just ten minutes went by, and then he saw several shadowy figures squeeze through a small gap in the gate that Thimbosa's truck had come through. As soon as all the men were through, ten men in all, they fanned out in different directions around the camp. The activist took out a small flashlight. He flashed in Morse-Code to the Delta Force squad leader. He messaged *A-One Ready to Go.* The squad leader saw his signal and flashed back *Head to L-Z.* The activist stood up at the top of the ladder. He glanced in the direction of Thimbosa's building. None of the operatives had headed in that direction yet. He held on loosely at the top of the ladder as he climbed down a few rungs. Then he placed his feet to the outside and let loose of his grip slightly. The activist slid down the ladder and landed with a muffled *Thud!* He took off in a sprint to the terrorist leader's quarters. He could hear the faint *zip-zip* sounds made from the double-taps of suppressed rifles the soldiers were firing into the huts. He leaned up against the wall next to Thimbosa's doorway. It was now or never. He knew he had the advantage in vision with his night shades on, so he ran into the single room.

Mbeki Thimbosa was standing there taking his worn out clothes off, wearing nothing but a pair of pants. He was bare-chested, and had a look of absolute shock on his face at the sight of a black hooded figure standing in his doorway. The activist did not waste any time; he swung at Thimbosa, but to his surprise, was blocked away. The terrorist had a three inch height advantage, so the activist guessed he had a slight advantage in reach as well. Thimbosa lunged at the activist and launched a quick side-kick.

Since the activist was wearing Kevlar, he absorbed the blow but reached around to catch Thimbosa's leg. He tried to hoist the man up and into the wall, but Thimbosa brought a fist across the activist's jaw and stunned him – but only briefly. The activist was done playing with this guy; it was time to get serious. He let loose with a barrage of punches to Thimbosa's body, and then a sudden open hand smack to the side of his neck. Thimbosa dropped like a stone.

The activist quickly extracted a small throwing knife from a slot on the side of his shirt. He held the blade firmly under the jaw of Thimbosa as he held him in a choke hold. "I already know you speak English, Mbeki, so I am going to make this clear. You tell me who supplies all your money for guns, and feeding recruits, and gas for your trucks, and anything else your little group needs – and I might let you live."

The African terrorist tried to swallow, and as he gulped down, his throat caused a small cut to open up against the edge of the activist's knife. He said something in French that the activist was sure was some kind of insult, so the activist hit him square in the nose, and then sliced a line across his cheek.

"Perhaps you didn't hear me. I know you speak English. Tell me what I want to know, and I will make it quick; no pain at all. You're past the point of living now." He locked down his arm wrapped around Thimbosa's neck, and the man began to speak. "Okay, okay," he began with a heavy accent. "I don't know his name. All I know is he is supposed to be the holiest of holies from the American City, Nude York. Please – let me go." The activist pulled the large man to his feet as he got up as well. He couldn't help but notice a shadowy figure run past the doorway. He replied, "You know what – I believe you. That would be Imam Kareem Hassad – and it's NEW York. Thanks."

And with that, he shoved Thimbosa towards the doorway. He glanced at his AK-47 hanging on a hook on the wall next to his bed. He grabbed it and tossed it to Thimbosa. As soon as the man caught it, the activist front kicked him out through the doorway. Thimbosa stumbled out into the open and fell down. When he got up to face the doorway, he realized he was trapped by soldiers. There were ten men standing around in a semi-circle in front of him, along with a blazing fire that had started around the compound. Mbeki Thimbosa realized he could call for help, but it would never come. But he did not want to die without a fight. So he began to raise the muzzle of his gun. As the muzzle of his gun raised up, his body was riddled with bullets. From the darkness of the sleeping quarters, the activist watched as Thimbosa's body hit the ground. He waited until the men out front departed the scene because he didn't want to startle American soldiers armed to the teeth. As soon as they ran away from the fire, he decided to do the same. He was making his way past several of the burning huts, and as he ran, he noticed several young boys, ranging in age from 9 to 14, bound to several standing poles several feet out in front of the huts. Well, who says Delta Force doesn't have a heart? But the activist didn't think the boys would survive the smoke from the fire that was building up. He thought these kids might stand a better chance surviving the jungle, instead of inhaling smoke and perhaps getting burned. The activist ran up to each pole. He took out his KABAR and cut the bonds that held all the boys together and to the poles. He pointed in the direction of the gate, and the boys followed suit. He ran up ahead of the youngsters and pushed hard against one of the gates. He could hear the little feet scamper behind him as he rested to catch his breath. Once he was sure all the kids were out, he followed them into the jungle. He had a helicopter to catch.

****

The activist knew that the stretch of jungle wasn't too thick between where he was and the clearing for the L-Z. Nevertheless, he had to chop incessantly with his large knife at the vines hanging down. He really could have used a machete, but that wouldn't have been very practical to carry when he was hanging upside down under the truck earlier in the evening. He was almost to the clearing, and could even hear the whoosh of the helicopter blades, although several decibels lower than your average Blackhawk. Suddenly, he had a something attack from the brush and land on his back! The activist reached up with one hand to try and grab whatever wild beast was upon him. He scrambled around in a small circle, and when he finally caught hold, he realized a big cat – probably a leopard – was mauling his protective clothing. The cat had ambushed him, able to locate him by the frantic noises he was making as he had to chop through the foliage and undergrowth of the jungle. The activist was a strong man, so he was able to stand his ground as the leopard pawed at the black shirt and began clawing the fabric away. The Kevlar he was wearing underneath once again saved him; the jungle cat's claws had not reached the activist's skin yet. The man in black grasped with his left hand for any body part of the cat he could find. He found the back of the leopard's neck and flipped the cat's large body over by bending forcefully at his hips. As soon as he threw the cat through the air, the activist followed through with his knife, and he buried it into the back of the cat's neck as it landed on its feet. The leopard convulsed and hissed, but then fell limp under the weight of the activist. He got up and dusted himself off. He twisted and pulled his knife out of the leopard's neck and wiped it on some nearby vines, still breathing hard from the exertion. He could see an opening ahead to the clearing for the L-Z, and he broke into a run.

A highly trained member of the Delta Force unit named Paul Sorsky was the last soldier running towards the Blackhawk. He was about 40 yards away, when he heard some footsteps come up quickly by him and then he watched a hooded man in black, with ripped and tattered clothes, out-pace him to the whirly-bird. He wasn't that surprised; the guys from Delta were used to working with the black hooded figure. He just shook his head as he slowed to a jog and jumped up into the helicopter, helped up by the hooded man who had just beat him in a foot race. "Thanks!" he yelled to the man in black over the roar of the jet turbine. The activist just nodded in acknowledgement and sat down in the jump seat against the interior wall of the Blackhawk. He was tired, and he was going to have to get some rest before taking a trip to the Big Apple.

Fort Benning, Georgia
The office of Colonel Bob Thornton

Colonel Bob Thornton was the man in charge of the entire base at Fort Benning. Benning was where all the Army Rangers received their training. It was also a hotbed for all forms of special-forces training, as well as training by special-forces soldiers of recruits of the CIA. He wasn't a particularly tall man; probably only 5 feet 11 inches. But he had a voice that filled a room at the slightest word. He had a fruit salad of medals and pins on his chest, and had an impossibly correct posture that exaggerated proper form for a soldier. His booming voice would soon fill his office as he gestured to the two chairs in front of his desk. Agent John Knox and Agent Beth White from the FBI had come to ask some questions, and the Colonel had been more than happy to cooperate with them. The Colonel had heard that Agent Knox was a University of Alabama graduate, so when the two federal agents came into his office, he was beaming with a very welcoming smile.

The two agents were followed by a Major Mike Willis who stood at attention next to the Colonel's desk and announced the arrival of the guests, "Colonel Thornton, Sir! Agents Knox and White with the FBI here to see you, Sir!"

He clicked his heels and saluted, and the Colonel casually returned the salute and calmly replied, "Thank you, Major. Please hold all my calls but stand by in case I need you. Dismissed."

The Major saluted again and gave a quick "Yes Sir, Colonel Sir!" He then snapped around in a sharp turn and left the room. The Colonel sat down comfortably in his large leather office chair and looked over at Agent Knox. He smiled warmly again, and welcomed his guests.

""So good to see a fellow Alabama alum," he said as the agents entered.

"Sorry about the formalities there. Major Willis takes his job quite seriously as my aide. Sometimes he overdoes it, but I wouldn't trade him for anybody else. Now how can I help y'all out today?"

Knox had told his partner that he would be happy to do most of the talking, because he knew Beth always felt a little awkward when interviewing or speaking with high ranking military personnel. Her grandfather and father were both retired colonels in the Marine Corps, and she said it always made her feel like she was talking to another carbon copy of her dad.

Knox started in with the Colonel, "Colonel, thanks for meeting with us on short notice like this today. As I told you on the phone, my partner Agent White and I are investigating a crime that is sensitive in nature, and we have reason to believe the subject we're looking for has been trained by US military."

"I see…well, son, I don't mind telling you that there are plenty of other military installations around the United States that train our soldiers," the Colonel responded.

"Yes, Colonel, but the specifics in the training are what brought us here. It appears our killer has been trained in the art of…well, not being detected by other military personnel. The guy we are looking for does seem to have a knack for picking locks, breaking and entering, and other modes of tradecraft. We are interested in the agents of the CIA that you have trained here at Fort Benning," Knox finished.

The colonel was nodding his head. "Well, now that is a bit more specific. I am afraid I can't answer any questions on any of those trainees we have had here on post. However, I can get Major Carson over here from the Ranger school. Not only is he in charge of the training of our Rangers, but he also makes sure those spooks from the Farm are ready for the field."

The Colonel pressed a button on his phone and spoke into the air with his commanding voice, "Major Willis, could you get Major Carson to come over here to the office and meet with these agents? Oh, and bring our guests some coffee while they wait." Major Willis seemed a little less over the top on the phone.

He gave a customary "Yes, Sir" and the Colonel ended the connection by taking his finger off the button. The Colonel looked over at Agent White. "Agent White, you've been quiet. Do you have anything to add to what Agent Knox has told me?"

She glanced over at Knox, and he just shrugged. "Actually, sir, you might know my father - Colonel William H. White, II; retired. He was a colonel over in Vietnam. They put him in charge of an entire brigade of code breakers. And my grandfather did the same thing during World War II over in Japan." Colonel Thornton scratched his chin and glanced up towards the ceiling for a second, as if he were pulling out old files in his head. "Ah yes – Colonel White, out of Lejeune! One of those jarheads. I do seem to recall meeting your dad at one time. Helluva man. And how is your father?" the Colonel asked Beth.

She grinned and replied, "He's living it up on the Outer Banks with my mom. He lives a quiet life. I don't talk to him as much these days. But I will make sure I tell him you said hello."

The Colonel nodded and answered, "You do that, Ms. White – I mean Agent White. Tell him from one Eagle to another, thank you for his service."

About that time, Major Willis brought in a tray and set it on the corner of the Colonel's desk. He filled two coffee cups, and glanced at the Colonel.

"Would you like some coffee as well, Sir?" The Colonel shook his head slightly and waved the Major away.

"Thank you, Major. I'm sure our guests can fix their coffee how they like. Please let me know when Major Carson gets here." Major Willis saluted with another "Yes, Sir!" and walked out of the room. Then Agent Knox spoke to the Colonel. "Sir, if you don't mind me asking, how long before we meet Major Carson? I don't want to rush you, but we will need to check with another investigator working on the case with us. He is checking things out from the CIA angle at Langley," he finished.

Colonel nodded and answered, "Son, I am afraid Major Carson is as unpredictable as a soldier in his field is expected to be. But he follows orders, so he will be here." The Colonel then stood up and grabbed a small silver pitcher and looked at Agent White first; "Would you like some creamer in your coffee, Agent White?" Beth smiled in surprise but replied, "Yes, Sir, if you don't mind. Oh – and just one sugar cube, please. I think Agent Knox could learn some manners from you Colonel," she said jokingly. Knox just waved her comment aside. The Colonel then looked at Knox as he handed Agent White her cup. Knox nodded for the creamer, and added, "Three cubes for me, Sir. Thank you." The Colonel finished doctoring Knox's coffee and handed his cup to him after a quick stir.

"So what all does this case entail, Agents?" the Colonel asked nonchalantly. Knox took a sip of the piping hot coffee, but shook his head.

"Sir, I am afraid we can't give you too many details. We can tell you exactly which questions we were going to ask either you or Major Carson if you like."

The Colonel declined and replied, "Well no – if that's the case I can wait for the Major. But I will sit in if you don't mind." Knox looked at Beth and shrugged. "It's your base, sir. I guess you can pretty much be where you want when we talk to the Major." Then the Colonel's phone rang.

He answered it after one ring. "Hello. Already? Great – send him in, Major."

The Colonel hung up the phone and said, "Major Carson is coming in now."

The office door opened, and a rugged, muscular middle aged black man wearing fatigues walked in and stood at attention.

He popped off a sharp salute, and the Colonel immediately responded, "At ease, Major. Pull up a chair and join us will you?"

The Major fetched the only other chair in the room from the opposite wall, and as he was placing it closer to the agents, Colonel Thornton introduced them.

"Major Carson, I want you to meet Agents John Knox and Beth White – they're with the FBI.

They have a particular interest in the recruits from the Farm that you have overseen the last several years." Major Carson shook the FBI agents' hands and had a seat.

Now that they had gotten past the greetings, Agent Knox started things off again.

"Major Carson, thank you for coming on such short notice. The Colonel informed us that you were in charge of all the special-forces training here, including the recruits you train in weapons and self-defense tactics for the CIA. We were looking for a recruit in particular," – The Major interrupted.

"Agent Knox, are you aware of how many recruits those spooks send down here…every month…every year? That's a large list of people to remember."

Knox nodded in understanding, but continued, "Yes, Major, I am sure you've had your share of the 'spooks' come through here. But what I was going to say was we are looking for a recruit in particular that probably would have had specific political and religious views; probably conservative, and a known church-goer. We also have reason to believe that the subject we're looking for was probably military before the CIA got their hands on him."

Major Carson sat back in his seat, and glanced over at the coffee pot. "Sir, do you mind if I have some? I am a little sleepy from the hours of training I've been overseeing," the Major said to Colonel

Thornton. The Colonel smiled and started to get up to fix Carson his cup, but the Major waved him off and stood up. "Colonel, I'm a big boy- I got this," Major Carson chuckled. The Colonel just took it in stride and recovered his seat behind his desk. It was apparent the Colonel and Major Carson had a good report with one another.

Major Carson fixed a cup and added a small amount of creamer; no sugar. He began again, "Agent Knox, if I may ask…what makes you so sure this guy has all this training. Could you possibly just have an evil person who happens to be good at killing? I am assuming that is who you are looking for, right? A murderer?"

Knox confirmed his question with another nod and replied, "We're looking for a guy who took a chance at sneaking into a virtual fortress, filled with security systems, guard dogs, armed guards, and the like. Our subject also killed another person with other people in a house next door, and they were totally unaware of what was happening. Whoever our subject is, he committed these crimes with efficiency, with stealth, and with boldness. Doesn't that fit the bill for the kind of folks you train, Major?"

The Major nodded with his eyes closed for a second, sucking in his upper lip.

He responded, "Okay, I'll give you that. Sounds like at least a former soldier. Can you be more specific on religious – do you mean he was a

Christian? Because the Army has its share of those as well."

Agent White cut in this time, "Major, he hates Muslims. Whoever our guy is has given us very specific reasons to believe he hates Islam. That's why we have a working list of people who have trained here since 9/11. Because that's the day that everything changed, and we think our subject could have some kind of connection to that day."

Major Carson started to look like maybe he had the image of who they were looking for in his mind, but he still wanted specifics. "How many armed guards are we talking?" Knox shot back, "At least twenty." "Were there any signs that your killer had been at the incident location? I mean besides the obvious dead people." Once again, Knox fired, "Not a trace. It was as if a death angel came in and killed them." Major looked up at the Colonel. Colonel Thornton saw recognition in his training Major's eyes.

"Major, do you know who they are talking about? If so, help these agents out. They've come a long way," he told his subordinate.

Major Carson answered, "There was a man back in 2002 who everyone here at Fort Benning knew. We all knew him because he blew the doors off any training exercise we threw at him. He came in here as one of the spooks-in-training, and I knew he was military. Turns out he had gone to the CIA from the SEALS. The word was he decided to help the CIA with a new counter-terrorism team after his parents died in one of the Towers in New York. But I remember we had this one challenge in the woods that the recruits had to take on; we paired them up, and each set of partners had to have one of their team reach the mission objective in the course without being detected, after capturing at least one of the other pairs' flags. The deal was that one partner could try and capture flags while the other guarded their own. The only catch was that they couldn't use any weapons. Whoever reached the end point first would call in on a radio that was left there for the winner. This guy got 7 of the 9 flags, and reached the mission's end without anyone ever seeing him. Sure, his partner let them down and they lost their flag – but it didn't matter. I mean he was so good at disappearing that he earned the nickname around here as Ghost."

The Colonel had listened intently, and was nodding with familiarity of the Major's story. Agents Knox and White sat there in anticipation, until Knox chimed in, "Well…did this Ghost have a real name?"

Major Carson nodded, but then had a disappointed look on his face.

He continued, "His name was Chief Petty Officer Robert C. Brady, retired. He went on from here to head up a counter-terrorism team for Langley. Word got around that he and his team were good. But then, while on leave for some R&R, something terrible happened. Brady and his family were whitewater rafting down the Colorado River without a guide. They traveled into a bad part of the river and their raft overturned. When the raft flipped, they were caught in a strong undercurrent that pushed them under some rocks. Brady, his wife, and daughter all drowned. I'm afraid the only guy that we've had around here that could pull off what you are talking about – died about a year ago."

Knox shook his head. He couldn't believe that their closest thing to a lead took them to a man who was deceased. There had to be an explanation. He finished his cup of coffee and set it down and looked over at Beth. She had finished her coffee a while ago. She looked back at him, and he stood up and brushed his hands down his suit to shake out the wrinkles from sitting.

"Colonel; Major – thank you for your time. I am sure we will find some other way to track down our subject; looks like we hit another dead end here." Colonel Thornton and Major Carson stood up as well and both men shook the hands of both FBI agents. The Colonel spoke up one last time, "Well, maybe your cohort you mentioned earlier will have better luck at Langley. Nevertheless, good luck to you both. It was a pleasure to meet such fine representatives of the FBI. Please don't hesitate to call if we can be of some assistance in any other matters."

With the farewell and the handshakes out of the way, they left the Colonel's office and made their way out of the command post and back out to their vehicle – a shiny powder blue Chrysler Crossfire that had been given to Agent White from her father upon her graduation from the FBI Academy. She always let Knox drive whenever they shared a vehicle. As soon as Knox fired up the engine, he was turning his head to back out of the parking space when Agent White spoke up, "You thought we had something for a second there, didn't you?" Knox put the car in gear and headed towards the main gate. He replied, "Something just isn't right. We'll have to see if Malik has any better luck. In the meantime, can you do a rundown of anything you can find on this Chief Petty Officer Robert Brady? I don't guess a dead guy can be our man, but you never know if he might have had some subordinate try to follow in his footsteps." They left the base through the main gate and headed back to the highway. It was a long drive back to Detroit.

****

The Colonel watched from his office window and waited until the agents had left the parking area. He dismissed the Major and sat down in his big leather chair. He thought about the former soldier that everyone at Fort Benning had referred to as the Ghost. He had been given very specific instructions one day about nine months prior regarding the man known as Chief Petty Officer Robert C. Brady. The Director of the C.I.A. told the Colonel to personally call and inform him if anyone should happen to come asking for any information pertaining to the Ghost, a.k.a. Robert C. Brady – deceased.

The Colonel reached over and picked up the telephone and contacted the switchboard at Langley. "Yes, patch me through to the Director; this is Colonel Bob Thornton at Fort Benning. It is important." The operator sent the call through, and after several rings, a dry, Boston accent answered the phone.

"This is Director Marks, Colonel. What can I do forya?"

The Colonel replied, "Mr. Director, Sir – you spoke to me about nine months ago and told me to call you if anyone ever came to me inquiring about one of your own, Robert Brady, that passed way a little over a year ago. I thought you should know that the FBI sent two agents to speak with me today. They're apparently working on a case that involves a subject with a lot of training. Anyway, it caused them to ask about Brady."

The other line was silent for about ten seconds, and then the Director simply said, "Thank you Colonel. You've been helpful."

And then he ended the call. Colonel held the phone out and stared at it; "What a jerk!" he said to the phone as if it could hear him. The Colonel enjoyed his meeting with the agents; he liked nice people. He sure liked that Ms. White. He then thought maybe he'd look her old man up and give him a call. Perhaps they could reminisce, maybe talk about the old days, one eagle to the other.

Langley, Virginia
CIA Headquarters

Malik hung up the phone. That was the second phone call of the day. The first had been to his mother in Kuwait; he called her before leaving for the airport. He apologized for not getting to come see her like he had planned, and he told her he would make it up to her when he was finished with his current case. Of course he couldn't tell her what he was working on, so that limited his conversation a bit. He had left things in good standing with his mom by the end of the call, though, so he was off to Langley, Virginia. He didn't like the road trips like his cohorts, Agents Knox and White. He flew into Dulles International in D.C. and rented a car to drive the rest of the way. He decided he would make some calls along the way. His Interpol badge would help him get to some places, but he knew he would have to make some phone calls, first. His second call had been to Agent Knox. Knox filled him in on what they learned at Fort Benning. He told him to get in touch with someone in Counter-terrorism and ask about an agent who died in a terrible accident; a man named Robert Brady. Knox had given a brief summary of their interview with a training Major at the base, and basically said that their best suspect so far was deceased. Malik pulled into a gas station before passing Langley High School.

He googled the number for CIA Headquarters and pulled up the phone number for single point contact. He left a message with the person on the line, including who he was and with whom he had an inquiry. Then he hung up and waited for a return call. Two minutes later, his cell phone rang, and the Director of Counter-terrorism; Logistics Division was on the line. Apparently this was as far up the chain as he was going to get regarding counter-terrorism, but he decided it would have to do. Paul Rutter was the guy's name, and he sounded nice enough on the phone. Mr. Rutter gave Malik specific instructions, and said Malik needed to follow them to the letter, unless he wanted to cause an international incident. He sounded like he was only half-kidding about that last part. Malik parked his car in a large parking lot in a space simply marked VISITORS. He then reported to the security check-in station, flashed his Interpol badge, and signed off on a security badge that Mr. Rutter had specifically requested for him. The security officer informed Malik before entering that the badge would give him access to all points necessary for his reason for visiting, which had been entered through a computer by the person he was visiting. He walked through the main front doors and crossed over the Great Seal stretched out across the marble floor. So far, so good.

He went to the first elevator on his right like Rutter had instructed him. He scanned the temporary security badge; the door opened, and a robotic feminine voice spoke to him, "GOING TO – FOURTH FLOOR". He walked into the elevator, and the doors closed. They opened up on the fourth floor. The elevator opened facing a wall, and labeled the two hallways that could be reached to the right and left. Malik figured that the large rectangular shape of the building meant that the floor was basically like a city block, but one side was missing. To the left was 4A. To the right, you could reach 4B and 4C. Director Rutter had told Malik that his office was at the end of 4C. He took a quick right turn down the hallway, and was amazed at the length of the hallway. He was about to turn onto 4C, when he happened to notice an open office door as he approached. The man inside glanced up from his desk, and saw Malik coming down the hall. The man stood up and walked towards his office door. He was tall, with red hair and a very clean cut and trimmed red beard. He looked Irish, but had a slightly darker complexion than most people would expect from one of Irish descent. He made brief eye contact with Malik, and for a split second, Malik saw brilliant bright green eyes. Then the man smiled at Malik, nodded his head in a friendly gesture, and closed his door. Malik didn't give the random encounter a second thought as he saw that 4C was much shorter than 4B.

He got to the end of the hall and saw that the door to the office at the end of the hall was dead center of the hallway; it was standing wide-open. Inside, there was a short spectacled man with a small pooch of a belly and balding gray hair. Agent Rutter stood up from his desk and walked around to meet Malik.

He extended a hand and introduced himself, "Inspector Sharif, very pleased to meet you. I am Agent Rutter; please come in and have a seat." Malik grabbed his hand and gave him a firm handshake. "Please, just call me Malik. I like to be informal when it's possible. Thanks for meeting with me. I just have a few questions, and I hope I won't take up too much of your time." They walked into his office, with Rutter taking the sleek, ergonomic office chair behind the desk, and Malik sitting in front of the deck in a quasi-comfortable padded pleather chair with small armrests. Agent Rutter said, "Okay Malik, how can I help you today?"

Malik started off, "Agent Rutter, first of all, what exactly do you do up here? You don't strike me as a field agent." Mr. Rutter chuckled and answered, "A field agent, I am not. However, without our division, the field agents on the Counter-terrorism team would be lost. They would be thrown to the wolves, not knowing where the wolves are going to come from. I help lead the logistics division in all the practical details of understanding the organization of the terrorist cells; where their bases of operations are located; which assets are nearby; the best ways to communicate without having their cover blown – those kinds of things. You might say one can't exist without the other."

Malik nodded.

"I see, so you don't actually go with the field agents to most of these mission locations; you analyze a lot of the data that other field agents have gathered on the ground – from other divisions."

"That's correct," Agent Rutter replied.

Malik continued, "How much direct contact do you have with the field agents, Agent Rutter?" Rutter replied, "Me, personally? Practically none. You have to realize, Inspector – we have several team members broken into sub-units around the world. More of the analysts underneath me would have a chance."

Malik nodded. "By any chance, would you recognize a name of an agent who died while not in the field?" Rutter nodded his head at this question. "You must be referring to Agent Brady. Everyone heard about him and knew his name. I never met the man personally. I don't even know what he looked like. But he was so good on the Counter-terrorism unit that he still earned a black star on the wall downstairs. I am sure you noticed our wall for fallen agents?" Malik nodded, but looked puzzled. "I thought only agents who died in the line of duty earned a tile star." Agent Rutter nodded his head and replied, "Yes, that's usually the case. They made an exception for Agent Brady because the man and his unit were known throughout the agency as the best at what they did. Such a tragic loss for the Agency."

"So was it like the military reports to some feds that are working with me on a case; did he and his family die in a river rafting accident?" Malik asked. Rutter nodded again; "That's affirmative. There was a memorial downstairs, but those things around here are very brief, and the family and agent are not visually recognized; they're honored incognito in death, just as they were in life." Malik was fascinated by the way the C.I.A. worked. He had heard things when he was growing up in the Bronx, and while working over in Europe, but it was different hearing how they operate from the lips of an actual employee. He could imagine himself being one of these field agents Rutter described; it sounded more exciting than his job with Interpol…and Allah knew, he had plenty of excitement in his current job.

"What else can you tell me about Brady, Agent Rutter?" Malik wanted to get as much out of this guy as he could; he knew it wasn't often you had information given willingly by the C.I.A. Rutter answered bluntly, "I'm afraid not a whole lot. I know the guy came to us from the Farm with a nickname; the Ghost. It was said that he could virtually disappear; anytime, anywhere. Some of the other analysts who had the pleasure of working with him said that he brought the art of tradecraft to a new level; that being a thief or undercover agent came as naturally to him as swimming does for a dolphin."

Malik crossed one leg high on the other knee, and propped an elbow up, scratching his chin. "Do you happen to know if Brady had any prejudices? Was he right-wing; left-wing; Christian?" Malik continued with his questions.

Rutter had a look on his face like he knew he had some information of some use and answered promptly, "The word on the grapevine was that Agent Brady came from the Navy SEALS shortly after 9/11. I don't know if this is true or not, but it's said that he lost both his mom and dad in the World Trade Center. I don't know if he was a Christian or not…but being a red-blooded American, I seriously doubt he would like Islam after what those terrorists did."

Malik just nodded. He didn't want to be too quick to judge Rutter's obvious presuppositions on Islam; he knew just how hard the terrorist attacks hit Americans on that fateful day. He understood how anybody would feel – but the Islam he knew; the Muslims he was brought up to know in his mother's family – they were not like that. Malik had one more question.

"Agent Rutter – I know you didn't know the man. But in your working with the Agency in the last year, have you noticed or heard of any agents in the field that might be following in Brady's footsteps?"

Rutter sat and pondered for a second. "I can't say I am familiar with anyone as of yet. I am telling you – Brady was a legend around here. It'd be like Kobe jumping into the NBA right away and thinking he could hang with MJ step for step…it just didn't happen." Malik laughed to himself; if only Agent Rutter knew how much he admired Michael Jordan.

Malik suddenly stood from his chair. He extended his hand once again and offered, "Agent Rutter – once again, thank you for your time. I hope it wasn't too much of an inconvenience for you." Rutter responded in kind and shook his hand firmly, "Not a problem. It's not often we logistics people can feel of some use for anything else around here besides logistics – I hope I was helpful." Malik gave one more smiling nod and walked out of the office. Although at a distance it seemed like another dead end, Malik still felt like it wasn't a total waste of time. But he wished he had something more concrete to tell the FBI agents.

Langley, Virginia
Office of the Director of the CIA

Director Marks looked around into the faces of the serious men seated in his office. They were a very exclusive group of men who ran the top secret society within the intelligence community for the United States of America. The President of the United States was an honorary member of the group known only as the Activity, but had express orders carried down from Harry Truman himself to not actively participate in the Activity; a sort of historical plausible deniability that had been passed down since the inception of the CIA in 1947. The only rule the Activity absolutely had to follow was that nobody who was associated with the Activity could disobey a direct order given by the President. In other words, although the President was not to be aware of the everyday plans of the Activity, if he asked a question to the CIA Director, the truthful answer was expected. If the President discovered certain actions had been taken and wished for them to cease, they were stopped immediately. There were only a handful of people who were included in membership, and five of them sat in the Director's conference room now. The other six were the highest operatives and activists for the organization; they were the members who worked in the field, and they did not even know the entire truth of who they worked for.

The highest ranking generals (and one Admiral) in all four branches of the military were the other four who were guaranteed membership into the Activity. This is how it had been since post-World War II. When the CIA Director and Deputy Directors of Intelligence were the top tier positions in the CIA, the Director of Intelligence had been the knowing member; the Deputy was out of the loop. Once the positions were merged into the Director of the CIA in 2004, whoever held that position was the default member. The actual Director of National Intelligence was totally oblivious of the Activity's existence. Only the predecessors of these five positions in the American government would make the men new to their positions aware of the existence of the Activity. Every man presently in the room had been members of the Activity for over a year and a half.

The Generals and the Admiral paid close attention as Director Walter Marks cleared his throat. "Gentlemen, one or two of you might know why I called you in here today, but not all of you. So I am going to be frank with you. I have reason to believe we have a rogue agent in our midst." The military industrial complex-elite all looked at each other with some puzzlement in their eyes, but looked back at Marks as he continued.

"Men – the acting Colonel in charge of Fort Benning contacted me earlier today and informed me that the FBI is asking questions about one of our own. The Feds are looking into a case that involves a certain assassin that has eerie similarities to our most trusted activist."

General Greg Baumgartner, the highest ranking general in the Army, asked right away, "How do they know he still exists? I thought we covered that base last year." Director Marks glanced over at him from his spot at the head of the conference table and replied, "They don't as of yet. But his name has come up because one of your own was just doing his job and was very forthcoming and truthful with information. That is where it stops so far. We even had an Inspector from Interpol come to headquarters today and inquire about the Activist. He had to walk right past our man's cover office, and was none-the-wiser."

The only Admiral in the room, Admiral Grant Stokes, added, "Is there any possibility that the Ghost is the guilty party the FBI is looking for? And why is Interpol involved?" Director Marks answered, "That we don't know, as far as your man the Ghost. But Interpol is involved because the same crime that was committed here on American soil – happened in Egypt. I wanted to make sure we were all aware of the situation. And should the activist be involved in such unapproved actions, I am afraid you know what we must do."

General Steven Chase of the USMC responded, "Our man from the old Recon side of things will get the job done. He'll do what he does best, and clean the mess up." Marks carried on, "Hopefully it won't come to that. We have only had a rogue Activist one time in our history, and that was when Kennedy was President. And I think we can all agree that the Ghost is a little more capable than Oswald ever was." They all nodded in agreement.

"So here's what I think we should do – you guys jump in if you have a better idea- but I think we should keep our eyes and ears on the FBI case. If anything else drastic happens, especially if it could expose us, then we send in the Arbiter. Are we all in favor?" Marks finished. The military men looked at one another, and the Airman in the room, General Dwight Johansen, piped in, "I'll speak for the military here and say I concur. Let's keep our ears to the ground a little longer."

The men who knew each other and their families very well then proceeded to carry on in small talk and trivial matters as if it were no big deal if by some off-shot chance they had a rogue agent in the Activity.

New York City
Rockefeller Center

Imam Kareem Hassad was a famous man. He wasn't your typical religious figure; he loved the limelight, and perhaps was not as humble as his peers would have preferred. Due to the previous US president showing an affinity to Islam, and the media falling in love with his silver tongue, Imam Kareem Hassad had taken full advantage of the new and improved Islam - and was going to appear on the Today Show. The show was set inside the famous Rockefeller Center; a large skyscraper in the center of Rockefeller Plaza. The Imam was inside his dressing room in very elaborate and extravagant robes with a certain Arabian flair to them. He had to wow the public and fit the part all at the same time. Although the sincerity of the Imam's beliefs had been questioned by several of the more prominent Muslim leaders around the world, the man was financially generous to the cause of Allah – and he had thousands of faithful followers. He also played the part well by always saying the right words during the Salats – saying just about anything he could think of to show Allah in a positive light, including tempting promises of salvation; if they would only submit to the will of Allah. The Today Show was having the Imam as a guest because of the controversy of the large cross that had been included in the 9/11 Memorial Museum. There had been both Muslim and atheist protesters lining the streets near the museum, and it had caused quite a stir as of late. The Imam had informed both his security as well as Today Show staff that he needed some time alone in his dressing room to make supplications to Allah; he wanted Allah to bless him with all the right words. Unfortunately none of those parties were aware that he really just needed some time for his vanity. The narcissistic man could not help staring in the mirror and constantly adjusting his head dress and wrinkling the robes just the right amount for the camera.

In the meantime, the activist had become the assassin once again. A large man who looked like a hippie on steroids in something like a blue custodian's uniform - with his long brown hair and a long beard to his chest, walked up to the security guard outside Hassad's door. He was carrying a basket of what appeared to be Green Tea and some fruit in one hand; a clipboard in the other.

"Excuse me, dude – but the show sends its regards and thanks to Mr. Hassad, man. I need to give him this stuff and have him sign for it…k bro?" the stranger asked the security guard with a surfer-dude accent.

The large Asian guarding the door said, "Hold on; I will only take it if the Imam is willing to see you." He slowly turned around and knocked on the door. "Excuse me, your holiness – but the TV show has sent you a gift. There's a man out here who wishes to give it to you and watch you sign for it," the guard finished.

The hippie added, "Your guard can come in and have some of this fruit and water, too – Sir!" The Imam yelled to the guard at the door, "It's okay, Quan; let the man in; I could use some refreshment." The hippie smiled at the guard as he held the door open for him.

The guard still didn't completely trust this hippie, so he followed him into the dressing room. The man with the long brown hair walked right up to the Imam and presented the basket. "Sir – if you wouldn't mind – I'd like you and your guard here to try the Green Tea. It's got a special flavor; it's the latest craze in the studio, dude!" The Imam reached for one of the tea bottles, but his security guard stopped him. "Sir, I'll try it first." He glanced into the face of the hippie and noticed his green eyes for the first time.

He squinted his eyes at him ever so slightly, and reached for a bottle. He twisted the cap off and tossed the bottle back, and even swished the stuff around in his mouth before swallowing – all the while glaring at the suspicious hippie. He then looked away for a second and back at the Imam. He smiled and said, "Actually it's not that bad."

Suddenly his face turned a deep red, and he put both hands to his throat. The Imam stared at him in horror, then quickly looked at the stranger in the room. The hippie ripped off his fake beard and wig, and quickly grabbed the Imam and wrapped the parts of his disguise around his neck. He held him there and strangled him, as he had to stand there choking and watching his security guard grasp at his throat and scrape at it with his own fingernails as if he could scratch out whatever poison he had ingested.

The assassin said nonchalantly, "You know, you really shouldn't drink water laced with arsenic, snake venom, and sugar. It's some real nasty stuff."

He tired of trying to choke the Imam to death, so he stood the man up straight and reached far around the front of his head with one hand, and held the back of his head firmly with the other. With a great twisting motion and several pounds of pressure, he broke the man's neck. Quan the security guard still had some fight in him despite the fact that his throat was on fire, and swelling profusely. He reached out and grabbed the hippie assassin by the neck with one hand and rushed forward. The assassin reached over the top of the man's arm and ripped over and downward with his arm, twisting his hips, pulling the security guard's face down and forward. The assassin then elbowed the man square in the nose, and it was lights out.

The assassin dragged both bodies over to the counter in front of the mirror and left them in the floor. He leaned their upper bodies up against the cabinets underneath the counter. He placed them close together so that the bodies would hold each other up without falling over. He then took out two golden crosses. He placed one on the forehead of the security guard, and then struck his head very forcefully with an open hand. When he took his hand away, the cross was embedded in the flesh of the security guard's thick brow. He wasn't quite as violent with the Imam. He took the other gold cross and stuck it in the Imam's thick beard, sticking it out far enough to stand out, but burying its bottom just enough so that it wouldn't fall out of his beard. The two bodies on the floor made quite the pair. The assassin knew he wasn't out of the woods yet.

Right then, there was a knock on the door. "Mr. Hassad, sir – we're on in fifteen." The assassin heard footsteps grow fainter, and he knew he had to act fast. He unzipped the custodian's jump suit and climbed out of it, revealing a pair of khaki's and a green and white striped polo shirt. He had a small, home-made name tag clipped to the collar of the shirt, and he reached down to pick up the basket of fruit that he had set on the counter.

He opened the door to the dressing room just a tad, and peeked out into the hallway. He could see the hustle and bustle of the crowd back stage at the end of the hall. He saw that no one was looking in his direction, so he walked out the door and walked straight into the crowd.

One person wearing a set of head phones who looked like they were of some importance to the show stopped him and said, "Who are you?" The assassin put his best smile on and with his most feminine voice, he blinked several times and sucked his teeth one time. "If you will excuse me, sir – I need to get this basket of fruit to the producers back stage as soon as possible." The man with the headphones raised his eyebrows, but then shrugged his shoulders, moved aside, and headed back in the direction that he'd been going.

The assassin came to another turn in the hallway and looked back over his shoulder. The set of the show looked like pandemonium as they scrambled to prepare for the next take. The assassin saw that he was of no consequence to anyone, so he proceeded to the elevators. He casually pressed the bottom button of the two options placed in the middle of the silver pad on the wall. The elevator took several minutes to get all the way up to his location, but when the doors opened, he just walked in and turned around; looking like someone going on their lunch break. The doors closed and it was just another day on the set of the Today Show.

****

The man with the headphones knocked heavily on the Imam's dressing room door. No one was answering, and the man began to panic. He called his supervisor, and they asked him if the door was locked. He turned the knob, and the door started to open. He still had his supervisor on the phone as he walked into the dressing room. The supervisor was in the process of asking the stage hand what was going on when the man dropped the phone on the floor. He stared in awe at the blank stares on the faces of the men leaning up against the cabinets. Then the man screamed. He then floundered around on the floor and picked up his phone; he stuttered into the phone. "S-s-sir, you need to call 9-1-1. We have two dead men in the dressing room!" he screamed.

Several people ran down the hall to see what the stage hand's scream was all about, and the hallway filled with more screams. People flooded in and out of the crime scene because security hadn't even shown itself yet. Unfortunately there wasn't a soul in the place with enough common sense or shred of decency to secure the scene and keep nosy on-lookers and prying eyes out of the room. The place had been busy before because it was the set for a popular TV show; now it was an animal house. By the time security got to the room, people had gone in and out of the room with cell phones, probably taking video and screen shots with their phones and posting them on Facebook. Once the room was secure and nobody else could enter the room except law enforcement, it was too late. Social media and the internet had been filled with pictures of the dead. The gall some people had was deplorable to anyone with an ounce of respect for their fellow man – but this crime had taken place on a TV set; controversy and basic de-sensitization was the name of the game.

The assassin was long gone. The FBI and Interpol were aware of the matter in a matter of minutes once photos hit the internet. The stage had been set, and there was definitely going to be some harsh feelings between at least two very large sects of people in the country – no, the world. The headlines the next day were not going to be pretty. Pretty was not what the assassin was shooting for anyway. War was never pretty. Although he knew Christianity was going to take its lumps, he knew it would be worth it. He knew that he would have the world's attention, and he wanted the world paying close attention. He wanted the world to see that the people were waking up to the violence of Muslims. He hoped that he had the attention of the Muslims, too. If they kept seeing the gold crosses, perhaps they would get the message. What he didn't expect that day was to become a legend. That day, the legend of the Jesus Assassin was born.

New York City
Imam Hassad's Dressing Room

Knox and White got off the elevator and followed the hallways around to the backstage area of the studio. The door to the Imam's dressing room was standing open with a strip of yellow tape marked CRIME SCENE stretched across at chest level. The two FBI agents ducked under and came upon the Interpol Inspector. Malik was squatting down to get a close look at the two dead men leaning against the makeup counter. He had beat them to the crime scene from the airport. He turned his head to acknowledge his FBI counterparts, but stayed in his catcher's stance.

Agent Knox asked him, "So I guess our man is escalating his tactics. What do you make of that, Malik?" Malik scanned over the morbid scene before him, and he stopped at the bodyguard's forehead. He stood up and scratched his bald head. "I don't know what to make of the escalation, but I think we have a number," he answered his cohort.

John Knox replied with another question, "How could you possibly know that?" Malik grinned. "Well, my Christian ally – I am a Muslim. Let me tell you about the twelfth Imam." Knox and Agent White gave each other puzzled looks. Beth just shrugged, and Knox looked back at Malik. He continued, "In

Islam, there is the belief that one day, one of the great prophets from the Quran will return to this world. It is said – and I believe – that this twelfth Imam will be the savior of mankind who will finally bring about peace and justice to the world."

Knox replied sarcastically, "Hmm, sounds like another story I've heard…one that is a little older than Muhammad's." Beth punched him in the shoulder. Malik just shrugged his shoulders. "Mock Islam all you want, Knox; that's what the killer is doing."

Beth pushed past Knox and went over to the bodyguard's body. She looked at the small cross embedded into the guy's forehead. "You guys can continue your religious stories later. What I am interested in is why this guy is suddenly becoming more violent. I don't think he is your typical serial killer."

Knox shook his head. "That's where I think you're wrong. I think he is like half the serial killers we deal with; I think he thinks he is doing something righteous with these killings."

Malik nodded in agreement. "I agree with you; I think whatever he has against Muslims has made him angry. He might get angrier as he goes. I don't think he is like most of the killers we have dealt with that escalate just to see how much they can get away with. I think this violence is stirring from the fact that each assassination seems to make him madder. Think about it…first kill – silent but deadly; just one victim. Second kill – still silent, but more dead as collateral damage. This one – silent entrance, but two dead with a big statement. How we found out about it, for starters," finished the Interpol man.

"Tell me about it – this thing is about to bust wide open, right in our faces. That was intentional on our assassin's part. He wanted to create bedlam with the media to distract us from running him down," Knox added.

Beth also gave her input. "All the more reason we nail this guy before it gets out of hand. Regardless of the religious implications this un-sub has brought attention to, escalation means he will make mistakes. Mistakes mean we will find this bastard."

Knox began walking around the room. He was looking around the floor for any clues, when something out of place – and hairy – caught his eye. "Speaking of mistakes – what's this?"

He bent down to pick up what at first looked like a dog's tail. He lifted it up for both the other agents to get a good look. Beth spoke up and guessed, "Looks like we found how he got in here. Another sign of him escalating. Instead of darkness or virtual invisibility, he used a disguise."

Malik picked up a small bottle with a Green Tea label on it. "Look at this; there's some kind of amber liquid trapped in the bottom of this bottle. I don't know if he meant to leave this or not, but it's something."

Knox scanned the floor further, and saw a small puddle of a slightly colored liquid. "Let's get that fluid analyzed. I also think we need to process the bottle for prints – maybe even the crosses. If he wore a disguise including the fake beard and wig here, he might not have worn gloves. It's worth a shot."

The agents walked around the room a little longer and decided they had pretty much found everything of note. Their response to the crime scene was the first time they had been back together since they had left the Detroit office and gone their separate ways for SAC McCoy.

Malik looked over at Knox as they were walking and asked, "So did you guys leave anything out over the phone when I last spoke to you? Did that Colonel Thornton tell you anything else…or that training Major – what was his name?"

Beth piped in, "It was Major Carson. He told us that the most likely suspect to fit our profile was a former Navy SEAL before he was in the CIA. And he told us that this Robert Brady lost his parents on 9/11. That's when he quit being a SEAL and became a terrorist hunting agent." Knox shook his head, "Yeah, well too bad he's dead."

There was silence for a few minutes as they boarded an elevator that had to go down sixty floors.

There were several occupants already on the elevator; probably tourists returning to the ground floor after visiting one of the three observation decks. When they reached the ground floor, the three of them headed out to the street.

Knox said to Malik, "We'll see you at the hotel later…unless you want to join Beth and me for some site-seeing."

Malik shook his head. "No thanks – you guys have fun. I'll see you at the hotel when you get back. I have to catch up with my Chief Inspector back in Belgium. I know he is going to have some major questions once this assassin's handiwork gets broadcasted all over Europe," he answered.

Beth grabbed Knox's hand and fired back at Malik as they walked away, "Suit yourself, Inspector." Malik raised his eyebrows as he watched them walk away, shrugged his shoulders, and flagged down a taxi. He spoke to himself, "Who knew?" and he climbed into the cab.

****

Knox stepped down off the step of the pay-per-view binoculars and helped Beth step up to take a peek through the viewfinder. Knox had brought Agent White on a date to the 86th floor of the Empire

State Building. As she leaned forward to peer through the lenses, she gasped in surprise at the view that suddenly opened up to her that zoomed in on the horizon and other parts of the grand city.

She asked her still-new love, "John – how can God give us the ability to build such wondrous sites as New York City, but also give us the capacity for such evil acts like assassination and murder?" She pulled away from the binoculars and let Knox help her back down to the observation deck.

Knox's smiled turned into a confused look, "What brought that on?"

Beth continued, "Well, it's just right when I started studying more of the Bible verses you told me about, and I started wanting to know God – this so-called Christian man starts picking people off; one or two at a time. How does a loving God let that happen?"

John walked with Beth over to another part of the high fence that surrounded the observation deck. They both gazed out over the city and listened to some of the city noises far below.

John started again, "Wow – you sure start off with the hard questions, don't you? Leave it to the analyst," he chuckled, but continued. "Honey, I don't think you'll find any verses in the Bible that say God made us with the capacity for evil. What He gave us was free will. He gave us the freedom to *choose*

Him…or choose evil. Unfortunately, we tend to make the wrong choice pretty often."

Beth wrinkled her eye brows and still looked puzzled. "But if He is an all-knowing God, didn't he know all along that we would screw it up?" she asked.

Knox nodded, "Sure He did, but doesn't a parent always know that if they give their teen-aged kid the keys to the car and keys to the house, that their son or daughter is eventually going to make a mistake? Of course they do. But the parent has to give the child some freedom so they can eventually learn from those mistakes. If God didn't give us a choice, we would be enslaved; not free to choose. He gives us the chance to either choose wisely, or choose poorly. And when we make bad choices, we can learn from those mistakes."

Beth seemed to understand. "Hmm, I guess I never thought of it that way."

The two agents held hands and took in their surroundings. Agent Knox wanted to ask Beth if she had thought anymore about their discussions about salvation, but he decided not to push the issue. He was enjoying the company, and he didn't want to take a chance at spoiling the mood. He didn't know exactly where she was spiritually, but he knew she had not truly given her heart to God – not yet. What he did know was that he was falling in love. Beth White had everything he'd ever wanted in a girl. He loved the fact that she was intelligent, beautiful, strong, and athletic. He also loved getting to work with her. At first he thought it might complicate things at work, but so far nothing had happened at work to cause any awkwardness. He didn't know that she saw him as the ideal man to have as a husband and start a family. He also didn't know that Beth was wrestling with her beliefs. For the past few months, Beth White had come to a point in her life where she had this overwhelming urge to know more about God. She wanted to know more, because she was fascinated, but she still wasn't quite ready to take the plunge. It was as if she wanted God to give her as much evidence as possible that He was who He said He was – and then she would decide whether to become a true believer or not.

When they took their eyes off the breath-taking view and looked at each other, none of that mattered. The two investigators were not law enforcement agents at that moment. They both glanced around the observation deck and noticed that there were not that many tourists around. Knox gave Beth a knowing smile. She returned the smile with a slight blush in her cheeks, and then she surprised him as she pulled him down to her. Their lips were drawn together, and Knox embraced her with a hug that would have protected her from anything. For a fleeting moment, things like assassins, the military, outside agencies, crime scenes, and religion didn't matter to them. For that moment they had each other – and that was enough.

****

The three agents had checked into a condo in a high-rise hotel right in the heart of downtown New York. It had three small bedrooms, a small kitchen, and a living room that opened out onto a small balcony. Malik was leaning against the railing as Knox poured a glass of wine for him and Beth. Once he poured the two glasses of wine, he broke out a large plastic cup with ice and filled it with Coca-Cola.

Malik was curious and asked, "Agent Knox – you don't drink wine?"

Knox laughed and said, "No sir – can't stand the stuff. But I thought Muslims couldn't drink wine?"

Malik shook his head, "Well I told you I am not the most devout Muslim."

"In that case, you and Beth go right ahead; I know she likes it."

Malik nodded and held up his wine glass; "Fine by me, but let's have a toast just the same – Here's to finding our assassin."

Knox and Beth held their glasses up and tapped the rims with Malik's glass. Then they all turned their drinks back.

Knox asked, "So gang – what's our next step. You said yourself, Malik, that we needed the assassin to kill again. Well, he helped us out. I know we definitely need to keep following the CIA angle. But how?"

Beth answered, "Well I say we try to run down as much information as we can on Robert Brady. He may be dead, but it might lead us to someone else. Does anybody have any other suggestions?"

Knox and Malik both shook their heads, and Knox spoke up, "Okay – Malik, see if you can find out what Brady looked like…maybe our guy will be a big fan and look similar. Beth, see if you can find out who he spent his time with besides his family. I already know what I will be doing – brainstorming with McCoy tomorrow about how to handle the coming media storm."

He chugged the rest of his coke, then he made a great yawn that sounded like a bear roaring as he reached his arms to the ceiling. "You guys stay up as long as you like, but I am beat. We probably have a long day ahead of us, so I'm turning in."

Malik looked surprised, and asked, "Really Knox? You just downed about 16 ounces of coke. You're gonna try to sleep now?"

He just watched the back of Knox's head as he nodded and walked away to his bedroom. "Yep; not gonna try though. I told you – I'm tired. Good night." He stopped next to Beth, gave her a small peck on the lips, and headed to bed.

Malik looked at Beth as she joined him at the railing. She leaned on it, and he asked her, "You're not going to join him?" Beth just chuckled, then shook her head and shrugged. "Trust me – I've been trying to get in that man's bed for a month now. But he always just says 'not yet'. Man's chastity belt is tighter than Maid Miriam's!"

Malik almost spit out his wine as he was taking another swig.

She laughed again, and said, "What? I'm serious – that man is so set in his ways, and so stuck on his rules...but I think that is what I love about him."

Malik turned to face the city lights and horns beeping down below. "Knox is a man of strong convictions, isn't he?" he asked.

"He's the most moral law man I've ever met. I guess he reminds me of my dad, except my dad is Catholic and was in the military," said Beth. Malik replied, "So there's a difference between Catholics and what Knox believes?" Beth nodded, but answered him, "Yes, that's what John would say – but you'll have to get him to explain it to you. He's the son of a preacher man; not me." Malik stood there in silence for a bit.

Beth broke the quiet moment. "So tell me, Inspector...what makes Muslim terrorists do what they do?"

Malik put his back to the rail and faced Beth. "Please, just call me Malik. I think we're definitely past formality."

Beth shook her head and said, "Not being formal; think of it as my pet name for you; I just like saying the word – *Inspector.*"

Malik just grinned and shook his head. He started to answer her question. "Beth, the terrorists are a lot like the assassin, or even Agent Knox. They are driven by strong convictions. They think they are doing what is right; according to their beliefs. They take the word jihad literally and turn it into something that Muhammad did not intend. The Prophet meant an inward spiritual struggle when he said in the Quran that all Muslims must fight a jihad at some point in their life. It translates to Holy War. But Muhammad meant the inward struggle with choosing to follow Allah, or choosing one's own path."

Beth pondered over what Malik said. She could see that he was a good man. She knew that John and the *Inspector* had their differences, but they were both good men with strong convictions. She wondered if they could capture this killer. She wondered if John and Malik could use their similarities to their advantage. They were both smart men, and they were definitely after the same thing – a closed case. But Beth had other thoughts pulling at her heart strings. She was thinking about what Knox had told her at the Empire State Building. She thought about the words she had read in the Bible at the last hotel.

She was lost in thought when Malik waved a hand in front of her; "Hello – Beth?" he said. She shook her head back to the present and told Malik, "Well, Inspector – I am practically falling asleep standing up. I think I will call it a night as well."

She put her empty wine glass down and pat Malik on the shoulder, then went to her bedroom. She didn't even wait to hear him tell her to have a good night sleep; she was guided by a strange yearning to know more about what Knox had said. She went in the bedroom and shut her door. She stripped down to nothing but panties and a t-shirt. She pulled back the covers, but turned on the lamp on the nightstand. She opened the drawer and there was another Gideon's Bible – identical to the one she read in Virginia. She got partially under the covers, but stacked the pillows on the bed behind her so she could sit up and read. She opened up to the back of the book and looked in its concordance. She found a good place to start, and she turned several pages and found her page. She began reading, and read well into the night. Perhaps

Malik was right; everyone needs to fight their own personal jihad once in their life.

PART TWO

New York Times
Who is the Jesus Assassin?

Christians are supposed to be nice, right? Well someone out there was not very nice yesterday morning when they decided to sneak into the set of the Today Show, go back to a dressing room, and assassinate Imam Kareem Hassad and his bodyguard. Through an indeterminate number of leaks to the internet, photos of the two dead men surfaced through Facebook for hours yesterday before finally being taken down by the site. But those images were up long enough to burn the atrocity into the minds of viewers. The killer left two golden crosses at the scene. One was so violently placed into the forehead of the bodyguard, one has to wonder what the killer was trying to say. Kareem Hassad was the most peaceful Muslim in this city, and he was taken out of this world with extreme prejudice. Authorities have not commented on the exact cause of death, but one can guess by the position of the Imam's head in the Facebook photo that his neck was probably broken. What kind of person breaks a holy man's neck? An evil person – that's who.

The Christians like to consider themselves righteous. Well where was the righteousness in these murders? A peaceful man who was looked upon as a spiritual leader for many, and the man charged with his safety, were slain senselessly – conveniently before a guest appearance on a show on which the Imam was going to speak to the unfairness of the display of – yes – none other than a Christian cross at the 9/11 Memorial Museum. Christians like to say that the Muslims support a violent religion. They like to point out all the radical Muslims over in the Middle East. I for one am sick of the Christians and their Holier than Thou attitudes. It's that attitude that led to this violent criminal. The Christians will want to deny this killer as one of their own; they will call him radical, and say that he is not what Christ is all about. They might be right; but what's the point of allowing one symbol of Christianity to remain standing to memorialize the death and honor of those lost on 9/11 – when that same symbol was used to mark two innocent people for death? Who does this killer think they are? What gives them the right to take life at will, and then leave their own holy symbol to justify their actions? Was it someone that follows Jesus? If the symbol is any clue, than yes. Who are you, oh killer of holy men? Who are you, oh carrier of the cross? Authorities are not being real clear as to any evidence you may have or have not left at the scene, but they don't have a name for you yet. Well I do…and until you are caught and we can put a face with a name – I dub thee…the Jesus Assassin.

This editorial was written by local editor and chief politics and religion correspondent, Jim Marshall. Jim is the author of *Atheism Weekly*, and has a weekly column in the Times. If you have any comments or questions, please contact Jim at Marshall@NYTIMES.org.

****

"Un-freaking-believable!" Knox yelled as he slammed the newspaper on the small kitchen table and then kept his index finger pointed at the headline for Malik and Agent White to see. "Who puts an editorial on the front page of the newspaper, anyway?" Knox continued in frustration.

Beth had scanned the article quickly and got the gist of it before picking up the paper and passing it to Malik to read. All three of them stood there as Malik held the paper up and read the article. When he finished, he put the paper back down on the table and added, "Well, Knox my friend – controversy sells. That right there is about as controversial as it gets." Knox agreed.

"Well we can definitely agree on that point. But come on – even the Muslims accept Jesus as a holy man. No Muslim would ever put those two words together…Jesus Assassin – Please!"

Malik said, "Actually we Muslims see Jesus as the second greatest prophet, second only to Muhammad."

"My point is – you know he was never a killer. This article does nothing but mock Christians; all on account of one crazy man," Knox finished.

Beth chimed in, "Keep in mind, the author writes a weekly column for atheists. He isn't trying to win Christian friends over, Honey – I mean John."

She blushed a little as Malik just smiled, and Knox rolled his eyes. "I don't care if he writes for Satan, Beth. This news article was totally unnecessary, and the assassin will either go into hiding because of it, or accelerate his behavior. In the meantime, I am going to have to work with McCoy on making sure the rest of the case doesn't break open to public knowledge."

Malik replied, "Well, we can't lose either way…except for the chance of not being able to catch up to him. But if he stops killing, no more Imams die. If he accelerates the killing, we'll at least be on his trail soon." Knox grimaced, and said, "That's not helping, Malik."

They were all eating breakfast that they ordered from room service. Knox had a plate of three fried eggs, bacon, and two waffles. Malik ordered two poached eggs and some sausage and toast. Beth just had a bagel with some cream cheese and a banana. Malik sat down next to Knox and poured himself some orange juice. He took another look at the news article. He thought about how readers would be reading it like it was going out of style because of the cord it would strike with so many non-Christians. He thought of just how much attention the so-called Jesus Assassin was going to get from such an article. He figured this assassin would keep tabs on the public's reaction to his latest accomplishment. Then a light bulb came on in his head.

"What if we could use the newspaper to our advantage? What if we could bring a couple of things to light in some separate, anonymous letters to the editor? I think we could tempt the assassin to somehow get careless in his next act."

Beth and Knox looked at each other, and Knox said, "You know – you might be on to something. You gonna write this editorial?"

Malik shook his head. "No, I don't think I have the right background. I was thinking of someone a little more…Christian."

****

The three agents had gone their separate ways; Knox had stayed in the condo to have a video conference with Special Agent in Charge, Agent McCoy; Agent White had gone to a local café to use the Wi-Fi to research the structure of the Navy SEALS and how to determine who was in the SEALs with Brady; and Malik went to the library to surf the internet for anything remotely close to a photograph of a Chief Petty Officer Robert C. Brady. Knox was sitting on the couch in the living room at the hotel, with his laptop opened up and his boss calling in on a video chat through a secure site.

SAC Jones McCoy's face filled the screen on Knox's monitor. "Knox, my lad – seems like you've had an eventful visit to the Big Apple."

Knox just nodded. "Sir – I am not sure what steps you want to take, but I thought you might need me since I am heading this investigation," Agent Knox began.

The SAC listened, then replied, "Knox, this thing has already gone viral. Every country with internet access is going to know about the New York City murder. If we can keep the other two killings out of the press - that would be key."

"Sir, do you mean you need me to speak with the investigators of the other agencies involved?" Knox asked.

The SAC nodded on the screen and responded, "That's right. I know they will probably already know this, but it's imperative that we keep some kind of international incident from occurring by keeping the other details of the other assassinations out of the news."

"I'll get right on it, sir," Knox answered. McCoy went on, "So what else is in the works? I see your other two cohorts aren't in the room with you." Knox affirmed the SAC and said, "Sir, Malik had an idea. I am sure you read the big headline on the New York Times, right? Well, we were going to write some letters to the editor, regarding the religion and politics section – and we were going to give the assassin a follower. We thought maybe if the killer knows someone is there for him – in a sense – that we could eventually draw him out; maybe massage his ego a little bit."

"That's not a bad idea, John. Who thought of that again…Inspector Sharif?" McCoy asked. Knox nodded again and added, "Yes sir. Inspector Sharif – Malik – has been a huge help on this case. I know we are still stuck in a rut, but I feel like it is only a matter of time before we find another lead, and Malik has been an essential part of that. Honestly, sir – he wouldn't make a bad federal agent."

"Yes, well, I'm sure he is interesting to work with. Your differences in background haven't been an issue, I assume?" the SAC interjected.

"No, sir. I mean we've had our share of miscommunication, but for the most part, we've gotten along pretty well – all things considered," Knox answered.

"See to it that it stays that way, John. Now get to work on contacting those other folks; make sure they understand to keep a lid on everything – I mean everything!" his boss finished. Knox answered him one last time before terminating the connection, "Don't worry sir; consider it done." "Let me know where you get with the letter to the newspaper," – and then McCoy ended the connection.

****

Beth walked on the sidewalk, scanning her surroundings to make sure she didn't trip while at the same time picking up the sense that someone was following her. She casually walked over to a street vendor and bought a magazine; as she was about to pay she tried to glance over her shoulder and to her left and right to see if she could spot anyone suspicious. Seeing nobody that looked out of the ordinary or ducking for cover, she finished paying the vendor and moved on. She came to the Starbuck's she had seen earlier the previous day and knew they'd have Wi-Fi. She walked up to the counter and ordered a Tall Mochaccino Frappe. She picked her drink up and paid for it, and headed to a small wooden high table in the corner and sat down.

Shortly after she walked in, a tall slender man wearing sunglasses walked in behind her. He was just your average middle-class, Arab-American male –

wearing a collared Under Armor shirt and some 5-11's. He was about 6 feet, 1 inch; average frame (but exceptionally fit) – with absolutely nothing out-of-the-ordinary about him; except for the fact that ordinary people don't just randomly pick FBI agents to follow around and stalk, just to see what they are up to. Agent White was totally oblivious to this fact, and she did not even pay attention to the man when he entered. He ordered a drink and a pastry and walked over to the far corner on the other side of the partition that surrounded part of the section in which Beth was sitting. Beth had made the mistake of sitting with her back to the corner, even though she was facing the door to see people coming in. She had already booted up her laptop, and was peering at the screen when the stranger walked in; she might as well have had her head in a book.

The stranger sat in the background and pretended to be playing on his phone as he watched Agent White pull up information on her web browser. Beth was watching the screen, and as soon as she had the search engine open, she typed in *Navy SEALS* in the search box. She read through pages of information on the training process of the SEALs, and who gets chosen or recommended to try to cut it as a SEAL. She read about the number of teams there were available on any given day. She read some pages that were just misinformation entered by some wannabe on Wikipedia. She tried to find out just about everything there was to know about the Navy SEALs that had ever been printed on the internet, and she made brief notes along the way. The stranger sitting behind her couldn't make out any of her notes, but he was sitting close enough to see what kind of websites she was pulling up. Although the FBI agent didn't give away exactly what her next steps might be, the stranger had enough information to know that the agents might know more than they had let on with the Colonel back at Fort Benning. He made sure that the FBI agent continued to be absorbed in her work, and finished his coffee. He got up from his small table and walked out of the Starbuck's.

The stranger walked around the corner of the next block and then dialed a number. It was a direct line to CIA Director Marks. The Bostonian answered after the first ring. The stranger spoke immediately; he knew the Director needed no identification – his caller ID would have told him who it was, and very few people had the Director's direct line.

Marks answered, "Marks…what did you find?"

The stranger replied, "You may have a problem with your asset. No definitive proof they even know what he looks like, or that he is the one behind these dead Muslims. But the FBI is definitely interested."

Director Marks replied, "Well – we can't address the problem, if it is a problem, just yet. We have to put the Activist to work on another assignment that just came up. Forget the agents for now; your new target is the Activist. Tail him, and pack your bags; you'll be traveling. Find out whatever he finds out, and do not be discovered. We'll test his innocence while observing him on the mission."

The man who had descended from an ancient order of killers nodded on his end as he replied, "Understood. Where can I expect to travel?" Marks didn't waste any time as he shot back, "Baghdad – the capital of Al Qaeda."

****

Knox sat down on the sofa with the laptop and opened up a blank Word document. He thought for a second on how he was going to begin his editorial letter. He thought of how he could praise the actions of the assassin without putting too much controversial information that may discourage the paper from even printing the letter. Once he thought he had his thoughts in order, he began to type:

Dear Editor,

My name is none of your concern. However, the fate of our country should be. How you can sit there and insult Christianity just because of one man's actions is beyond me. You act like there is some huge cosmic communication link that lets all Christians know what the other is doing, and that they can control what one man does. And who says that this one man is so flawed in his judgment, anyway? His methods are definitely questionable – but are his motives? Islam is quickly showing its true colors around the world, and frankly I think it is about time the shoe was on the other foot. No, I don't think we should be selecting random targets of the Muslim religion. But I do believe we need to send someone over to that Al Qaeda nation they are building over there in Baghdad to show them who's boss. So how about you stop trying to pick fights with the Christians who are here at home, and concentrate your bashing on the real enemy plotting to invade our shores and destroy our country. And by the way, this title you gave the killer – the Jesus Assassin; it is offensive. I can speak for many church-goers when I say that those two words should NOT be together. As for the cross used as a memorial for the fallen from 9/11…it stays! You atheists and anybody else don't have to like it, but you better accept it. One man's misguided embrace of a symbol does not mean the symbol's true meaning is any different from its original intentions. Jesus died on a cross and rose three days later. He is our only hope. That's the Truth, whether you believe it or not. So, Mr. Editor –

don't bad mouth our cross, and don't bad-mouth Christians. And Mr. Assassin...how about going over to the Middle East and taking care of business.

Sincerely,

A Concerned Christian

Knox read over his letter and decided it didn't link him or his identity to the writing in any obvious ways, unless of course the reader was someone like Beth White, who knew him like a book. He decided he was satisfied and saved the file. He attached the file to an e-mail and sent it to the editor's address that had been offered in the New York Times article. He'd have to wait and see if the editor had enough guts to print it.

Shenandoah Valley, Virginia
Brady's Cabin

Entry #30 – May 1, 2016

 Lord, forgive me for not having the foresight to see the sacrilege that would be spewed from the national media. They are calling me the Jesus Assassin after my latest mission was accomplished. Unfortunately, Father, I took a chance by going after the Imam right before he was in the national spotlight; I did not think about certain writers' opinions of my work. I was simply trying to make the work I am doing known to Christians and Muslims alike; for the Christians I want to be a sign of hope, but for the Muslims I hope to be heralding their doom. I at least know I am not alone in my fight for you, Lord. The New York Times put a response letter in the editorial section today. The response was from a fellow Christian. Thank you for further assurance for what I am doing. I pray you sway others to your side, Lord. I intend to stay the course. I have dispatched three of your enemies now. Please stay with me and protect me long enough God, so I can carry out my mission and take out the last nine. Show me the way to the next enemy, and I will quickly deliver him to the appropriate place. Thank you again for all your guidance.

Amen

The activist finished his journal entry and put it away under the coffee table. He got up and left the screen porch. He walked out to his habitat shelter for the snakes. He grabbed several vials of the Black Mamba venom, and then he walked around to the back of the cabin. He had another shed in the back yard where he worked on his tactical gear and weapons. He had been working on applications for the venom with his crossbow. He had set a target up approximately 40 yards away. The target was made of a special foam that would indicate whether the tip of the crossbow bolt expended its poison into the target or not. The activist attached a modified head to the end of one of the crossbow bolts; it was fully loaded with concentrated Black Mamba venom. He primed the crossbow and readied it to fire. He placed the bolt into its slot and drew back the bow until it made a small click. He then said a short prayer; extracting the venom was a tricky procedure, so every bolt head was as valuable as gold. He had to make this shot count.

Once he loaded the bolt, he put the stock of the crossbow up to his shoulder just like he would a rifle. His crossbow had a high-tech scope with a laser site, so his chances of missing his target were slim to none. He aimed down the top of the crossbow, and he saw the bull's eye on the target down range. He focused on the site picture in his scope and lined the crosshairs up with the center of the bull's eye, and squeezed the trigger. He wasn't too concerned about missing the shot; he was pretty sure of his accuracy due to years of training with virtually every hand-held weapon known to man. He was more concerned with the effective delivery of the venom from the new bolt heads. As soon as he squeezed the trigger, he paused just long enough with the crossbow aimed down range as if he was following his shot with his eyes, even though no human eye could keep pace with a crossbow bolt fired from a Tenpoint Stealth SS crossbow. He ran down to the target and saw to no surprise that the bolt hit close to the center of the bull's eye. But what he was looking for was a yellow stain to expand directly outward from the tip of the bolt – and after he removed the bolt, that is exactly what he found. The small improvised bolt head had a small explosive mechanism inside its tip that was designed to force the liquid contained inside it to explode forth in a blast cone due to a pressurized blast of air caused from the impact at the front of the bolt. The internal damage to a living body would be devastating.

The activist's pager went off in the holster he was wearing on his belt. He picked it up and looked at the small green screen. The small digital message that flashed across the screen simply told him to report to Andrews Air Force Base in Maryland by eighteen hundred hours that evening. That gave the activist about four hours to get his duffle bag packed, get a couple hours' sleep, and pick up his 'little black bag' from the office at Langley. The activist got a few last minute things together and secured his tool shed with a Fortress padlock. He didn't know where he was going just yet, but he was sure they would brief him at the base. He got an extra sidearm pistol out of the cabin before he headed down the road to Andrews. He would have to make a pit stop at his Langley office for his 'Activity Gear'. The activist didn't know it, but in about twenty-four hours, he was going to infiltrate the new inner sanctum of Al Qaeda.

Andrews Air Force Base
Hangar 31

The activist noticed the normal Delta Force team sitting in the first two rows of metal chairs that had been set up for a mission briefing before the Activity team left for Baghdad. There was an AC-130 parked behind the chairs with its ramp down. Three men who looked to the activist like Air Force pilots were standing at the foot of the ramp, and there was an Army Major waiting to address everyone seated in the chairs. The activist was in a seat on the back row, in his token black outfit, with his hood pulled over his head. In all the nine months the Delta Force team had been working with the activist, none of them had seen his whole face. He was a character shrouded in mystery, and they left him alone for the most part – except for those times when the best way to cope with violence around them was meaningless banter.

The Major was Major Thomas Dozier – a long time special-forces hero, whose very reputation preceded him everywhere he went in the corridors of the military. He was a short, stocky but well-built fellow. He had a friendly countenance when he looked his men in the eyes, but that was only meant to fool those that wanted to test him. Underneath the southern gentleman and country niceness was a mean-as-a-snake, ornery Tasmanian devil that happened to have a 4th degree black belt in everything from Muay Thai to Tae Kwon Do. His physical discipline and experience in hand-to-hand combat is what got him this far in his career, and really what made him famous among his men. The Major cleared his throat to make sure his audience was listening.

He spoke with a southern drawl mixed with a bit of a country accent, "Gentlemen, I know this is different from the norm, and that you haven't received any intel in advance on this mission. The reason for that was to make sure there were no leaks about this mission; so the enemy wouldn't have time to prepare," he began.

"We have intelligence that suggests a very cunning Al Qaeda terrorist cell has been carrying out secret meetings right in the heart of the civilian population. This cell is rumored to have several heavy hitters as its local members – one Aziz al-Zawari, who is said to be the guy calling the shots for this particular cell. We also have reason to believe that they have intentionally surrounded themselves with Iraqis who are very opposed to jihad. The cell members pretend to love the West during the day, but then plan our destruction at night. Once you are on the ground at one of our outlying air force bases over there, you will wait for confirmation of all of this information from the activist."

The Major looked at the activist on the back row. He then started speaking directly to him; "You will go in by cover of darkness, stealth Black Hawk, almost as soon as you land in Iraq. We need you to find out where these meetings are taking place, and which big name targets are present. Text what you find out to a pre-programmed number in this satellite phone. Be careful; these guys are supposed to be tougher than they appear at first glance."

He tossed the activist a small, black, sliding smart phone. The activist caught it, slid the top screen back to reveal a small keypad underneath, then closed it and stuffed it in one of his many pockets.

The major finished addressing the whole group, "Once details have been confirmed, you'll receive new orders, and you will be prepared to infiltrate the terrorist cell despite the immediate presence of civilians. I'm not going to lie to you men; this could end up being a very difficult mission; depending on what the activist finds and when he finds it. You will have to use absolute discipline when it comes to determining whether you are about to shoot a civilian, or a terrorist. But listen up gents – if you nail some of the bastards that we think are located in the neighborhood, you will have made a major dent in Al Qaeda's new hold on Baghdad. Now I'll be goin' with you over there for the de-briefing, but of course you know this old codger can't hang with you young scrappers in the field anymore. Good luck to each of you. That is all men – carry on." He watched the men all stand up and come to attention, and he snapped a genuinely sharp and crisp salute to the other men; they all returned in kind.

****

Thirty minutes later, they were all airborne; two pilots and a navigator up in the front of the plane, and everyone else was in the back. Although they didn't expect to have to use the large gun on board (An M102 Howitzer mounted in the side of the plane), three of the guys on board could use the weapon in their sleep if the time came where it was necessary to take out enemy targets below. In the meantime, everyone had gotten settled in their jump seats and began accepting the normal clatter and rattle of the walls as they approached 30,000 feet before crossing the Atlantic. Casual conversation was taking place in the cockpit of the gunship.

"So, you're a new navigator around this plane; we're used to Senior Airman Phillips. What brings you aboard the Hercules?" the pilot asked the navigator seated behind the pilot and co-pilot seats.

The new face in the cockpit smiled and responded, "Name's Smith...Carey Smith, Sir. I am just following orders; you know, when your Captain tells you that you need experience being closer to the black operations and tells you to meet a certain plane at a certain base – you do what the man says. So here I am."

The pilot just nodded. He added in a joking tone, "Well just don't get us lost. I am not sure I know where to turn once we cross 'the pond'."

The navigator laughed in return and then waved off the comment. "Well, if we get lost, I can always give you directions to the best town to find some good Mediterranean food," the navigator said sarcastically.

Little did the two pilots know that the man giving them small changes in headings along the way was not a navigator at all. Although the man had experience navigating in several large aircraft in his past, that was not the man's true mission on this flight. "First Sergeant Carey Smith" was planted on the flight crew by none other than CIA Director Marks. He was the Arbiter. He was the same Arabic-American male that had followed Agent White back in New York. The Arbiter was sent to keep tabs on the activist, and his mission started as soon as the activist had been seen sitting outside the Hercules. So far he had seen nothing out of the norm. As soon as they landed outside Baghdad, things might pick up. The Arbiter was there to make sure that the activist was not a rogue agent. The Arbiter was also going to 'fix' the problem if he discovered otherwise.

In the meantime he would play the part of navigator. He and the two pilots told cockpit stories, and shared little anecdotes about family back home. Of course it was all a lie for the Arbiter; his lifestyle and occupation would not coincide with family life, but the pilots didn't need to know any of that. He was strictly acting out his assigned part, and playing it well. By the time they were about to re-fuel at an air force base in France, he fit right in with the crew. All the while the activist sat in the back of the plane with the Delta Force soldiers; shaking, rattling, and flying along. The activist didn't know it yet, but he was about to let someone else in on his little mission for God.

****

The stealth helicopter had dropped him down a climbing rope over the heart of the largest residential area in Baghdad. It was two-thirty in the morning, and the neighborhood appeared to be in a state of rest. The houses and apartment buildings stacked up around each other in large city blocks, and all the buildings were made of white and tan brick and concrete. It was a mostly middle-class neighborhood, but the equivalent of a lower-class area back in the United States. The only crime in these areas was petty theft, auto-theft, and of course crimes associated with terrorism (you know – kidnapping, murder, torture, etc.); but most of that stuff happened in daylight hours. The activist scanned his surroundings as the Blackhawk quietly flew away after he dropped off the rope onto the roof of a three story apartment building. It was strange how the entire city seemed to be like a ghost town late at night. The helicopter had dropped him in an area that intelligence resources had indicated some of the top dogs in Al Qaeda were hiding.

It was said that they were pretending to be Iraqis who embraced western culture, and this neighborhood was supposed to be the home of the biggest American-wannabes. The activist's main target was a high ranking Al-Qaeda leader by the name of Aziz al-Zawari. There were several other minor terrorists that had been rumored to be here, but Al-Zawari was the main guy that had caught the attention of CIA informants. Al-Zawari was known to be a big fan of American sports, so any sports team logos in the middle of Baghdad might be a good indicator of his location. The first thing the activist was going to look for were signs of obvious Americana.

There was an old rusted, miserable excuse for a ladder that had small handrails that came up over the ledge of the roof. The activist made his way over to it and climbed down to the ground. He stepped off the ladder into a dark alley between the apartment building and what appeared to be the back entrances to several small housing units. There were short little walkways that led up to low hanging archways made of brick, which covered the entries into small courtyards and patios. The activist had never seen this side of Middle-eastern life; it was a hidden treasure among the other old-fashioned desert buildings. The first one he came to, he slowly crept under the archway and into a courtyard with a small fountain and goldfish pond. There were signs of western influence in the shape of the patio furniture, as well as several small bits of yard art. There were some interesting pieces of pottery in the shape of flamingoes and eagles, and a patio table and chairs, with an umbrella. There was also a small tricycle parked over near a set of sliding doors that marked entry to the house.

The activist moved on to several others of similar character and scenery. As he got further down the alley after seeing several pieces of property that looked the same, he heard a smattering of voices two more houses down. He kept his back against the outer walls of the houses, and quickly slipped across the next two yard entries covered with archways. As he slowly edged his way across the wall of the last house, he could hear the clear sounds of an American football game. Although he found that to be a real head scratcher, he kept going. When he thought he was close enough, he slowly peeked his head around the last entry way. To his surprise there were several Iraqis sitting around a large patio table, drinking beers. They were at least speaking some form of Arabic, so they weren't totally Americanized…but this scene let the activist know he was probably in the right vicinity. Although he figured the men gathering in that particular backyard may just be trying to emulate neighborhood life in America, the activist decided to explore more of the immediate area. The activist thought he probably wouldn't be able to send a confirmation to Delta Force until he had positive ID of at least one of the terrorist targets during the day, but he thought he might try to find other examples of the Iraqi terrorists, maybe trying a little too hard to be 'Westerners'.

He could see four Iraqi men in the courtyard, and there was a big screen TV sitting outside, with a cord running back into the house through a sliding back door. One of the men went back in through the door, probably to get another cold beer. The other men seemed to be remotely interested in what was obviously a replay of an NFL game on the TV. The activist knew he could take all four men out, but they didn't come across as the terrorist-type. He quickly slid across the entrance below the archway, and the other three men didn't even notice. He went around to the side of the wall and found another ladder that went to the roof of the house. He climbed the ladder to the roof and found a small storage house with a water heater, the connected pipes running out of the storage house and down through a hole in the roof. He could only assume the pipes ran down into a bathroom or laundry room of some sort on the floor underneath.

He looked over the edge of another side of the roof, and saw a window to whatever room was under the water heater. He took the black rope that he always wore around one of his shoulders and tied it around the water heater. He held on tight as he hung over the side and unraveled several loops of the climbing rope, and then he lowered himself down the wall by repelling down beside the window. He held on with one hand, and used the other to test the window. He pulled up on the bottom, and it slid open. He pushed it the rest of the way up and shimmied with his feet down past the window. He grabbed on to the bottom ledge of the window and pulled himself up and into a small bathroom. The bathroom had a southwestern motif, as in southwestern United States. There were pictures of cow skulls and canyons on the wall. The activist was really starting to feel like he had stepped into the twilight zone.

The activist could hear the faint sounds of the TV out on the patio downstairs, and a couple of voices laughing, probably belonging to a couple of men who were getting more drunk by the minute as they enjoyed the American custom of drinking beer and watching football. The activist made his way out of the bathroom and into a hallway. The hallway was dark because none of the rooms upstairs seemed to have their lights on. The activist slipped on his night vision shades and set them to the best lighting. There were three doors along the wall on the right before coming to a set of steps that led downstairs. The activist decided to enter the first door on the right. When he slowly pushed the door opened, to his relief, it didn't make any loud creaking noises. He looked into the room and noticed large pictures on the wall. He carefully walked all the way into the room and then pulled the door closed behind him. He could tell through his night vision that the pictures on the wall were large maps. He took a closer look and realized they were maps of Texas. There were several small towns near the border between Texas and Mexico that were circled. There were also long lines of highway highlighted on the maps that followed all the way to the interstate system. In the middle of the room was a ping pong table. The activist had walked into some sort of map room that doubled as the terrorists' rec room.

On the table was a single American newspaper – a copy of the USA Today. The headline on the front had a big red star that had been drawn there to emphasize the importance of the article; it read *Top Muslim Brotherhood Imams to Meet in NY to Address the UN*. The activist read on to discover that the imams of the largest mosques in Yemen and Saudi Arabia were the men selected to speak to the UN. They were set to meet with the UN within the next few weeks. The article said that the imams wanted the United Nations to play an active role in capturing this Jesus Assassin that had now been confirmed to have killed three of their Muslim brothers. The activist had stumbled onto his next two targets for his mission, and never even would have had to come to Iraq to discover the information. He took the front page of the paper, folded it into a neat little square, and tucked it away into one of his pockets. However, he still had a mission to finish now. After all, his country needed him just as God needed him.

The activist still needed to locate their main target. He had a good feeling that al-Zawari was downstairs watching football, but he had to make visual confirmation before summoning the cavalry. He eased his way out of the bedroom and back into the hallway. He thought he would snoop around a little more since the men downstairs seemed so distracted. He went into the next room just as quietly and closed the door behind him. This time he stumbled into a major cache of weapons and bomb making materials. The activist imagined this is where the terrorists kept all their weapons for defense stashed, in case their location was ever discovered and compromised. There were several boxes full of

AK-47s, hand grenades, and even some RPGs. The activist wrinkled up his nose as he caught the faint smell of some of the chemicals used to make explosives. He knew he would have to text the team of operatives soon; this was some seriously dangerous stuff, and these terrorists could not only be storing some of these things up to use against Americans back home, but also some of the soldiers that were still in and around locations in Iraq. The activist left the weapons room and still saw that the hallway was dark. He decided to by-pass the last door and get a closer look at the men downstairs. One of them had to be al-Zawari.

As he came close to the bottom of the steps, he could see one of the men outside through the back door. His face was a bright glare because of the activist's night vision glasses, and the reflection of light from the TV screen. The activist removed his night vision glasses, and immediately recognized the man as one of Al-Zawari's lieutenants. He had all the key players' faces committed to memory, and he knew this was one of the big fish. He quickly took out his satellite phone and slid the keypad open. He began texting: *ACTIVATING LOCATION SIGNAL UPON SENDING OF TEXT. AT LEAST FOUR TARGETS...REPEAT – AT LEAST FOUR TARGETS. HAVE NOT CONFIRMED AL-ZAWARI, BUT –*

Suddenly the activist was grabbed from behind, and before he knew it, a very sharp, very handy KABAR fighting knife was held to his throat. The assailant was very quick, and strong. He pulled back on the activist's head to expose more of his neck. The activist couldn't believe he let someone get the drop on him; it was the third door – he made the mistake of walking right past the third door in the hallway. But he hadn't lost his clarity of thought yet; he went ahead and hit the send button on the phone at the same time that he slowly raised his hands – all in the same motion. The attacker yelled down to the other men in Arabic, and suddenly the activist had three other men scrambling into the house to assist the large man who had him in a very tight chokehold. Before the activist re-considered whether or not he would resist, despite having a blade at his throat, the attacker's buddies all grabbed a limb, except for the one that his attacker had pinned up in the air as part of the chokehold.

The activist found himself being lifted off the steps, then carried upstairs back to the first room with the maps. The attacker's friends were much bigger than they appeared outside in the dim patio light. The men who had appeared to be so sluggish and drunk earlier were now thriving on a surge of adrenaline – and they knew what they were doing. They quickly forced the activist down into a chair near the ping pong table. Two men continued to hold his legs down, while Al-Zawari's lieutenant ran over to a small cabinet in the room and took out some duct tape. He quickly began taking the start of the tape off the roll, and then quickly began wrapping the activist's limbs and body into the chair. It had been executed so efficiently, it was obvious to the activist that these men had done this before. Horrible flashbacks of the video of his wife and daughter played in his mind as he realized the predicament he was in. The man who had held the knife to the activist's throat went over to the wall and turned the light on.

"Who are you? How did you get here, and who sent you?" the large Iraqi terrorist leader barked. It was heavily accented English, but the activist knew the speaker.

He knew he didn't stand a chance trying to fight the men holding him captive in the room now; not when he was completely taped to a chair and rendered pretty much immobile. But he also knew he had been able to get the message on the phone sent. All he had to do now was stall them; he sure hoped the Army's new stealth motorcycles were as fast and silent as he had heard the Delta Force guys brag about on the flight over. They had described the motorcycles as being fast like a crotch rocket, but quiet like a remote control car. The plan all along was for him to send confirmation of the target, and they would come riding into town like ghosts, do their thing, and take him with them when they go. In the meantime, he was in quite a pickle. Al-Zawari pulled the activist's hood back to reveal his white face and red hair.

His big green eyes met the eyes of the terrorist leader as he answered directly, "I was sent here to find you. The people I work for wanted to know if you'd be interested in buying some girl-scout cookies." That smart comment earned him a backhand slap across the face.

Al-Zawari glanced over at the ping pong table, and noticed a bright orange paddle. He set his KABAR down and snatched up the paddle in his right hand, and struck the activist hard across the face with a wicked backhand. The strike immediately opened up a cut across the bridge of the activist's nose.

The other terrorists in the room giggled and laughed, and one even had the nerve to make a comment in accented English, "Hit him again, Aziz; I think he said it tickled." The activist looked over at the man who just spoke and noticed his position in the room...closest to the fatal funnel and a prime first target for special-forces soldiers clearing a room. He smiled and spoke back, "You're first to go."

That earned him another solid backhand with the ping pong paddle. Al-Zawari was getting tired of playing games (except for his backhand; the activist was beginning to think he favored the backhand in ping pong). "I told you American – I want to know who sent you! There's never just one of you. You travel in packs like cock roaches when you come to our country. Where are the rest?"

The activist knew he needed to say anything he could think of for the next few minutes; he had to stall him until Delta Force came. As he had a brief moment of silence, he heard the sound he was waiting for…the sound of what seemed to be remote control cars coming to a stop outside. He noticed that none of the terrorists reacted. They must not have heard what he heard; but then again, they didn't know what stealth motorcycles were supposed to sound like. The activist knew better. With him knowing escape was close at hand, he couldn't help but talk a little smack.

"I tell you what, sports fans. Let's play a game. How about 'Who's the dumbest terrorist in the room'?" That earned him a forehand this time; good to know the terrorist leader was multi-talented.

By this point, the activist's face was looking pretty messed up, but he knew that if he could just get un-taped from the chair, he'd be alright. He just had to wait a little bit longer. Suddenly, a small metal cylinder fell in through the door and the lights were turned off. As soon as the cylinder hit the floor, it went off like the loudest cherry bomb in the world. Knowing that the Flash-Bang would temporarily de-pressurize the room, the activist held his breath and squinted his eyes at just the right moment. Delta Force excelled in what the military likes to refer to as 'violence of action'. As soon as the flash-bang went off in the room, the squad of soldiers clad in their body armor and night vision methodically came through the door one after the other, each double-tap of suppressed M-16's signifying one more for the good guys. The squad leader ran over to the activist and pulled his knife out as he set his rifle to the side.

He began cutting away at the duct tape, but couldn't resist a jab at the activist, "Well here we are once again – busting in to save your butt! You look like crap."

The activist rubbed his sore jaw and stammered, "Hey, at least I got them all in one place for you." He walked over to al-Zawari and took the ping pong paddle from his cold, dead hand.

He walked over to the funny man who enjoyed watching the activist's head get used as a ping pong ball, who of course was the first to get shot. "And for the winner of the 'Who's the dumbest terrorist in the room', you get the golden paddle." He reached down and put the paddle in his hand.

He signaled the squad leader to hold on, and he ripped two of the maps off the wall and folded them up and put them in his cargo pocket with the front page news article he had found earlier.

He looked up at the squad leader and gave him thumbs up; the leader spoke into his radio mic, "Ok team…that entrance was supreme, but we made a lot of noise, and better get the heck out of Dodge.

Main target was hit – I repeat…Main target was hit and is down. Leave the bodies, and let's ride!"

With that, the activist and the other soldiers quickly ran out the back patio into the alley. Several lights had been turned on in the neighborhood, but most of them were in the front of the buildings. Each Delta Force member picked up their bike and cranked it up quietly. Apparently, the folks at DARPA spent so much time working on the stealth technology and performance of the engines, they forgot to add a kick-stand.

The activist quickly climbed on the back of the squad leader's bike, and right before they left he whispered, "I always wanted to ride one of these." Although curious eyes saw the group leave, none of the other terrorist cell members in the area knew who they were, and didn't know quite how to respond. Without their leader, their organization would start to crumble – especially with US soldiers camped out nearby. The activist was proud to accomplish another mission; now he just had to make plans for the UN building.

****

A short time later, inside a hangar on an air force base at a non-disclosed location somewhere near Baghdad, the Delta Force Team was sitting down to de-brief the mission with Major Dozier. Since the mission was a success, the Major had invited the pilots and the navigator to sit in on the de-briefing. As people were in a hurry to get the meeting over with so they could get some shut-eye before heading back to the States in the late morning, the navigator bumped into the activist who was still wearing his black outfit. Although he had his hood drawn over his head once again, so as to conceal some of the punishment his face had taken while being interrogated, he looked up for a brief moment. The navigator, who unknown to the activist was the Arbiter, caught a quick glimpse of the activist's green eyes. The activist showed no expression, but shrugged off the glancing blow of the navigator's shoulder into his, and found a wooden seat on the back row of the several chairs set out for the small gathering. The navigator started to say 'Excuse me', but by the time he had the words on the tip of his tongue, the activist was already seated, and the Major was giving his customary throat clearing sound to get everyone's attention. 'First Sergeant Smith' quickly sat in a seat in the back corner as Major Dozier began. He was standing next to a large table with a map of Baghdad spread out before him.

"Fine, fine example of how to get things done, men! As you all know, what you are about to hear in this hangar stays in this hangar – but I want us all to get an understanding of what just happened so you can get a firm grasp of what it means for our combat theatre over here for the rest of our boys in desert cammies."

The Major pointed out the Squad Leader and briefly introduced him. "Gentlemen, this is Squad Leader, Captain Charlie Parson. Captain, what were the results of your team's little bike ride, Sir?"

The Captain piped in, "Sir, we eliminated the leader of the main al-Qaeda terrorist cell in Baghdad. He was killed with two gun shots to the head, and we left his body as a message for the other bad guys, just as the mission required." "Outstanding news, Captain. I understand you found something while you were infiltrating the house?"

The Captain shook his head, then pointed to the activist sitting in the back row. Then he added, "Not us – he did. Our asset located maps in a rec room upstairs in the house. I am not privy to what those maps entail as of yet, but he can probably show us." The Major motioned for the activist to approach. Although the Delta Force team knew he would sometimes joke around under pressure, nobody expected him to talk – and he did not disappoint. He walked up to the major and nodded, then took out some papers that had been folded several times from a large pocket on the right leg of his BDUs. He spread the maps out on the table, right over top the map of Baghdad. He waved his hands out over the maps as if to say 'Here you go', and walked back to his seat. Although nobody else noticed, 'First Sergeant Smith' noticed a separate, smaller folded piece of paper fall to the floor behind the activist as he sat down. The Major just nodded in acknowledgement of the activist's contribution, and told everyone that they were both maps of Texas.

The Major was ready to wrap things up, and he knew his men were tired. "Gentlemen, although I can only speculate as to what they were planning with these maps, I don't get paid enough to determine that. But what I do know is this; each person in here did their part today – and now al-Qaeda's influence here in Iraq will begin to crumble because of what you accomplished today. So good job, everybody! Now, y'all need to go get some R&R before we leave for home at eleven hundred hours later this morning…dismissed!"

As everyone got up to find their way to their barracks, some of the men got up to look at the maps before leaving the room. The Arbiter kept an eye on the activist and watched as he got up to walk out of the hangar. He waited until the activist was out of sight, and made sure nobody else was looking as he wondered over to where the activist had been sitting. He bent down and picked up the piece of newspaper that had been folded several times over. He walked around some crates stored in the hangar that hid him from view of the rest of the team as they were leaving. He unfolded the page and looked on with a puzzled face as he read the headlines and the first part of the article included on the title page. He folded the page back up following the same creases made by the activist. As he made his way to his bunk, he found a new sense of direction as he realized his next stop would be New York City; right after he was finished playing the part of navigator First Sergeant Carey Smith.

New York
Hotel Room at Holiday Inn

Malik was pacing back and forth outside on the porch outside the sliding glass door, talking on the phone with Chief Inspector Holcroft back in Belgium. There was nothing quite like listening to an angry Belgian on the phone.

"I want to know how you let it get to this point Sharif! This Jesus Assassin mania is going to make Interpol look bad!" He was shouting with his typical German accent.

Malik tried to reassure him. "Chief, we will reign him in using this media attention. Trust me, this guy Knox is one of the smoothest feds I have met over here. Give us time, and we'll have this assassin before you can say Belgian Waffle."

Malik thought by adding some humor to the conversation, it would lighten his boss's mood. He was wrong. "Don't get smart with me, Malik! I gave you the assignment because I trusted you to get the job done. The powers that be are breathing down my neck about this assassin. I don't care who you are working with – just get it done. Catch him soon, or I will have to pull you from the case."

With that Holcroft hung up on his end, and Malik was left standing there rubbing his temple. He walked back into the living room area of the hotel suite, and Agents Knox and White were sitting next to each other on the sofa waiting on him.

"So, trouble back home there, big fella?" Knox asked him. Malik smiled casually and said, "Oh, you heard that? Yeah, that was headquarters. My chief is none-too-thrilled about the media attention our case has received. You guys have any more luck?"

Knox went first, and told Malik that he had some luck speaking to the law enforcement powers-that-be in New York and Dearborn to keep a lid on the facts of their cases regarding dead imams in their cities. The press had already had a field day spreading flames on an already tumultuous war in religious philosophy between Christianity and Islam. News agencies like Al-Jazeera and others in the Middle East were excited to know and portray that the shoe was on the other foot for Christians now, who were so used to seeing the violence initiated by Muslims in different terrorist attacks around the world. So far, Knox had been able to stem the blood flow of ink on the pages of news across the country to only include the third assassination. If the assassin were seen as a serial killer, they might have a real religious panic on their hands.

He finished telling both his cohorts, "I'm just glad McCoy didn't want me to try to talk to your boss, too. From the look on your face, he might be a hard man to work for."

Malik nodded and answered, "Oh he is a hard man, alright. But Chief Holcroft knows what he's doing when it comes to running the show in Brussels. Make no mistake about it, he's just putting on the pressure because it's been put on him. He still has faith in me…or should I say us? Anyway, he was just hammering the point home. What about you, Beth? You get any ideas of where to go next with your look into the Navy? Because I couldn't find anything about Brady…not one single factoid or hint on the internet that the man ever existed."

Beth shook her head, "Nope, I thought maybe we could follow the enlisted trail, and I could find out who was in his class at the naval base near Chicago, at Naval Station in Great Lakes, Illinois. Came up empty like everyone else. Suddenly there is no record of Robert Brady ever being trained as a Navy man."

The three of them sat there and said nothing for a few minutes. Then Knox stood up and walked into their hotel room's tiny kitchen and opened the fridge. As he stood there and stared into the refrigerator, he spoke up, "This calls for a drink."

He took out a Coke and set it on the counter, then grabbed two bottles of beer and tossed each one to his partners. He sat back down next to Beth and twisted off the top to his soda, tipped the bottle back, and took a long swallow. The other two agents gave their beers a glance, and both shrugged their shoulders and followed suit.

Malik finally asked, "So where are we? Did anything ever pan out with your letter to the editor after our beloved Jesus Assassin debut?" Knox nodded and replied, "Well, they at least printed it. I don't know if it will make him want to stay his course or not, but it definitely rallied some folks to his cause. There have been several additional letters in response to what I wrote. No offense, Malik buddy – but a lot of Americans don't have a high opinion of Islam. Doesn't that bother you?"

Malik answered, "Sometimes it does. But I am settled with the fact that I am not like those evil men who committed such madness back in 2001. I can't blame those people who feel loss and anger; especially for not knowing everything there is to know about Islam."

Knox continued, "That's the truth; there is a big difference between true Muslims and the radicals we all hear and read about. I have known that for a while. But you still have to wonder about a religion started by just one man – and its very foundation all based on a book written by that one man."

Malik rebutted calmly, "Jesus was just one man – and look what happened from his teachings. And Islam was not started by one man, but by Allah himself after he saw that mankind was behaving like a spoiled teenager."

"Jesus was more than just one man, Malik; He was the Son of God," Knox added. Malik was about to come back with something else when his wrist watch started beeping. Glad for the interruption, Beth asked spryly, "What's the alarm for? Time for your beauty sleep?"

Malik smiled and said, "Nope." He then put his beer aside on the coffee table and went to the kitchen. He thoroughly washed his hands, and then began rubbing water over his face and forearms. He dried off and then walked to the glass door. He slipped off his shoes, and went out on the porch. He closed the door behind him, picked up a small *sajadah* that he had rolled up and placed on the small patio table. He faced the setting sun, and he began his ritual kneeling and standing and bowing in the required order.

Knox and White looked on from inside the hotel suite, and Knox said to Beth, "You've got to admire his devotion. Here we were just telling him how wrong his religion is, and he sticks to his guns in the middle of a debate and focuses on Allah."

Beth replied, "Um, you were the one telling him how wrong he is. I always just sit and listen. Although I'm coming around, you might want to cut him some slack. You and I both know he is nothing like the jihadists."

"I know Beth, but you didn't get to hear the rest of what I was going to ask him. What is more believable – a story about God that is inconsistent throughout because the core of its message changed with the mood of its writer, depending on what the writer was going through at the time…or a story about God that has stood the test of time, consistent throughout, despite being written by several men spread out over a thousand years?" Knox asked.

Beth had a puzzled look. "What do you mean about the Koran? Muhammad wrote the entire book?" Knox simply said, "Yep".

Agent White piped back, "So Muhammad wrote his message from God over a long period of time?" "Oh yeah," he replied. "Even devout Muslims will tell you it took him around twenty-two years. They will of course tell you that he didn't write it, but Allah himself wrote it."

Beth just nodded and said, "Oh – who knew?" Just about then, Malik walked back in from outside and slipped his shoes back on. "Sorry guys – I guess I should have excused myself. I told you I'm not devout – but I try to stick to my prayers during the day when I am not in public. I know I should be more consistent, but – well, like you said…not all Americans are comfortable seeing a Muslim praying."

Just then, Knox's cell phone rang. He picked up on the second ring and answered. "Knox here," he said. He sat there nodding his head several times, and kept saying, "Yes, sir." Finally when he hung up, he looked at Beth and Malik. "You guys read the paper yet? McCoy said we should take a peek."

Malik reached over to the coffee table and moved some of the pertinent papers and file folders that had found their way to just one more piece of furniture the agents could clutter with their work. He found the New York Times and spread it out. The front page told them what McCoy wanted them to know. *Imams from Saudi Arabia and Yemen to Speak to UN Tomorrow* were the words across the top of the page. "Well, gang – I guess we know where we'll be hanging out tomorrow," Knox said with sarcasm.

Beth responded, "You guys really think our man would attempt to take both imams out in the same place?" Malik added, "It does say they are presenting a case for the UN to assist in catching the Jesus Assassin. I don't think our killer needs a better reason."

****

A few hours later, Agent Knox laid there in bed engrossed in a crime novel, when a faint knock came to his bedroom door. Before he could say anything or get up to open the door, Beth quickly opened it just enough to slip her small frame through and pull it closed behind her. She started, "I couldn't sleep." She leaned back against the door briefly and pressed her palms against the door behind her as if to make sure nobody else would come in. That's when Knox noticed she was only wearing a very short t-shirt and black underwear. The shirt clung to her curves, and despite her short stature, Knox couldn't help but notice the amount of long legs displayed in front of him.

"Um, Beth – you don't have on any clothes." She walked over and sat on the edge of the bed on the same side where he was already halfway under the covers sitting up. She leaned over and gave him a small peck on the lips, then replied, "Well that's the idea, genius. I was sitting in bed, thinking about all you and I have talked about, and I don't know…I just feel like I want to have this moment with you because I don't know what's going to happen tomorrow."

Knox just hung his head and let out a sigh. "Honey, you know how I feel about this. It's not that I don't want you; quite the opposite. I still want us to wait. I've been down this road before, and I just think there are reasons the Man Upstairs put certain rules in that great big book that you've been reading lately."

Beth climbed up and sat on top of the scholarly looking man, wearing a set of reading glasses and a white under shirt to sleep in. She removed the glasses and leaned over to put them on the night stand. She turned off the lamp at the same time. He couldn't help but admire her muscular, well defined shoulders and neckline. "John, I know what you've said, but I just don't want to have any regrets.

If something should happen to one of us on this case, I don't want to squander the chance we had together"- Knox pushed down on her lips with his finger and shushed her. He looked into her eyes and bent down to kiss her. He sat back up one last time and whispered, "Okay – you twisted my arm. No regrets."

They started slow at first, but in no time, Beth had kicked down the covers that had been pulled over Knox, and the room temperature became pretty hot and heavy. Agent John Knox had been intimate with only two other women before. He had always been such a boys' scout with Beth ever since they'd started dating, and he always told her the same thing about rules, and reasons, and how he already felt guilty for not waiting for marriage. But after he saw Beth sitting there straddling him in the dim light that came in from a window with the shades partly drawn, all his reasons and morals figuratively went out the window. The Boy Scout was just going to have to chalk this one up to the sinful nature of man.

New York City
United Nations Building

The agents had taken their places in various places around the outside of the building, awaiting the arrival of a short motorcade that was to be carrying the Muslim leaders of two prominent countries in the Middle East. Imam Adad al-Bahrain of Saudi Arabia, and Imam Mohamad ibn Alsabadhi of Yemen were to arrive with a Secret Service Escort to meet with world leaders and persuade them to take an active role in a manhunt for the Jesus Assassin. The leaders and their followers believed that FBI and Interpol were both run by Christian heretics, and they wanted the UN to level the playing field and catch this assassin. The imams had no clue that the FBI and Interpol already had officers all over the place. Although they had objected, the US ambassadors and the UN representatives themselves had insisted that the imams welcome the use of the Secret Service to insure their safety at this meeting. The Muslim leaders had been reluctant, but went along with the suggestion because they realized the US would never want anything to happen to embarrass their precious Secret Service; and they had a pretty strong track record for the past several decades when it came to protecting their President.

Agent Knox had taken up a position directly across the street from the main entrance, sitting in a Chevrolet Impala FBI car along the curb. Malik was waiting inside the front lobby, and Beth had claimed a spot further away at a street corner a block away. She was trying to keep an eye out for any signs of sniper activity. There were other FBI agents in place at various locations around the building at the request of Agent Knox, and Malik had made a similar request to his Chief about having Interpol counterparts in the vicinity as well. They were ready for just about any attack - from the outside. The Secret Service had already done their prep work and had a pre-planned course for the imams to follow into the UN Building that would keep them separated from the expected crowd and on-lookers.

Knox picked up a radio that he had clipped to his belt. "Fed Team, Knox knocking– radio check…over," he spoke into the radio.

"White as snow…reading you clear as a bell – over," Agent White replied.

Finally Malik spoke up on his end, "Sheriff Sharif copies as well."

Everyone seemed as ready as they were ever going to be, and all agencies anxiously awaited the limousine motorcade. Meanwhile, the scene on the street in front of the building was being monitored by one more individual; the agents and law enforcement officers unaware of his presence. The Arbiter was camping out up in a high perch from one of the tall buildings down the street. He had a high powered 30-06 long rifle, with a clean and pristine scope mounted on the top of the gun. He looked down through the scope now from his spot on very high ground to check its clarity and settings. The rifle he was using would shoot at this distance with certainly enough velocity to be lethal, but not so much pressure and force around the bullet; therefore limiting collateral damage. Now the Arbiter would play the waiting game like everyone else.

Finally two large black armored limousines came around the corner, flying each of their respective country's flags as they approached the front of the building. The limousines were flanked by two large, black SUVs. As the vehicles approached, agents and officers were talking to each other; everyone was on high alert, and snipers and people on the ground were searching for any hint that the assassin was close. The Arbiter focused his sites on the area near the curb where the limos were pulling up now. Once all four vehicles came to a full stop, several men in suits, wearing shades and ear buds, got out of the SUVs and formed a wall of people along the curb in front of the two limousines. The passenger in the front seat of each limousine got out and opened the rear door for their assigned Imam to exit the vehicle. Although the Imam from Saudi Arabia was in the first limo, and the Imam from Yemen was in the second, both men had decided they were going to walk in together, so the Yemeni caught up to Imam al-Bahrain of Saudi Arabia.

The two Secret Service Agents who rode with them formed up in front and behind the Islamic leaders. The man in the front had short brown hair and shades, a very muscular build, and a thin mustache. He must have been the one who had been through this before, because he led the way up the sidewalk and into the front of the UN Building. The Agent behind the imams was a very fair-skinned bald man with a similar build to the man up front, dressed in the customary suit, shades, and ear bud. As the small group got closer to the front doors of the building, the human wall of agents that had been in front of them had separated off into two lines, one on each side of the entering party, to fight back the crowd of supporters and on-lookers that had already gathered. While walking into the building, none of the agents, investigators, or even the Arbiter could find anything suspicious. Shortly after passing through the front doors, the imams and their entourage headed to one of the elevators. Unfortunately, they were only going to present their ideas to a small panel and committee; not the whole of the United Nations, so they were going upstairs in the tower to one of the smaller conference rooms. The UN had planned it this way in order to prevent so much fanfare.

As the elevator doors opened, the imams and their Secret Service agents boarded the elevator while their human wall lined up again in front of the elevator doors to prevent anyone from following. The doors closed and the elevator began its ascent.

After he saw through the small crease between the doors that they had passed five floors, the bald Secret Service man suddenly got the other agent's attention and asked, "Wait a minute…did anyone hear that?"

Just as his cohort was raising his hand up to his mouth to speak into his hand mic, the bald assassin sprang into action and struck the real agent's hand down and caught him with a quick throat punch with the other hand as he pushed the hand holding the mic down past his face. The imams were stunned as expected, and the elevator was still in motion. The assassin took no time pulling one syringe out of his pocket. He hit the imam from Yemen behind him with a series of sharp elbows to his torso and face, and then stabbed the other imam so many times with the hypodermic needle it was like a blur. The agent clutching his throat wasn't out of the fight yet. He kicked out at the assassin, attempting to hit him in his common peroneal nerve to incapacitate him. The assassin put his elbow down at his side to block as he squatted down slightly. He knew he was running out of time, so he caught the Secret Service man in the temple with an elbow. The man went down and fell limp on the floor of the elevator. The imam whom had all the needle strikes applied to him was convulsing on the floor, while the other was carrying on in Arabic about how much pain he was enduring and yelling in English for help. The assassin struck the remaining imam in the head with a hard knee. As the imam fell all the way to floor, the assassin grabbed another syringe out of one of his pockets. He jammed it into the remaining imam's neck and pressed the plunger home. The Imam had the normal expected reaction, and in a matter of seconds, took his last breath. While the Secret Service man still laid there unconscious, the assassin took two gold crosses and placed them in each Imam's right hand.

Robert Brady waited until he saw a small open area through the crease between the doors, then pressed the emergency stop button as the elevator approached the 20th floor – five floors below the location of the meeting room where several key world leaders awaited the Imams' arrival. He quickly stripped out of his Secret Service disguise, and was wearing a dirty old polo shirt and wind pants underneath. He shook a small apron loose out of his front pocket and tied it around his waist. He left the suit, ear bud and thumb mic, and Secret Service badge in a pile on the floor of the elevator. He also took a small pocket knife out of the inside pocket of the suit jacket, and he started cutting into the base of his neck line. Brady had been wearing a false flesh-colored skull cap made of a flexible polymer that gave the strong appearance that he was bald. He sliced a thin line of where the false bald head was attached to the inside of his undershirt, and then peeled the rest of it off – revealing his red hair underneath. He picked up the small walkie-talkie that had been attached to the ear bud and mic, and he quickly took off the clip that slid into place on the back of the radio. He wedged the small hard plastic into the crease between the doors, and wedged the elevator doors open slightly; just far enough to squeeze his fingers in between them. Brady was not a small man, and was able to pull and then push the doors open the rest of the way with brute strength. He knew that once the emergency stop had been activated, he would only have a few minutes to clear the elevator and escape to find another path back to the ground floor. The elevator had stopped a few feet above the 20th floor. Once the doors were open, Brady sat on the edge and squeezed through the gap between the elevator floor and the ceiling and dropped to the hallway on the 20th floor. As soon as he hit the floor, he checked the hallway intersection at the elevators and ran towards a red exit sign he saw at the end of the hall.

The assassin made it to the corner stairwell and entered just as another elevator beeped back at the intersection he'd just left. There was no sign of interference coming from below, so Brady took the stairs as quickly as possible, sometimes three or four steps at a time. He went all the way down to the maintenance level and headed out the maintenance door. As he exited, he realized he had come out to the side of the building. He had a fake hot dog vendor's cart waiting for him up closer to the front of the building, but across the street. He ran over to a crowd of tourists exploring and examining famous sculptures and statues scattered on the grounds of the UN Visitors' Center. He weaved through the crowd, catching some curious glances but losing their attention after blending in to bodies of moving people. He saw his vendor's cart across the street and made a run for it. Although all hell had broken loose inside the UN, the assassin got to his cart and began slowly pushing it up the street.

****

Malik was waiting in the lobby near the elevators, when he realized there was a commotion among the Secret Service agents standing in front of the elevators. He radioed in to Knox, "Sheriff here – seeing a disturbance with Secret Service. Gonna go check it out and find out what's going on."

Knox responded, "10-4…let us know what you find out." Malik ran over to the closest agent, holding up his badge and introducing himself. The Secret Service agent replied, "Inspector – we have a serious problem. I know you guys have been working this case. Come with me."

Malik followed the agent to the elevator, guessing he knew what he was about to see. They got on the next elevator and he saw the agent hit the button for the 20th floor. On the way up, the agent filled the inspector in on details of their last few radio transmissions, and told him that the Imams' elevator had been stopped in between the 20th and 21st floors. He went on to tell him that they discovered their problem when they were able to make contact with one of their agents who had been assigned to the Imams' protection detail. The elevator opened, and the man from the Secret Service led Malik to the elevator next door. The elevator doors were open, and Malik immediately noticed the Muslims in their robes, each sitting up against the back wall of the elevator holding crosses in front of them - looking well rested and at peace with the world.

Malik then noticed another Secret Service man standing to the side, rubbing his temples. "What happened?" he asked the special agent as he flashed his credentials and the man's cohort nodded to him in approval.

"Inspector, the guy was new to our detail. I had never met him, but we aren't paid to question orders from above, so I was just going through the motions. The other agent was bald, muscular, about my size, and highly trained in hand-to-hand combat. He still had shades on in the elevator, before he busted me up on the head pretty hard. I honestly don't remember anything after catching his last elbow."

Malik glanced back into the elevator and saw some miscellaneous items on the floor. He saw a flimsy piece of rubber that looked like the upper half of a volley ball. He bent down and picked it up and realized it was the top of a bald head. He took his radio off his belt. "Knox…White…He's struck again. And he's long gone by now." There was silence on the other end of the radio.

****

The Arbiter watched the pandemonium in the streets below, and he scanned the crowd through his scope for any signs of someone bolting against the flow of people. He could only figure that his target had struck from the inside, and if that was the case, he'd probably be making his escape. He took a step back from the window he was perched in and got a glimpse of the bigger picture. He looked all around the city block and the surrounding parts of the UN property for anything out of place. He was slowly trying to piece together the way he would probably escape if he were going to kill someone inside the UN Visitors' Center, simultaneously peering down through the window and looking for a brief sign. Out of the corner of his eye, he saw something moving more slowly than the crowds had been moving at the UN. There was a small silver cart with wheels being pushed along by someone under a red and white umbrella. He watched closely as the man and the cart made their way to the end of the block and began a slow turn around the corner. As the man had moved farther along, more of his head and face were finally revealed as he made his turn. The Arbiter finally realized that the man had red hair, but also noticed that the man was about to make it to a copse of trees. He stepped back up to his weapon to get a better look, and as he did, the man with red hair suddenly stopped and turned around. As the Arbiter watched the redhead scan the horizon, the man's gaze stopped in the direction of the Arbiter's location. The Arbiter zoomed in on his scope to get a better look at his new target. When the redhead's face came in to clear view, the Arbiter saw a man staring back at him; his green eyes suddenly squinting, as if he were trying to focus in on the Arbiter's position. The Arbiter hesitated for a brief moment as if to take a double-take. He had seen those green eyes once before – in a hangar somewhere near Baghdad! He bent back down to his scope and was ready to fire and eliminate his mission objective; it was no coincidence that his target to follow was in the same place as the location of two fresh assassinations. But as he looked back through the scope, the redheaded man was gone…he'd vanished - just like a ghost.

****

Brady casually looked back over his shoulder as the crowds in the UN plaza were scrambling and panicking over the apparent news of assassination. He was across the street and down about half a block away, slowly meandering along with his hot dog cart. Nobody seemed to pay attention to some white guy trying to make his living selling hot dogs on the streets of New York, so there was no suspicion aimed his way. He approached a tree line as he came to the next corner and enjoyed a cool breeze that flowed in from the nearby river. Just as the wind was cooling him off, he felt a small tingling in the back of his neck. It's said that those who experience fight-or-flight situations on a regular basis develop a sixth sense, kind of like eyes in the back of their head – that make them sense danger before it happens. Brady had perhaps experienced more danger than most, and his senses were sending him that warning now. He stopped pushing his cart. He slowly turned to scan the buildings in the distance, and in the far corner of a large tower, he noticed an open window. It wasn't the window that caught his eye; it was a small glimmer of light in the middle of a small dark space. Brady, of all people, knew the glint off a scope of a rifle anywhere. He knew he had a fraction of a second to react. He didn't know who was behind that scope, but he wasn't going to get to try and find out if he didn't leave the vicinity fast. Just as he expected to hear or see a round hit the pavement behind him, Brady ran as fast as possible for the trees and shrubbery around the next bend. The report of a rifle never came.

New York Times
The Jesus Assassin Strikes Again

Well I hope you Christians are happy! I recently received several of your so-called articles of concern, and even gave you the courtesy of allowing some of your work to be seen in print. Do you still think this Christian assassin is a good guy? Is he really doing us a favor? Yesterday, our beloved hero murdered two imams in cold blood – inside the United Nations Visitors' Center! Are you seeing what I'm seeing, folks? Because from where I sit, this is some pretty violent action taken by someone who is supposed to believe in a Prince of Peace. The two imams were set to meet with members of the UN, to ask for help in hunting down this international criminal – they never even made it to the meeting! And don't get me started on our friends at the FBI and Interpol. These guys obviously couldn't catch a cold...let alone an assassin. I for one think after this embarrassment on our own soil, we should give the UN a chance to step in. Someone has to catch this guy. It is the least the UN can do, since they never got to hear the Muslims out.

As for the FBI, they might as well pack it in. This guy has killed four people that we know about, and they obviously aren't getting any closer to finding *out who he is. Whatever part Interpol has in any of this, they might as well go back to Europe; they might have better luck catching the Pink Panther. This kind of bumbling over a religious fanatic is exactly why I'm so against religion in the first place. If you want to find out more about how we can make it in this world WITHOUT God or Allah or Neo (Insert godly title here), then check out my weekly postings in my column, **ATHEISM WEEKLY.** IF you are the Jesus Assassin – please stop the senseless killing. You are only reinforcing the very principles I write about every week.*

This editorial was written by local editor and chief politics and religion correspondent, Jim Marshall. Jim is the author of *Atheism Weekly*, and has a weekly column in the Times. If you have any comments or questions, please contact Jim at Marshall@NYTIMES.org.

****

Knox's reaction to the Jim Marshall article was not quite as heated as the first time; it was more of a sign of resignation. He finished reading the paper and passed it over to Malik, who was enjoying a cheese Danish brought in by room service for breakfast. Beth had just finished freshening up and came out of her bedroom to sit with Knox and Malik. She could tell by the look on her man's face that things weren't good. She reached out and put a hand on his. Knox looked up and smiled, then got up to get his phone. He dialed up the SAC.

Jones McCoy answered on the third ring, and surprised Agent Knox with calm words. "How are you and Beth holding up, John? I read the article this morning." John stayed on the phone with McCoy, but re-joined Beth and Malik at the small kitchen table.

He spoke up, "Sir – I'm sorry we've failed the agency. I don't know what to say." McCoy cleared his throat on the other end of the line, and replied, "John, it's not your fault. It's obvious this is happening from within. This assassin has some really good connections if he can pull off impersonating a member of the Secret Service. Those guys are vetted and checked more than you and I were before working for the FBI. This guy is good – too good. I want you and Beth to take a break from this thing."

Knox's eyes got bigger as he tried to reply, "But, sir" –McCoy cut him off. "I mean it. You, White, and that Malik fellow need to take a step back. Come back to Detroit for a few days, step away from the case, and re-group. That is a direct order." Knox started nodding and looked over at his partners with a calming expression. "Yes, sir. We'll do it. And thank you, sir. It probably will be good to take a break from it all."

Knox hung up his phone, and Beth said immediately, "Let me guess – the boss says we need a break?"

Knox nodded, and Malik shrugged his shoulders as he finished off his cheese Danish. He added, "Probably not a bad idea, considering we just took a major step backwards. We might as well start again."

Beth shook her head. "I still think we were going in the right direction with the CIA, and this just confirms my suspicions."

Knox said, "That's what McCoy was saying. The only way for someone to infiltrate as deep as the Secret Service is to already be part of the IN crowd, as in Intelligence. But Beth, we don't know where to go. Even if Brady or some friend of his were doing this, we have no way of finding him, or even proving that he is still alive. Heck – we don't even know what he looks like."

Malik chimed in, "Well, I can tell you he's not bald."

They all chuckled at that, and Knox finished, "Well, I'll make our travel plans, and we'll go back home. Maybe some days at home will refresh our minds."

With that, they all went to their separate rooms and packed their things. It was time to take a step away from the Jesus Assassin.

Virginia

On the Interstate near Blacksburg, VA

The Arab-American man called CIA Director Marks as he was driving down the interstate towards his target's home. Marks picked up on the other end, "You better have good news for me."

The Arbiter replied, "It's Brady. I had visual confirmation at the location of the last assassination; I almost took him out as soon as I was sure – but I lost him. I am on my way to his residence now."

Marks continued, "Be sure you fix this. That was quite a spectacle he gave us back in New York. I was hoping you would have him before that last little snafu happened."

"How was I supposed to know he would sneak in as a Secret Service agent – seeing as how he didn't look anything like himself, and I still wasn't 100% sure he was our killer? Don't worry – all connections will be severed."

He hung up, and concentrated on the road. The Arbiter was ready to end this job; the activist Robert Brady had become quite a thorn in the government's side, and if he were to continue his religious quest, he would bring more than embarrassment to his country. He might bring war. The Arbiter couldn't help but wonder if his target was sitting at home, perhaps planning his next assassination. If he was at his old family home, the Arbiter would at least send him off in a place that was important to him. He felt some respect for his upcoming adversary; the man was a highly decorated Navy SEAL, and responsible for the capture and elimination of an untold number of terrorists who had been enemies of the State. It would be honorable for him to die in a place he cherished. According to GPS, the Arbiter's destination was only five miles away. He figured that gave the activist a good twenty minutes before he met his end.

****

Entry # 31   May 25, 2016

Heavenly Father – I fear this will be my last written prayer to you. I was able to defeat two more servants of Islam for you, Lord. Thank you, Father, for protecting me and giving me safe passage from my last objective – but I think I have been discovered in my mission for you. I sensed it back in New York City as I was escaping the United Nations building. I know not who pursues me, but I pray you have prepared me for whatever I am about to face. Lord, I have not yet completed my task, but I am almost halfway there. Please remain with me throughout this quest, and protect me from those who would try to stop me from completing the mission. Lord, I know I can succeed, but not without your almighty hand. If I should fail, God it will because I turned my back on you ---

His writing was interrupted by an alarm sound coming from somewhere on the eastern corner of his property. The assassin had wired alarms all around his property, in case anyone ever came snooping around. One of his alarms was going off now, and he knew that this was the unknown evil force that was out to thwart his mission. Brady got up from his desk in his study and ran to the porch to grab his little black bag. All his essentials were still packed; he knew he had enough to survive for a little while as he tried to come up with a new plan to complete his mission. But he wasn't going to complete anything if he didn't escape his pursuer. He was just about to head back into the house from the screen porch to retrieve his journal, when he heard a loud crash at the front of the house. Then he heard the clatter of suppressed machine gun fire in several short spurts, and he knew he would not be back inside his home. The assassin had to make a run for it, and he knew the front of the house was out of the question. He didn't want to give away his position, so he crept out the back screen door of the porch and ran to his reptile shelter. He ignored the containers holding all his reptiles, and went straight for the reserve stockpile of snake venom. He quickly gathered up vials and put them in his bag. He then checked back outside, and saw a clear path to the work shed. He made a run over to the shed, and on the way he glanced back over his shoulder towards the house and saw a silhouette of a man with an assault rifle pass by the kitchen window. He ran faster, and made it to the door of his shed. He flipped the light switch, went inside and grabbed his crossbow, or rather his crossbow parts; he had broken it down for easy storage for his next mission, so it was ready to go. Just before heading out to his car, he grabbed all the modified bolts for the crossbow and stuffed them into the bag as well. He had everything he needed and ran back out of the shed. When he couldn't see a sign of the intruder, he made a break for his car.

He climbed behind the wheel of his SUV, a large blue Jeep Commander, and cranked the engine. As soon as he did, the screen door was just about knocked off its hinges as his heavily armed assailant came out of the screen porch and fired shots at the vehicle. Holes riddled the windshield, but Brady was already ducking as he slammed the transmission into Drive and sped away from his house and up his winding driveway that lead out of the valley. The Arbiter did not give chase because he had parked his vehicle further away in order to catch his target by surprise by sneaking in on foot. He had a feeling

Brady would have alarms set up around the property, but he had no idea they would be so hard to detect. He was just going to have to catch up to his target later. As he saw the tail lights of Brady's SUV pull off in the distance, the Arbiter scanned his surroundings. He decided since he had full access to Brady's property, he would take a closer look around.

****

The Arbiter was already outside, so he walked around the house, and he was finally able to spot several booby traps and alarms that had been rigged by Brady. He then noticed a small wooden shed, and he walked over to the large door in the front that had a padlock hanging through the latch, unlocked. He realized that the activist, Mr. Brady, had been in that shed most recently, and had left the door hanging slightly open. He must have grabbed things in a hurry, which meant there might still be things of importance in the shed. He pulled the door open and stepped into a small work area. Brady had left in such a rush he left the light on in the shed. The Arbiter looked around at Brady's work area. He saw empty gun magazines; small brass casings scattered about on the floor near a reloading machine; long arrows that looked to either be arrows for a professional archer, or possibly even large crossbow bolts. He also saw an assortment of tools spread out in organized fashion hanging in holes on the wall behind the work bench. Several hooks were empty – probably some important tools that Brady had grabbed before his escape.

The Marine Recon government 'fixer' had seen enough of the work shed; there was nothing else of note for him in there. He walked back outside and saw a larger building with a flat roof. He knew it wasn't quite large enough to be a guest residence, but the building was large enough to contain an office or two. He walked over to a black door on the long side of the building. He tried to turn the doorknob and found it to be unlocked. He pushed his way in, and immediately felt the difference in temperature between the interior and outside. The inside was hot and humid – almost like being in a jungle. As he crossed the threshold, a motion sensor made the lights turn on and illuminate a long room full of shelves containing large plastic crates and large glass tanks. As he made his way down the row of shelves, he came upon the first glass tank. As soon as his face passed the front of the tank, he heard the unmistakable sound of a small rattle. He peered in and saw one of the largest Eastern Diamondback Rattlesnakes he had ever seen. The next glass tank contained a long, slender serpent, smoke-gray in color, with a small head and large black eyes. When the snake struck at the glass as the Marine waved his hand in front of it, it displayed the inside of its mouth; a deep, bluish black color that gave the Black Mamba its name. The Arbiter had heard from Director Marks that the Jesus Assassin, a.k.a. Robert Brady, had used snake venom to kill his targets. He could only assume that either one of these two snakes could have been the culprits the assassin used to extract venom. He also assumed that the other large boxes and crates in the room contained more venomous snakes. He would have to remember how dangerous and resourceful Brady was when he confronted him; he very well could face some kind of weapon of Brady's that puts the venom to use.

After seeing what he wanted to inside the reptile house, the Arbiter went back to the cabin. He walked through the quaint but somewhat spacious cabin and wondered room to room, observing family pictures and newspaper clippings that had been framed and placed on various walls in the house. It was obvious that Brady loved his family. There were photos of various sizes throughout the house; some containing pictures with his wife and daughter; some with just his wife; some of just his daughter. He was hoping to find a photo containing Brady himself, but he was coming up short. He eventually came to the living room, and saw a silver TV, sitting in an entertainment center that was pretty bare – with the exception of a DVD that was simply marked '**My Reasons'.** Having peeked his interest, the Arbiter turned on the TV and put in the DVD. It was a grainy video, but the Arbiter could definitely tell what was going on. The speaker in the video was your stereotypical terrorist, rambling along about America, and Allah. Then the camera panned to two females strapped down into chairs. The Arbiter immediately recognized the wife and daughter of Robert Brady – two people with very beautiful faces; the mother with her big blue eyes, and the little daughter with her bright green eyes. The Arbiter realized the terrorist was back in the picture, rambling on some more with his anti-American rhetoric. Then the scene included both the girls again, and the terrorist was handed two scimitars. Suddenly the terrorist in the video swung the scimitars down through the air and made a sweeping arc to abruptly end the lives of Brady's little family. Even the Arbiter flinched at the gruesome sight, and immediately turned off the TV. He had seen enough.

He shook the images away and walked into the study. He was looking for something to help identify the assassin; the Arbiter had an idea that might help him catch up to the Jesus Assassin quicker. He had just about given up, when he saw several old military photos scattered about on the floor in the corner of the room. He walked over and ran his hand through the pile. He found several pictures of different soldiers posing together, but Brady had to be the redhead standing in almost all of the photos. They were definitely photos of a younger Robert Brady, back when he was a SEAL. The Arbiter picked up a picture that had Brady posing all by himself, standing next to a patch of bamboo trees. He had a full head of red hair, a full beard that he obviously kept trimmed close, and bright green eyes that were almost cartoon-like. The Arbiter gathered up a couple of the pictures. Although he wanted to erase the images of Brady's family from his thoughts, he couldn't help but understand why Brady was doing what he was doing. He headed out the door and took the photos with him. He had a feeling they would come in handy later. He didn't notice the small leather-bound journal sitting on the desk as he left the cabin.

Detroit, Michigan
Agent White's House

Agent Knox stood at Beth's front door, waiting for her to come in response to the doorbell. He held a bouquet of red roses behind his back. Beth came to the door and gave herself a look-over and patted her clothes down as if to fix herself up one last time before letting Knox see her. She opened the door and smiled. She was wearing a perfume that smelled like a combination between mountain flowers and vanilla sky; Knox couldn't quite decide which one.

He returned the smile, then swung the bouquet of roses around from his back and said, "I picked these up on the way…couldn't help but think you needed to know I can be romantic every now and then." Beth's eyes lit up, and she planted a short, wet kiss on his lips.

She took the roses from him, and as she did, she said kindly, "Thank you so much, John. Let me go run and put these in a vase with some water – then we can go."

Knox just waited out on the front porch with the front door left open, and heard Beth moving around the house near the kitchen, opening and closing cabinet doors, and running some water to fill up a vase. She rushed back out front, and pulled the door closed behind them. She hit some buttons on her cell phone and her door automatically locked.

"New alarm system?" Knox asked. Beth nodded and answered, "A girl can't be too careful these days. So, where is my knight in shining armor taking me for a romantic dinner this fine evening?" "Well, you know I don't cook...but I know good Italian when I taste it. We're going to this new place over on Elsie St. It's called Cardone's, and I swear they have the best calzones and fried lasagna in the world." Beth was getting hungry, and she was glad that she and her man both loved Italian food.

They rode to dinner in Knox's big cherry red pickup truck. Knox tried to play the part of a gentleman, opening Beth's door for her both when they left her house and when they arrived at the restaurant. The place wasn't crowded because the usual dinner crowd had already left. Knox and Beth both ordered fried lasagna, and Knox added an order of Italian potato soup. The conversation was kept light, and the two agents just enjoyed one another's company. They had both decided before Knox came to pick Beth up that they would not talk about work; conversation about the Jesus Assassin was strictly off-limits. Instead, Knox asked Beth about her likes and dislikes, and she asked him about his family, and his days at the University of Alabama. Finally the talking became a little more serious.

"Honey, I've been thinking…about our special night back in New York," Knox began. Beth grinned at him and replied, "Funny you should mention that. I was feeling – well – guilty about it. I mean it was my fault, John. I know what a weapon seduction can be, and let's face it; I seduced you that night."

Knox nodded with a blush, "Well, that you did. But that's not what I am getting at. I don't want you to feel bad or guilty. I just want you to think about the meaning. I've been pouring my heart and soul out to you about my spiritual life, and trying to tell you why I try to walk a straight and narrow life. And then as your mentor I go and sleep with you! I am the guilty one here, Beth. I guess what I'm getting at is – did it mean enough to you, that if we didn't do it anymore for quite a while…say, 'til we're married…would it be okay?"

Beth looked puzzled. "Married?" she asked. Her eyes brightened and she said, "You really think we're ready for that?"

He answered, "Well – no, not yet. But I never would have given in to your seduction if I hadn't considered it." She was only quiet for a brief moment. Then she spoke up, "Well, I wasn't going to go there, but since I know you feel that way, you might as well know I love you. I have been falling in love with you ever since we started the assassin case. And about that night, if you're asking if it meant a lot to me, well - of course it did. John, I just meant I felt guilty in a sense that it didn't sit right with me after we'd done it. I mean something *inside* told me we were wrong.

Knox raised his eyebrows. "So, you're saying you didn't feel guilty because of your knowledge of my beliefs about what we did…but what you believe? Beth, don't take this the wrong way, but that is good news."

The waiter brought the check and put a short, awkward break in the conversation. Knox got out some cash and folded it up in the small receipt book. He handed it to the waiter and said, "Keep the change." The waiter nodded and walked away.

Beth caught Knox's eyes as he got up and pushed his chair under the table. "I should have known it was bothering you…but I am serious. It has been like someone telling me that I messed up; almost like my dad's voice, but I feel it; I don't just hear it." Knox nodded as they walked out to the parking lot. He opened Beth's door for her once again, and he gave her a heart-warming look and said, "Beth…it's all the time you've been spending in the Word. I have been telling you. It's more than just pretty words. Once you apply those words to your life, you *feel* them. I'm happy for you."

He walked around and climbed up in the driver's seat. He cranked up the big Turbo Diesel and it roared to life. Beth sat there and began thinking to herself as Knox put the truck in Drive and pulled the big pickup out of the parking lot of Cardone's. The two sat quietly for the first part of the ride back to Beth's place.

Just before turning the corner to Beth's street, she asked Knox, "So I guess when you drop me off, you're not going to stay, are you? I mean, I can't blame you. I know you're not going anywhere anyway."

Knox pulled the truck into her driveway. He got out and walked around to Beth's door. She couldn't help but smile to herself when he would open doors and pull out chairs for her; it was always good to know chivalry wasn't dead. Knox walked her up to the front door.

They turned to face each other, and he bent down and gave her a passionate kiss that lasted several seconds.

When he looked into her eyes again, he answered, "One day, Honey. One day we'll have plenty of nights together like that last one. By the way, I never got around to saying it back." Beth's short term memory had gone blank. "Say what back?" Knox planted one last kiss on her and stood back. "I love you, too." They started walking apart as he turned to go, when his cell phone rang.

"John – I'm sorry to bother you at this hour. But he's done it again," McCoy's voice said on the other end of the line. Knox replied, "We'll be in shortly. Agent White is with me."

Beth punched him in the shoulder and mouthed that she couldn't believe him, telling their boss that they were together after hours like that. Knox laughed as he hung up.

"Well, sweetie…let's get back to work."

Detroit, Michigan
24 Hour Gym at Hotel

Malik was punching a 100 pound bag that had thoughtfully been mounted from the ceiling of the 24 hour gym only accessible to hotel guests. He would occasionally throw in a quick knee or disguised elbow, sometimes leaning back and grabbing the top of the bag as he did so. Malik had been taught Krav Maga by one of the finest Israeli instructors when he lived with his mother in Kuwait before being accepted into Interpol. He was in really good shape through years of practice, and he was almost 'in the zone' when his cell phone rang. He didn't recognize the number, but he answered it anyway.

"Hello?"

The caller's voice replied, "Malik...that you? Son – it's been too long!" Malik started taking his gloves off as he held the phone up to his sweaty cheek.

"Dad? Allah be praised, how are you? How are you getting to call me?"

Malik's dad was in a federal prison for a crime that he had committed back when Malik was in high school. He had been caught driving a truck for some drug dealers out of New York and smuggling the shipment up north to Canada. Malik even knew back then that his dad did it because they were under hard financial times, and his dad's skills as a truck driver had been the only thing that had kept them afloat in the US once he had retired from the Army. Malik had spent time in Kuwait until his dad was shipped back to the States. His dad had married a sheik's daughter in Kuwait, but when both parties agreed to an amicable divorce, Malik's grandfather had been understanding with the boy's wishes to see where his dad had come from – so long as he kept the mother's last name. So he traveled back to the Bronx in New York, and attended middle school and high school in the Bronx. Although Malik's grandfather offered for the boy to come live in Kuwait with his mother, Malik had always admired his dad's work ethic, and decided he wanted to try and make it on his own. Arrangements were made for Malik to go back and visit his mother whenever he requested, and he lived out his high school days with his Aunt Teresa, his dad's sister.

"Malik, I've been blessed with a work detail that allows me full access to a cell phone, but all my calls are monitored. But I had to go through some crazy channels to get your number."

Malik laughed, "Whoa – you didn't have to speak with the Chief, did you? I can just see his face now, trying to understand your jive talk." His father answered, "Was he the guy that sounded like Arnold? If so, he's a pretty serious cat. But he gave up your digits – so here we are. Have you talked to your mom lately? How is she?" Malik nodded and told his dad about his last talk with his mother. He also told him how busy he'd been overseas and here in the States with his last two cases. He mentioned that he was on the Jesus Assassin case with a guy from the FBI.

"What'd you say that agent's name is that's helping you go after this guy?"

Malik repeated, "Knox…Agent John Knox. And Pops, you wouldn't believe this guy. He is the opposite of what everyone overseas thinks when they think about Christians; especially Christian Americans. He's down to Earth, and he really has his head on his shoulders." Malik's dad, sometimes affectionately known to others as simply, The Sarge, piped in, "Sounds like you really respect this guy. Well if he's so sharp, and they have someone as gifted as you going after this assassin, than this Jesus Assassin must be really good."

Malik confirmed his dad's statement, "You're right about that, Pops. But Knox thinks like him, and he might even be able to use that to guess what the killer is doing…but only if we get a few more leads first."

"You guys got a suspect yet?" he asked his son. Malik said, "Not exactly…we think someone is possibly a copycat, as far as military and espionage go. But we could be wrong about that, and our original suspicions could turn out to be right.

Something is just fishy about the first guy that matches our killer's skillset to a tee."

The Sarge continued, "Well, sounds like you guys have your hands full. So besides work – how have you been doing?" Malik thought about an appropriate answer his dad was looking for. "I've been trying to be consistent with my prayers; work consumes most of my days, and exercise. But when I'm not doing either one of those, I have my alarm set for the five prayers every day."

His dad responded, "So you're still following Allah? Hmmm, I thought all that time in Europe might have changed your mind."

"Of course not, Dad. You taught me well. Don't worry so much about me." Malik told his father.

The Sarge just answered, "Son, let's just say, my eyes-"

Just then Malik's call waiting was beeping in on the line.

"Dad – I've got to go. Agent Knox is on the other line. But thanks for calling. I will come visit as soon as this case is over."

The Sarge just replied, "You do that boy…you better just do that. I love ya!"

Malik hung up and answered Agent Knox, "What's up, sir? It's only been two days. Do we have something?"

Knox replied, "Pack your bags again – we're going to Virginia."

Fairfax, Virginia
Fairfax Center for Islam

Brady was waiting near the small city mosque. It was on the outskirts of the downtown area of Fairfax, Virginia. The last prayer of the day had just ended, and several people were leaving the mosque. He was concealed behind some shrubbery across the street, ducking down behind some holly bushes as the loyal and religious Muslims left to go home to their houses and prepare to get up the next day and practice their heresy all over again. He despised them; he knew they had nothing to do with his family's deaths, but he hated them just the same. He abhorred anything Muslim. He had come to the conclusion that if Islam did not exist, his parents, and his wife and child, would still be with him today. He would still be Robert Brady. He would still be a SEAL, fighting the other forces of evil for his country. This hatred had led him down this road, and there was no turning back now. He saw the last of the Islamic followers' cars leave the parking lot, and saw that there was only one car left. It belonged to Imam Abrahim al-Sunni. Al-Sunni was a peaceful man, only trying to make it along in this world by teaching as many people as he could about Allah and his prophet Muhammad. He harbored no ill will towards Christians, Jews, Hindus, or fellow Americans in general. Although he was considered by many to be a lonely man, he always knew he had Allah.

The small framed, somewhat pensive looking man walked out of the front door of the mosque. He didn't have the slightest suspicion that anything dangerous was lurking outside the doors of his mosque. Why would a killer like the Jesus Assassin want to kill an imam like him; he was insignificant in the great big scheme of things. He had zero ties to terrorists, and he had no evil wishes towards anyone. Yet here he was, in the crossbow sites of Robert Brady. It was because Brady had grown desperate. He was on the run, even though he was sure that authorities had no clue as to his current position. But with an organization like the Activity, and the intelligence resources at their disposal, he had to rush his mission. All he needed were 12 imams; he had convinced himself of that. In his twisted view on Islam and Christianity, he could set things right with the world by reaching the twelfth imam. Mr. al-Sunni would be number six. Brady let the imam get all the way to his car door. Just before he stuck the key in the door of his little red Toyota Corolla, the assassin fired his crossbow. The bolt twisted through the air, accelerating until it hit its target; center-mass, stopping the imam in his tracks. It was a death dealing blow, but the imam did not die as fast as some of the assassin's other methods had done to others. He turned around and leaned against his car. He slid down and sat up on the ground, wondering what just happened. Surely Allah would not end his service this way. He had been so diligent; so devoted. Then the figure in black approached him from across the street.

Although the imam's body was shutting down and burning from the inside out from snake venom, his brain was still functioning – albeit in a state of shock. He spoke up to the assassin, "Why? What did my people ever do to you? Why would you be willing to serve Satan in this manner?"

Brady looked upon his target with some regret; he was a puny man; Brady was definitely the bully on the street. He responded regrettably by taking a small gold cross out of his chest pocket.

"Mister, I don't even know your name. But I know you preach blasphemy. Jesus is the answer – not Allah. Your religion has done more harm to this world than good. I am simply aiding our race along the way, until He comes again."

The imam's breathing had become more labored, and he wheezed as he finished, "And what do you think your Christ would think of your handiwork? I am…afraid… you are the blasphemer."

He coughed one more time, and then his head slumped forward. Once Brady knew there was no more life left in him, he placed the cross in the imam's right hand. He had heard the imam's words. A tiny part of him asked the question, "Did I kill an innocent man?" But his resolve did not falter. He had just eliminated another Muslim. That was one less threat to the spreading of the devil's religion in disguise; that's the way he saw it.

****

He was speeding down a two lane highway at around 75 miles per hour. As he contemplated his next move, he thought it was worth a shot contacting his old boss, despite his unsanctioned hits. He knew the Activity had to be the only group that had even come close to catching him. He knew that the ruthless, persistent soul who had attempted to kill him at his cabin was one of their hunters. His only hope to end that hunt was through the head of the Activity. He had almost forgotten he had a direct line to the man. He hoped they hadn't shut that perk off to him just yet. He was surprised they never tried to reach him; maybe to set up a fake meeting just to trap him for the easy kill. He hit send on his cell, and waited.

Director Marks picked up after several rings. He answered groggily, his Boston accent even stronger in his exhaustion.

"This better be good – I was sleeping."

Brady cleared his throat.

"Sir, back when we arranged this whole thing – you told me to call you if I was ever having an emergency. Well – one of your hunting dogs almost had me back at my cabin, and I am begging you to call him off." The Director recognized Brady's voice right away, despite being sleepy.

"Mr. Brady – so good to finally hear from you. If you'll recall, I never assured you of anything if you ever broke protocol. Unsanctioned hits on non-US targets are extremely forbidden. You know I can't call off our dog. You've brought way too much potential attention to our organization. I wish you had come to me after your first mistake. But mistake after mistake; well I am afraid my hands are tied. The other leaders in the Activity even agreed to have you eliminated. I am sorry Robert."

The man formerly known as the Activist calmly replied. "Well then send him if you must. But know this, sir. No matter how bad he wants me; no matter how skilled your hunter is – I will not stop until my mission is complete." Marks pretended to laugh on his end. "Robert, I am afraid we selected the Arbiter for a reason. You may have been the best spy in the business. But I guarantee you the Arbiter is the best hunter out there…and you are his prey."

Brady, who was normally a man of few words, simply replied, "Catch me if you can, *Directa.*"

Annandale, Virginia
Cemba-sacur Muslim Center

He drove his Jeep Commander just six miles down the road to a town called Annandale. The highway going into town – the Little River Turnpike – made it a straight shot from Fairfax. On his way into the town, there was a sign for the Northern Virginia Mosque. Although it was past nightfall, Brady followed the sign's directions and headed down the next road for about two miles. He pulled into the parking lot of the small brick Islamic center of worship and saw some light coming from several lamps inside the small windows along the wall. There were also two cars in the parking lot. Brady had no idea what he would discover inside, but he knew only the leader of the mosque would still have the building open this late at night. He parked in the parking lot, right in the front of the mosque. He grabbed his crossbow out of the backseat, and he headed to the front door. To his surprise, it was unlocked, so he slowly pushed the door open and crept inside.

As soon as he entered, he was in a large, open room, with several neat rows of prayer rugs on the floor. On the very back row, there was a woman on her knees; her face and head were prostrate to the floor. At the front there was a black man in the same position. However, he had noticed the man in black come into the mosque, and stood up abruptly.

"This is a house of God, sir. You have no business here…I know who you are."

Brady held up the crossbow. He was close enough to the imam to not have a need for the scope. The imam was tall as he stood up; an African American male, with robes and head wear of African design. He would have been an imposing figure in his youth, Brady thought to himself. Brady answered him as he saw the woman at the back look over at him and hold her hands up. She was not very tall, and had a petite build. She was also wearing the customary black vail over her face, along with her head dress.

"Allah is not God; Allah is just Muhammad's fabrication of a god that conveniently taught him tenets to write down in a book, that just so happened to go along with his political views of the time period."

The imam glanced over at the woman and motioned to the door for her to run, but she was frozen in fear.

Brady spoke up again, "She has nothing to fear. Chances are, she was coerced into this faith anyway, therefore not entirely to blame for her sins. But you"- Brady pulled the trigger, aiming higher on the chest on his target this time. The crossbow bolt hit its mark and the imam hit his knees.

"You know exactly what you are doing. Satan has all sorts of servants...and you are the worst kind. Pretending to bring something good to spread throughout the world, then preaching that all the infidels must die in your next breath, the moment people get with you behind closed doors!"

The imam was struggling to catch his breath. The crossbow bolt protruded from the highest part of his chest cavity, just under his collar bone. He felt like his insides were on fire. He was trying to put something into words, but his internal organs were fighting a losing battle, and finally he had a massive heart attack. He grasped at his chest and the crossbow bolt, and then slumped over forward from his knees. At least death came relatively quickly. The woman lost all fear for a brief moment and ran over to the imam's body. She was oblivious to the assassin's approach to the body as she knelt over him, grabbing one of his hands and crying over his death. As she finally noticed the assassin standing off to the side, she looked up at him. She tore off her vail and yelled at him.

"Get out, you monster! Just get out! You said you wouldn't hurt me – just go! Please – my child is outside in the car waiting for me. Please just pass him by, and go!"

Brady was going to leave a cross with the imam's body, but ever the man for adapting and adjusting, he stopped and turned for the door. He was walking out with the crossbow slung over his shoulder, and looked back at the woman. She had resumed her crying; not bothering to call 911. Brady shrugged his shoulders and walked out the front door.

On his way back to his car, he came across a small African American boy looking for his mommy; probably around six years old. He looked concerned and determined, until he noticed the large crossbow over Brady's shoulder. Brady motioned with one hand that he was laying the weapon down, and he put it on the ground. He reached into an inside pocket and took out one of his gold crosses. He called out to the boy and motioned to come a little closer. "Don't worry kid. Your mom is fine. She told me to tell you to wait in the car. She didn't want you to leave the safety of the car, ok?" The little black boy looked confused, but finally nodded as if he understood. "Hey, kid. Before I go, I want you to have this." He knelt down on one knee as the boy cautiously stepped closer. He reached out to hand him the gold cross. The boy took it reluctantly, and then ran to his mom's car. He opened the back door, jumped in, and slammed the door. Then he pushed his little face up against the window to watch the assassin as he picked up his crossbow and walked back to his Jeep. Brady didn't look back at the child, or the car, or even the mosque. He just put his SUV in gear, and headed for his next objective.

****

JESUS ASSASSIN HITS SMALL TOWNS
Annandale Monitor

First the murderer hit Fairfax and took out a local imam...then he went straight down the turnpike to Annandale, and murdered another imam probably an hour later. It all happened last night between the hours of 8 and 10 pm. Although a predominantly Christian area, folks are starting to worry about this Jesus Assassin. Authorities still don't know exactly who they are looking for. There were two witnesses at the crime scene in Annandale. Unfortunately both a mother and her 6 year old son described him as a large white man dressed in black, wearing a hood. That is all they could give the police, and investigators have been stumped for weeks now on the identity of this killer. First he made the infamous hit on the Today Show backstage, and took out a well-known peaceful imam from New York City. Then he attacked two holy men from foreign countries, with every major agency in the US and UN on high alert. Now he wants to invade small town America! This is an unprecedented government conspiracy if you ask me. Who else could get away with so much murder...so much chaos – but an American Assassin gone rogue? I hope you are paying attention, people. This assassin is killing at will, and the authorities don't even know who they are looking for. In case you didn't know, that has secret agent written all over it. So if you are a Muslim in the United States, you might want to hide your wife and kids. And if you are a Christian in the United States, you better hope you aren't in cahoots with this assassin...because let me tell you – once the government catches up with him and knows who's doing this, they are going to bring down the hammer.

Article by Bobby Jones of the Annandale Monitor writing team. Comments or questions, email Bobby at BJAM@Monitor.net.

The agents and inspector all had Deja-vu after Knox finished reading the article out loud. The team was sitting in a Waffle House, on their way from their hotel to meet with the county sheriff, since both murders were committed just outside city limits of both Fairfax and Annandale.

Malik finished the last bite of his omelet and replied to the reading of the article, "Now the assassin takes the cake. I could almost understand if the imams are somehow connected to terrorist organizations, which I sure some are. But not on this level. These were peaceful men, worshipping Allah the way it was meant to be done. Our assassin is once again escalating his behavior."

Knox gradually nodded, but scratched his head and said, "What if the author of the article is right? I am sure he is another conspiracy nutcase, but what if someone is covering this up? What if someone higher than us is after the assassin, and that is why he has accelerated the killing?"

Malik looked shocked. "You seriously feel something for this guy, don't you?"

Knox looked puzzled. "What makes you say that?" Malik looked hard at him and said. "Here we just read an article about two totally innocent men who got murdered in cold blood – and you want to make excuses for him and give him a legitimate reason to kill?" Knox looked to White for help, but she looked just as puzzled as he was.

"Malik, you've got me all wrong, brother. I think what he did is heinous, but keep in mind, he left a mother and child unharmed at one of the crime scenes. I think he thinks the ones who spread the word of Islam are the bad guys…that's why he's picking them off. I am in no way saying it's right, and just because I think the government at some higher level might be after him – does not mean I condone his sudden progress."

Malik shrugged and apologized.

"Sorry I snapped at you like that….sleep deprivation, you know. I am just tired of not knowing who Robert Brady is. We need something that includes him in a photo somewhere."

Across the street, the Arab-American man peered through the binoculars and watched the team of investigators from his parking spot across the street. He was in a rental car, and it conveniently came with tinted windows. The Arbiter was about to break protocol, but he was ready to pull out all stops against Brady. He knew that if he didn't get the agents to help track the assassin down, he might never catch him. Sure, Brady might mess up along the way and get caught, but if it took too long, his identity could eventually be tied back to the existence of the Activity. The Arbiter was aware of the investigation and steps they had taken so far; he had information sent to him via e-mail from the Director through classified channels. He had to admit…the team of law enforcement officers were pretty good, considering they did not have the knowledge with which the Arbiter and Director Marks had been given access. The Arbiter thumbed through the photos and picked the selfie Brady had taken, with the trees in the background. He thought that one was the best portrayal of what he remembered seeing through his scope in such a brief instant at the United Nations Visitors' Center. He took a snapshot of the picture with his cell phone and attached it to an e-mail. He typed on the small screen a message to none other than the lead investigator, Agent John Knox. When he finished typing, he sent the e-mail, and then he sat and waited for the team's reaction. He knew they'd take the bait and somehow track down Brady quicker once they had the same knowledge he did. He knew the Director would not approve, but he wasn't worried. He would fix the problem – and the evidence – once the investigators led him to the Jesus Assassin.

Knox was standing up at the cash register, using government money to pay for everyone's breakfast. Suddenly, his phone beeped and showed he had a new urgent e-mail. Knox opened up the e-mail on his phone as he handed the cashier the credit card. He read over the text and then looked at the photograph, and his teammates watched his eyes open wider. Knox handed his phone over to Malik.

Malik immediately said, "Hey – I know that guy from somewhere." Malik put his put his finger to his temple, but he couldn't think of where he had seen the man in the photo. Knox took the receipt from the cashier and filled out a generous tip, considering the revelation of facts in the e-mail. He then looked over at Malik, who handed the phone to Beth.

Knox almost sounded like he was rubbing it in as he asked Malik, "Still don't believe in government conspiracies? I don't know if these people are after Brady or not, but the message also says LAST SEEN IN BLUE JEEP COMMANDER. That seems pretty specific to me. I guess we can at least get Virginia law enforcement a decent description of a white male with red hair and green eyes, and a make and model of the vehicle."

The investigators went out the front door of the Waffle House, and all piled in Knox's rental sports sedan. The vehicle backed up, and took off quickly in a Northerly direction. As the car made some distance up the road, the Arbiter pulled out from his spot on the opposite curb and followed them. He knew they were headed to a certain cabin in the woods.

Richmond, Virginia
International Islamic Center of Virginia

     Brady didn't know anything about the article in the local Annandale newspaper. He just knew he was one target closer to the 12th Imam. He also knew that the largest mosque in Virginia was coming up on his right. It was the middle of the day, but he was willing to take the risk. He knew that it was common for mosques to hold Friday prayer at some point in the middle of the day. He didn't have time to calculate when the sun would be at its zenith (the time when Muslims carried out traditional midday prayer), but he knew he was early. He found the mosque quite accommodating for convenient parking; he was able to pull behind the mosque, and pull right down a ramp that led to the dumpsters. The way the ramp sloped down behind the building, passersby would have a difficult time knowing that a car was parked down there. He had passed several lots that were already full of cars on his way in. He thought that people were already getting comfortable and in places for the salat, so he went ahead and left the Jeep near the dumpsters. He got out and once again grabbed the crossbow. He grabbed several bolts, and even took out a quiver to wear on his back to help with carrying the bolts for the crossbow. Since he had already observed so many vehicles on the way in, he decided to scout out the mosque a little more thoroughly. As soon as he wondered around to the side of the building, he observed some Muslim worshippers gathering near a side entrance. As the small band of people finished entering for the prayer, Brady saw there were two large men guarding the double doors. They closed the doors behind the last stragglers and assumed an intimidating stance in front of the doors. Brady backtracked and went around to the other side; he saw two more guys guarding the other side entry. It appeared as though the guards all had radios. These men were looking around cautiously, as if they expected something bad to happen.

Brady was going to have to weigh his options. He could only assume the front of the mosque was just as heavily guarded as the side doors, if not more so. Brady decided he was going to have to take out two of the guards at the side. He couldn't tell if they were armed security or not – he would just have to assume they were armed. There was no way he could take out one guard without the other one making at least some kind of noise on the radio. Brady was quick, but not that quick. He was going to have to find something to distract them. Before he could do that, he would need to move his car. He had a plan, but in case any communication did get out among the guards, Brady needed to have a failsafe. He couldn't chance someone getting a vehicle or tag description to authorities. He went back to the hidden parking place near the dumpster and drove out of the parking lot and pulled the car off the road into a small patch of woods. He hoofed it back to the area with the dumpster, carrying the crossbow; this is where he would make his distraction. He had noticed that the large dumpster had huge lids that flipped over the top of the dumpster. He had heard the sound of that type of lid on a dumpster slam shut before. If he could make the lids slam down just right, it would almost sound like a gunshot. The small sloped drive-in area near the dumpster was closer to one side of the building than the other; the assassin was pretty sure the building itself would keep the goons from the other side from even hearing it. It was worth a shot. He went around to the narrow space behind the dumpster and the concrete wall on one side of the sloped entrance. He climbed up at a spot where one of the lids was already down. There were still three large black lids flipped open and backwards toward the wall. It was time to make some noise.

Jazeer and Amad were standing at their post at the side door, being watchful as instructed. Brady couldn't have known beforehand, but the International Islamic Center for Virginia was always heavy on security. Although the deaths of two local imams raised their eyebrows, they offered this kind of protection for their imam, Jafar al-Mirak Mohammed, every Friday during the Midday Salat. Mohammed demanded such security because he stirred the pot in the area; calling out the local atheists and Christians in the area for their false beliefs. So because it was just another Friday for the two guards, they were startled by the loud BOOM! The two guards gave each other a glance, but instead of calling in on the radio, the two geniuses decided to just head in the direction of the loud noise at the back of the property. They rounded the corner of the building and began a slow, cautious walk down the sloping driveway to the dumpster. As they approached the dumpster, they began whispering something in Arabic. Three of the lids were closed, but there was one more that was wide open against the wall behind the dumpster. They came within fifteen feet of the trash container, when suddenly the last lid came crashing down hard. Brady jumped out towards the men, and as he was falling towards the ground, he launched two throwing knives right at their throats. The two Arabs were just too slow for the Jesus Assassin. They both collapsed to the ground with hands immediately thrust against their own necks, attempting to stem the blood flow. Brady casually walked back around behind the dumpster and picked up his crossbow. He hung it over his shoulder and started a slow walk up the hill.

He watched cautiously as he came around the corner to the side doors the two Arabs had been guarding. There was no sign of extra security; he had been right in his pre-assessment that the two security guys were amateurs. He snuck in through the doors and came upon an empty hallway. As soon as he crept into the hall, the sounds from the main room of the mosque echoed throughout the building. As he stared at a set of steps at the end of the hall, he decided that this must go up to a balcony. To his relief, everyone was enthralled in the almost hypnotic effect of traditional Muslim prayers. When he crested the top of the stairs, he saw an empty balcony. So far - so good. He slowly made his way up close to the railing of the balcony. He peered over the edge and looked down upon hundreds of Muslims, prostrating themselves to the floor; he could only assume in the direction of Mecca. The Imam stood up at a podium of sorts at the front of the room, chanting and making Middle-Eastern utterances not understood by the assassin.

Brady sat back down with his back against the wall of sheet rock that made up the railing. He withdrew a bolt from his quiver, and he locked back the bowstring of the crossbow. He then took out a small sheet of paper he had folded in his pocket, along with a sharpie magic marker. He scribbled a brief message on the paper, and placed it on the floor close to where he was going to take his shot. He then placed a gold cross with the note. The Imam was really cranking out some prayers, because the Arabic he was speaking came out in what seemed to be endless, indecipherable gibberish. Brady put the stock of the crossbow up to his shoulder as he barely stood up over the rail. The Imam was speaking to the crowd with his eyes closed; or maybe he was speaking to Allah for the crowd. Brady didn't really know or care. He aimed through the scope, placing the crosshairs right on the center of Mohammed's chest. He pulled the trigger and let the bolt fly; and chaos followed.

The bolt struck the Imam mid-sentence, and took the wind from his sails. The Imam staggered backwards, and his security immediately knew from which angle the arrow or bolt came. One of the security team members ran to attempt to render first aid to the Imam, but because of the distance the bolt traveled, the acceleration of the bolt, and the impact of the modified bolt head – the Imam was dead in seconds. But as the rest of the guards in the room looked up at the balcony from the ground floor below, there was nobody to see. The assassin had taken off back down the stairs, up the hallway, and out the door. Security teams had scrambled out the front and side doors and scrambled around the property, but found no one. Up in the balcony, a security guard picked up a small note and the cross that lay with it. The note simply stated, 'Whatever he's saying, it ain't true.' At the same time that two more security guards discovered the two dead men at the dumpster, a certain man dressed in black was peeling off in his rental car, out of the woods and onto the main road. Only four more to go.

Brady's Cabin
Midday, as the Jesus Assassin strikes the 8th Imam

The three investigators opened the doors to their rental SUV and got out in front of the picturesque cabin. Although it was a hot day, most of the area around the quaint home was shaded by trees. Knox approached the front door somewhat carefully as he looked around for any signs that the man or a relative might still be around the home. Seeing nothing to cause alarm, the other two joined Knox as he knocked on the door. When he knocked a second time, the door slightly opened. Someone had forgotten to lock the door the last time they were here; at closer inspection, the deadbolt had been knocked clean through on the other side.

Malik spoke up as he drew his weapon, "So much for needing a warrant; someone's been here." The FBI agents drew their guns simultaneously, and the three agents methodically checked doors, sliced the pie, and gradually cleared the house, room to room.

Once they realized whoever had been in the cabin was long gone, they holstered their weapons, and Beth was the first to speak, "Well I don't know about you guys, but I'm going to take a look around."

Knox decided he would go explore outside. He went through the house and out the kitchen through the screen porch. He tried to see anything lying around, and he realized one of the screen doors had been forced open on one side of the porch as well. He looked outside in the backyard, and he saw the awesome view of the trees and mountains as a backdrop behind the peaceful pond. Off to one side of the yard, he saw a building that looked like it might be climate controlled, and he decided to go check it out first. As he came up to the door, he thought he saw something out of the corner of his eye. When he took a moment to look, whatever it was wasn't there anymore. He shrugged to himself, opened the black door, and walked inside. As he entered, he noticed the intense humidity at the same time that the motion sensors turned the lights on. Once the lights were on, Agent Knox was able to see a long line of containers; some large, plastic green ones; others made of glass. The glass tanks were obviously more telling of what was kept in these containers – snakes. As Knox walked past the first glass tank, he heard the rattle before he saw it. Obviously the rattlesnake inside was not too fond of his sudden presence in the room. The grumpy little snake got louder as he tapped on the glass. He moved on down the line of shelves, thinking it was probably a bad idea to open any lids on the green containers. He came upon another glass tank, but couldn't see the resident snake – or any place it could hide in the tank. Although he thought this was odd, he kept going. Finally he came upon some containers at the end that were labeled. One said KING BROWN SNAKE. The other one next to it said INLAND TAIPAN. And finally, the smoking gun, or dripping fang…so-to-speak – which was labeled BLACK MAMBA. Knox wasn't about to lift the lids on any of these boxes; he would just take the written words for what they said. Satisfied with his discoveries so far, he decided to proceed to the other small building in the back yard. He weaved his way around several roots in the yard, and made his way to the shed. He noticed it was unlocked as well, but when he walked in, he had to flip a switch to turn the lights on. As soon as he did, he saw large compound bows, long guns of various caliber, handguns hanging up on one of the walls, and a machine for loading one's own ammunition. Over in a corner on a work bench – there was a pile of syringes. They contained some kind of amber fluid inside; he could only guess that it was some kind of snake venom. Agent Knox had enough to suspect whoever was using this cabin was the assassin. He decided he'd go check on the others' progress; if they weren't looking for Brady, they were at least looking for someone who'd been using his property.

While Knox had been outside, Malik had been searching for photos of Brady himself. He had been through almost every room, and all he had been able to find were pictures of the photogenic girls in his life…his wife and daughter. Brady had pictures of his little ladies plastered all over the house. Malik still needed to see more pictures of Brady; the one he saw on Knox's phone struck a chord of familiarity, but he wouldn't mind seeing the man photographed from a different angle. Finally he came to the study. He saw that there were several pictures in a pile; they looked as if someone had gone through them recently. He picked up several of the pictures, and noticed the man from Knox's phone in several of the pics, posing with fellow SEALs. He picked up one picture in particular where the sunlight hit his eyes just right; he was standing next to his wife and some other SEAL who was obviously a close family friend. But in the perfect shadow and light, the man's green eyes jumped off the picture at Malik's memory, and he yelled out, "Aha!"

He went into the living room to tell Beth what he realized, when Knox came in through the kitchen and almost bumped into Malik. "Find anything, partner?"

Malik nodded, and said "I realized where I've seen Brady before…he's alive, Knox. And he's been right under our noses since I visited Langley! We've got to go back and nail him." Knox was about to tell him what he'd seen in the buildings out back, when Beth yelled to her partners, "Guys…in here!"

When they found her in the living room, she was holding a small leather-bound book open, diving into the handwriting on the pages. Beth was already known to the guys as a speed reader, and she expounded on what she'd already read. "You guys – this tells us everything. This tells why he's doing it…it tells us about the twelve imams; it has mock plans that match some of what has already happened to a Tee!" She closed the journal and laid it down for a minute. "Now that I have skimmed through some of that, I think I want to take a look at something I thought I saw earlier." Beth walked over to the TV, and she turned it on. She turned the DVD player on as she grabbed a small DVD case and showed Knox and Malik the title… 'My Reasons.' She hit play on the DVD player.

The DVD had started in a place that the Arbiter had either not cared to see or just didn't know was there. But at the beginning of the video, there were short clips of Brady swinging his daughter up in the air, holding her in his arms, and spinning her in circles. The video montage moved onto times when the beautiful little girl was older, and the redheaded father was seen pushing her down the driveway on her little pink bicycle, letting her go and watching her little redhead coast the rest of the way until she crashed into the bushes…with her mother to the rescue. It continued to a later time when the daughter with the matching green eyes, along with Brady and his wife, were posing out in front of the pond for live video shots of their little family. Brady kept coming and going from the shot, trying to get the video camera to get just the right shot of the three of them. Then there were shots of Brady and his beautiful wife, kissing passionately, not realizing until it was almost too late that their daughter had been capturing the whole thing on camera.

Finally there was a shot of just the women in Brady's life, sending him a message; probably recorded and sent to him overseas when he was a SEAL. His wife started, and could be seen and heard on the video saying, "Hey Hon…just wanted to send you a message to tell you how much we miss you around here. The bed is awfully empty without you in it…and Jessie misses you something fierce. Speaking of fierce, here she is." Brady's daughter entered the scene, holding a black rat snake, speaking in a false Australian accent. "Now you can see as I handle the black rat snake, he sticks his tongue out time and again to taste the air. If this were a black mamba, I would literally be 'sweating bullets." The video showed more of the two little ladies laughing and joking, and then yelling to Brady, "Come home soon!"

Then the video went to static for a split second before it cut to a terrorist with his head wrapped in a checkered kafia. The two FBI agents and Malik looked on as the TV screen showed the tragic scene of the terrorist's rant - and the horrific execution of his little ladies. Before the ultimate gruesome scene hit them in the face, Knox reached out and cut the TV off. The tension in the room could have been cut with a knife.

Malik finally shook his head and said, "That's not Islam. That's just barbaric homicidal maniacs!"

Malik had to walk away from what he just saw, and wandered outside. Meanwhile, Knox looked at Beth, and her eyes were so full of tears. She stopped holding it in, and she at least needed to wipe her eyes with some Kleenex nearby. Knox even had a hard time not letting a tear fall himself, but he wanted to be strong in front of Beth. He ejected the video and picked up the journal and put them in his inner pocket in his sports coat. Then he went back out to the shed and snake house to take pictures of everything. Several minutes later, Knox, Beth, and Malik headed back to the car. Everyone walked away from the house in an awkward silence.

They were all walking to the rental car when a long, slender gray streak of movement lashed up and out from the bushes out in front of the house towards Malik. Knox's pistol was out in a flash, and bullets riddled the gray serpent until it was a dead mass of scales sizzling on the ground. Agent Knox had almost emptied a whole magazine to make sure that he didn't miss the black mamba that had reached out for Malik with blinding speed. The sudden break in the somber mood was a welcome change.

Malik spoke up after his heart stopped racing, "Well, I guess I owe you one, Knox."

Knox laughed, "Well, at least I know why one of the glass tanks in the snake house was empty."

Malik eventually got to tell them where he had seen Brady before, and that easily made up Knox's mind.

He put the rental in Drive, and said, "Well gang…next stop – Langley!"

PART THREE

Durham, North Carolina
Local University's Football Stadium

It was a small football stadium for a Division I school, but it didn't pose any problems for Brady as far as blending into a crowd was concerned. It was around seven thirty in the evening, and the liberal University had decided to allow a large gathering of The United American Muslims to meet inside their stadium. Brady had donned some loose robes held in place with a large black and white sash tied around his waist. He strolled around the top perimeter of the upper deck around the stadium. The stadium was set up like a giant bowl, and the top deck was at ground level, where all the vendors and merchants sold refreshments and fan merchandise during football games. Brady considered his presence here a blessing from God; he just happened upon a sign advertising the event as he drove into the North Carolina town of Durham to stop for lunch. He was amazed at the sheer volume of people in attendance – he had no idea that Islam had spread so rampant among Americans; especially in the South! Brady had acquired his current outfit by 'borrowing' it from a student outside the gates of the stadium, shouting out blasphemous messages about Allah, and how He will judge the United States soon. It didn't take the assassin long to take a small, discrete detour with the student behind some trees and shrubbery – where he just happened to beat the student within an inch of his life, stripped him of his robes, and casually broke his neck.

Brady was not sure what his target looked like, but he knew he would have a large audience. The assassin decided he would recon the stadium and its layout, and assassinate the featured American Imam when he had his biggest crowd of spectators. Brady was up for a challenge; he thought he had gotten away from the mosque in Richmond way too easily. He was ready to fight his way out of the stadium if he must. He had no qualms about harming these dysfunctional, brainwashed Americans who had supposedly 'found Allah'. Brady couldn't help but laugh to himself as he observed the many students and other American citizens (mostly white Americans) walking around wearing robes and turbans. Brady thought it looked like some kind of bathrobe convention. He could hear whisperings and conversations around him in both English and Arabic. It never ceased to amaze him how people who were born in the USA with certain inalienable rights in a country blessed by God – could turn on that God and worship a false god made up by a false prophet. In Brady's mind, worshipping Allah was no different than worshipping Satan himself.

Brady turned a corner and started making his way down by rows of spectators. As he began to see more of the football field, he could see the stage about three quarters of the way back from the front entrance to the stadium. The stage was surrounded by large frames to hold up stage lights, and the sides of the stage were divided from the rest of the surrounding stadium seating by a large black curtain to either side. A podium sat in the center of the stage, and several cameras aiming towards the podium from various angles in front of the stage. They had also set up two large TV monitors in front of the black curtains, so crowds sitting farther away could still see the Imam once he took the stage. Brady was fascinated by the spectacle of it all; one could tell these were truly American Muslims because of how Americanized and elaborate the whole show was going to be. True Muslims would not waste such money and energy on the entertainment side of Islam. But then again – it obviously turned out the big crowds. Maybe this was how Islam was going to take the US by storm. Brady made it down to the bottom row of the stadium bowl and made his way out onto the field; security was not very tight at this facility.

That is where Brady saw their weakness…the liberal University would spend an arm and a leg for security during college football season; but when it came to the United American Muslims having to provide their own, it was very limited. Brady doubted very seriously anyone in the place was armed besides him. He did think this group was *trying* to portray the more pacifistic side of Islam. That didn't matter to Brady, though. Blasphemy was blasphemy.

Brady surveyed the stage, and realized that the metal framework for the lighting stretched up a good 20 feet above the podium, with metal crossbeams holding lights and speakers in a straight line across the top of the stage. Brady could tell by looking at all the equipment that the framework would easily hold his weight. He could visualize his attack in his mind as he traced over the layout of the metal tubing and crossbars on stage with his eyes.

Brady just had to make it close enough to the stage to get behind the curtain, shed the stupid robe he was wearing now, and climb up the metal frame of stage equipment to wait for the precise moment to strike. He had on his token black outfit underneath the robes; he would need it to blend in with the black curtain as he made his ascent and moved across the bars. He nudged past a few robed figures that acted oblivious to his presence. He knew the type of people he'd be dealing with as he would fight his way out of this place; as long as he didn't get over-zealous and try to take on too big of a mob, he would leave the stadium with nothing more than hard breathing. He got close to the black curtain and peered around his immediate vicinity to see if anyone was paying him attention. Seeing nobody of interest, he dove in through a gap in the curtain and pulled it over behind him. There were no backstage workers because this wasn't a rock concert. There would be no groupies trying to get behind the curtain, or any roadies attempting to hang out with the band as they warmed up.

The assassin ducked down into the shadows behind the curtain and removed the hideous bathrobe. He pulled his black hood over his head. He didn't need his night vision, so he left the night vision glasses in his chest pocket. He peeked around a large post holding up one side of the curtain; there was a tall, lean white man with red hair, similar to the assassin's own hair. He also had a full beard and a small, dark gray turban. The man was Karim Alah-ah Ahkmed, and he was about to address the whole congregation of Muslims in the stadium. The assassin didn't know if he was going to simply offer prayer (It was not Friday at Midday) or deliver some kind of speech. He saw a woman who looked like some kind of event manager speaking to him, pointing in different directions, but having a questioning look on her face, like she was asking the Imam permission for something. He didn't wait around to find out what she was talking about, and instead found an inconspicuous place to begin his climb. He made sure he moved through a dark corner of the curtain as he made his ascent backstage. He was slow and deliberate, making sure his large body didn't shake the metal tubing and bars in any pronounced fashion. Hand over hand, knees slowly pumping in alternating motion, he moved up the metal frame of the lighting like a spider stalking a fly caught in its web. The structure had only shown signs of shaking once or twice, but he made it all the way to the top with ease. As he came up just past the top of the curtain, he realized that the crowd probably wouldn't see him if he stayed on top of the structure because the sky was already dark, and all the light in the place pointed at the center of the stage.

There was a loud squeal through the speakers as the Imam approached the podium carrying a small, black microphone. He moved it further out and attached it to the mic stand at the front of the podium, and he cleared his throat. It appeared he was not there to offer prayer; he began addressing the entire crowd in English. The assassin listened for a short time, with some interest. "Ladies and gentlemen – fellow Americans…Thank you for coming tonight. This marks a new era in our nation. This is just the beginning of a movement that I intend to help spread like wildfire throughout this country. Folks, we are here tonight to show the world that America is ready to embrace Islam. There is no will but Allah's, and Allah has made it possible for us to assemble like this, in the United States…in the South, no less! I am here to tell you all, blessed followers of Allah, that we all must submit to Allah and his will. His will is to spread the news of his almighty power, and share the word that there is no alternative but to submit to Allah." After hearing the words 'submit' and 'Allah' too many times in one sentence, Brady had determined that it was now or never. He shimmied his way out over the cross support over the Imam's head. He hoisted himself up where he supported all his weight on his forearms as he peered down below to make sure he was lined up with his target. Just as he heard someone shriek up at him, as if he were about to attack them, the man dressed in black dropped down upon the Imam's shoulders. The 240 pound assassin made the 190 pound bean pole (Ahkmed was 6 feet, 6 inches tall) collapse like a house of cards. Although he knew his descent probably broke several of the Imam's bones, he withdrew a syringe from one of his inner pockets and planted the needle right into the man's neck.

He leaned in close to the Imam's ear, and whispered "How's this for Allah's will?"

He pressed the plunger all the way in, and then dropped the Imam's head like a sack of potatoes. He observed the short gasps for breath as the fast-acting snake venom raced straight to the brain. He took out a gold cross, and flung it on the floor next to the Imam. He had no time to waste, and he ran towards the back of the stage. The front side of the stage sounded like pandemonium, but several of the crowd knew the assassin was the famed Jesus Assassin who had killed so many imams already. He already had people running up to the stage as he jumped over some equipment and then pushed it down behind him as he began his escape.

Although Brady knew he had to evade the on-coming crowd of outraged Muslims in order to complete his mission, he let rage drive him forward. Just the mere thought of Islamic terrorists and the harm they had brought to his entire family made him keep pumping his arms and legs. As he used his arms to boost himself over the wall before climbing the rear steps of the stadium to the top of the bowl, a crazed follower of the Imam grabbed at his ankle. He ruthlessly kicked the guy between the teeth as hard as he could, seeing the instant gap in the top row of teeth as he fell back down to the field. The assassin reached the steps in between rows of seats, and began the fastest stadium run ever. There were loyal Muslims true to Allah's cause who were banking in on him as they had cut across the rows of seats. Brady batted one away with an elbow to the forehead. He jumped and kneed one would-be attacker up under the chin, ending his state of consciousness. Brady started to take three, sometimes four steps at a time, and he kept running. The crowd kept coming as well. As Brady reached the top row, he made a turn into a crowd of six robed men by planting two hands down on the top of the chair and then swinging his legs around in a circular whirlwind of motion, as if he were an Olympic gymnast. Four more men discovered what it felt like to get knocked out, and the other two lost their desire to catch this mad man known as the Jesus Assassin. Brady found open space and made a run for it. Although he got quite the head-start on the crowd watching the stage, just the large number of spectators swept him into corners of the top deck, and he knew he needed to exit the stadium before he was trapped and pummeled by the mob.

Brady saw his way out as he approached the fence where tickets were usually collected on game day. He boosted himself up and scaled the fence like a ninja, and the on-coming crowd hit the fence and almost came to a dead-stop. That gave the assassin the momentum he needed to run to the parking lot. By this point, campus security had heard about the commotion, and a small golf cart with headlights began bearing down on Brady's position as he cut through the large parking lot. He split down one row, ducked down and rolled under a pickup truck, and temporarily lost the security officers. He got back up and took off down the same row on top of vehicles; he could see where he parked his Jeep Commander. The security officers made a sudden U-turn in the golf cart, almost flipping in the process. Brady found his Jeep at the last second, jumped in, and fired that puppy up. Just as the golf cart pulled up next to his Jeep, Brady swung the Jeep into reverse in a wide arc, punched the gas pedal to the floor, and left the guys in the golf cart wondering if anyone ever caught that license plate.

Langley, Virginia
Outside CIA Headquarters

Malik told Knox as he stood outside the front doors of the CIA headquarters, "Let me try my contact I made the last time I was here. He worked just down the hall from Brady; he probably doesn't even know it's Brady." Malik dialed up the phone number that Agent Rutter had given him the last time.

"Rutter here. Who's speaking?" Malik re-introduced himself, and Agent Rutter acknowledged him, "Oh yes, Malik...good to hear from you again. What can I help you with today?"

"Well, I'm outside with two other agents and we wanted to talk to you in person; ask you some more questions about someone that works on your hall." Rutter told him to check in with the security personnel, and he would have three scan cards made for them. The agents all scanned into the building, and then scanned their cards again to get on the elevator. Knox and White just followed Malik; this was his show since he had been here before. Once they arrived on the fourth floor, Malik immediately turned to the right and walked confidently down the hall, like a man on a mission. Instead of turning around the corner to the left and going to Rutter's office, Malik made a bee-line to the office at the corner of 4B and 4C. He walked straight up to the door, turned the knob, and walked right in. He came right back out, then headed right to Rutter's office. Knox followed behind, with Beth on his heels. "What gives, Malik?"

Malik ignored his cohort for a moment and immediately addressed Agent Rutter with some concern. "The man who was in that office last time I was here...where is he?" Rutter shrugged, and replied, "You mean Maxwell? He transferred to a different department. That's all I was told. One day he was here; next day – he and his things were gone."

Malik looked over at Knox and explained, "He was here when I was, Knox. He was in that office, and he and those deep green eyes – he looked right at me. Son of a...I could have had him."

Rutter jumped in, "Excuse me...could've had who? Maxwell? He was in logistics, just like me. He worked for me, or under me anyway. What'd you need with Maxwell?" Malik finished, "Agent Rutter – I know you said you never saw him, so you wouldn't know...but his name wasn't Maxwell. That was Robert Brady, and he's our assassin." Rutter took a moment to digest the information.

In the meantime, the agents all walked back to the old office previously occupied by 'Maxwell'. The office was so clean and bare, the three of them could have sat down and eaten a meal off the floor. There was no trace of the previous occupant. Malik pointed out that he had at least noticed a large Bible sitting on the corner of the desk before Brady had gotten up to close the door that day. Knox shook his head and bit his upper lip.

Beth knew that perplexed look. He didn't worry often, and Beth was one of the few that could tell when he was worried. She asked, "What's wrong?" Knox responded, "Somebody bigger than the FBI doesn't want us finding this Brady character. If I were a betting man, I'd say they already have someone trying to take care of him as we speak." Just then, his cell phone buzzed. Coincidentally, so did Malik's. They looked at each other strangely as both of them answered to the glorious sound of upset supervisors.

McCoy asked as soon as Knox said 'Hello'. "Agent Knox...have you been watching the news? Have you been checking your e-mails? Better yet, have you climbed out from under that rock you and your cronies have been hiding under?!" the SAC finished erupting.

Knox tried to add with a calming effect, "It's Robert Brady, sir. We know it's him. We have evidence that proves it's him. That's where we've been sir. We found his family cabin. We found the snakes. We found everything sir...except him."

The SAC seemed to be absorbing the information slowly on his end of the line. Finally he sounded more relaxed, but still concerned. "So that's why you weren't at the crime scenes of the small town assassinations?" Knox nodded and answered, "Affirmative, sir. We've kept abreast of media information, but we got a clue sent to us by an undisclosed informer."

McCoy fired back, "Undisclosed informer? Is this guy working with someone else? Why would someone want to help you catch this guy, but not identify themselves?" Knox thought for a minute.

"Sir – there's more. Malik had seen Brady the last time when he was here…back when White and I went to Fort Benning. He was posing as some analyst. Well, now his office is cleared out and he has vanished without a trace. Sir, I think this is bigger than you and me."

The SAC took a second or two to take this new info under consideration.

"Nevertheless, follow the course he's on, John. Catch this guy…put a stop to him. You probably missed this last assassination; being as busy as you guys have been. You near a TV?"

Knox asked Rutter if there was a TV nearby, and he motioned the team to his office. Meanwhile, Malik walked and talked with his boss. The Chief, Holcroft, stated plainly, "Sharif – what is the meaning of this. Your killer is running amok in the US!" Malik tried to reassure his Chief Inspector.

"Sir, we almost have him pinned down. We know his identity. His name is Robert Brady"- Holcroft cut him off in a thick German accent. "I don't care if he's Mickey Mouse – Catch him before he kills again!" Holcroft once again hung up abruptly, leaving Malik worried about being taken off the case if they didn't catch this guy soon.

He paid attention to his team, and they were all looking up at the TV screen in Rutter's office. The headline that rolled across the bottom of the screen said it all: *JESUS ASSASSIN KILLS IN FRONT OF THOUSANDS ON TV BROADCAST.* Those words kept scrolling across the screen underneath some disturbing footage of what looked like some modern-day ninja storming through a crowd of people, injuring them as he went. The scene then cut back to the video clip that caused the headline. The television showed the same black figure drop from the scaffolding that held up the stage lights, right onto the Imam standing below him. It also showed the man bend down and inject something into the Imam's neck…and then again jumped to the scene of panic in the football stands. The investigators all stood there staring at the screen, when Beth finally spoke up. "So that's in Durham, North Carolina…right?"

Knox nodded at the screen. Beth continued, "I know Virginia pretty well; as well as North Carolina. He is following the Interstate 95/85 corridor. If we can look at a map, or even the internet – maybe we can guess the next large Muslim site in his path."

Malik snapped his fingers and added, "You've got it. I've got a road atlas in the car." With that, the agents left Agent Rutter standing there, dumbfounded and asking himself what just happened. Before they rounded the corner, Malik yelled back to Rutter, "Sorry – almost forgot. Thank you for all your help, Rutter. You helped more than you know."

The team left and went to the SUV. Beth opened the road atlas, and the next major city in the path was Greensboro. Knox googled the city, and specified the search to Muslim mosques in Greensboro. Once several choices popped up on the screen, Knox and Malik perused the images and words for each location. Finally, Knox pointed at one in particular, and Malik nodded; if they were trained killers of imams, that's where they'd go. It was time to find the Jesus Assassin.

Greensboro, North Carolina
Islamic Mosque of Greensboro

Brady put the Jeep Commander in park, with its beat up fenders and a windshield riddled with bullet holes. It was about ten in the morning, and he found a hidden alcove of trees along a gravel path not far from the mosque he intended to stake out. Brady knew whoever the Activity had sent after him was well behind him by now, so he had time to prepare. He parked just far enough away from the main roads to remain inconspicuous. He decided that he would stalk and hunt down the next imam at the mosque nearby, just outside a heavily populated part of the city of Greensboro. He knew the place and area would be new to him, so he would observe the coming and going of the various people at the mosque throughout the day. Brady was a master at finding a place to hide, in almost any conditions and environment. He would treat this like any other mission – like he was trained to do. He felt like a novelist who was almost finished with a story; the end of his mission was within sight…and he could hardly contain himself due to his excitement. It would be rewarding to possibly help bring about Christ's return by putting all these cogs in motion for the Lord. Brady had considered himself God's tool. The way he saw it, God used his mission objectives to bring more spiritual unrest between God's people and the rest of the world. If he could get the rest of the ungodly world angry at Christianity, Jesus would have to come back in order to save His people one last time. Brady also thought about the reward that mattered most to him, personally. Brady just knew that a merciful God would allow him to see his wife and daughter, and parents again – despite the sinful actions he had been forced to take along the way.

Brady crept through the trees that lined a frontage road to a minor highway. He looked at the GPS on his cell phone, and could see that he would have to make his way around a sewage treatment plant to get to his objective. He used the satellite picture application on his phone to zoom in on the layout of both the property of the mosque and the plant, and visualized the path he needed to take as he lightly touched the screen. He saw on the map a thin trail that cut a path between the properties through another copse of trees. He got his bearings and headed in that direction, finding the trail about two minutes later. Brady was getting closer to more civilization; he could hear the traffic from a nearby convergence of main thoroughfares into and out of Greensboro. He was getting close.

As he came to a clearing at the end of the trees, there it was; the Islamic Mosque of Greensboro. It didn't look like the typical mosques you see and read about in the Middle East – but it wasn't exactly small. It was built in similar fashion to an American elementary school from the 1980's. It was a large, spread out, one level complex - but with obvious high ceilings inside. Brady looked to the other side of the parking lot and saw that the Mosque was about to grow. He wasn't sure what was under construction until he noticed a construction company's large white sign, showing a depiction of the completed project and labeling it COMING SOON: MUSLIM SCHOOL OF GREENSBORO. There were several buildings and structures of two to three stories, with some structures more complete than others. What a great place to hide….once the construction workers had left for the day.

Brady ran to a corner of the building, and saw two large air units that would keep him concealed during the day, provided nobody needed to mess with the air conditioning that day. He looked around and saw a few cars pulling into the distant entrance to the parking lot. They must be coming for the Midday prayer. He waited until the cars parked and were facing away from him, and made a mad dash for the large air units. Once again, Brady would play his waiting game. Snipers had been practicing this for decades now…finding a hide, and waiting for their target to reveal themselves; sometimes waiting days at a time. Brady had no intention of sniping this imam, though. He would wait for the moment to strike when he was alone and vulnerable. Now he would become a people watcher...and wait.

****

Malik pulled into the parking lot of the mosque. The International Mosque of Southern Muslims was not expecting a visit from the FBI today, but Knox figured it was as good a place to start as any. They were just past downtown Greensboro, and this mosque was the one they found on the internet that was in the most direct path down Interstate 85.

Knox spoke to the group. "Okay gang, I contacted all the local authorities, and I also have North Carolina's FBI office in with us. They are putting out extra patrols on all 15 public Islamic sites in a 30 mile square radius of Greensboro. I thought that would raise our probability of finding Brady. What we'll do here, and every location we come to, is separate and spread out and search for any signs of Brady, and speak to anyone we encounter along the way that thinks they saw anything suspicious. We've been grasping at straws, guys...but Beth's hunches have gotten us further in this investigation than anything else."

Beth slapped Knox on the back from the back seat, "Aw – that's a sweet thing to say." Malik offered, "Um, hello? It's true. Beth, you've been the brains of this operation from the start. May I just say, I am honored to have worked with both of you on this."

With that, he abruptly exited the SUV and walked towards the mosque itself. Beth pulled Knox back in his seat from behind with one hand and planted a quick kiss on his lips. "That really is sweet. But you guys have contributed just as much. Now – let's find this whacko."

She opened her door, and started heading to the far side of the complex and began a walk around the perimeter of the building. Knox decided he would monitor the parking lot. While waiting, he couldn't help but ask himself, 'Is this assassin really whacko? Is he really that different than me? If I lost everyone I loved, my temper would send me after the killers for sure. If that lead me into a crusade against an anti-Christian religion, so be it. No,' he decided. 'He's not crazy. He's just as misguided as all of us.' He decided that he was going to approach this assassin with caution, but also understanding. That little video at the cabin had more of an impact on him than he thought. Of course, to approach the assassin, they would have to catch him first. Little did he know that this would be the first of a few stops that day where they would come up empty-handed. He didn't know what the day had in store for them. He also didn't know that they were being watched.

****

He watched from across the street in the supermarket parking lot. He saw two of the investigators get out and go their separate ways to explore inside and outside the mosque. The Arbiter could only assume that their leader, the one to whom he had sent the e-mail, was waiting and watching from their rental car. The Arbiter didn't think they would find their target here; it just didn't feel right to him. His only close encounters with Robert Brady, a.k.a. the Jesus Assassin, had been in the attack at the cabin, and his brief meeting in a makeshift hangar - on an air base in Iraq. But he had read *all* of Brady's file. He probably knew Brady better than any one of the three investigators; he was surely a better match against Brady in a fight than the agents. But this mosque; its location; its convenience; its simplicity…it was just too easy. Brady liked a challenge. If something wasn't much of a challenge, Brady at least wanted things to appear to be a challenge at first glance – so he could always make people say, "He did what?!"

The Arbiter had faith in the sleuthing ability of the agents, though. He knew the assassin might be too much of a match for them if they ever caught up to him, but he wasn't too worried about that. He would take care of the problem real quick. Yes, the Arbiter could feel the end in sight, just like Brady. It was only a matter of time before they clashed. Although, if the Arbiter had things his way – there would never even be the need for a clash…if he could take care of the problem from a safe distance.

****

It was almost dusk, and Officer Lovelace was cruising the vicinity of the sewage treatment plant and the nearby mosque. He was good at his job; always extremely observant, noticing little things that common people would never pay attention to. That's why when he slowly drove past a copse of trees, he happened to notice what he thought was a red reflector shining his alley lights back in his direction as he passed a small gravel path, just wide enough to drive a vehicle. Lovelace drove a little further down, and then whipped into a U-turn after making sure there was no traffic to oppose him. He came back to the gravel path and pulled his patrol vehicle onto the little trail. He followed it back a few yards and around a small curve. As soon as there was a clearing, he knew he had something. The A.P.B. (All Points Bulletin) that had been put out to his platoon had been for a blue Jeep Commander. He immediately got on his radio and called in the approximate location, and requested backup. All units had been advised to approach the vehicle with extreme caution because there was a possibility that the owner was the now infamous Jesus Assassin. This Jeep looked like it had been through a small war zone, and Lovelace shined his spotlight right into the rearview mirror in case it was occupied. He got out quickly and drew his sidearm and flashlight. He wasn't about to take any chances with a known assassin. He had already made up his mind as he got out of his car that if the assassin was in the Jeep, and made the slightest overt move, he would empty his magazine into the bastard.

As he got closer to the vehicle, he touched the rear tale light just as he was always taught…in case the worst happened, and the assassin killed him and got away; at least there would be a Jeep Commander somewhere with Officer Lovelace's prints on the rear tale light. He aimed his flashlight and the muzzle of his weapon into every visible part of the vehicle as he walked up to the window, but realized the Jeep was empty once he got all the way up to the driver's side window. He cautiously scanned around him for any signs of an ambush, but once he realized he was alone, he re-holstered his weapon. He kept the flashlight out and looked around the vehicle for any signs of where the assassin had gone. He wasn't about to track this guy down alone; he would wait until backup arrived…and possibly a K-9 unit.

****

Knox, Malik, and Agent White were just leaving the parking lot of their fourth mosque of the day, when Knox got the call from the night shift captain. He put the call on speaker phone so his teammates could listen. Captain Bo Reynolds was on the other end of the line, and had good news for the agents. One of his boys in blue had come across a suspicious vehicle; a blue Jeep Commander parked within one mile of a local mosque. Knox looked right at Malik and winked as the captain added that the Jeep looked like it had been shot several times. Knox informed the captain that they would be on their way, and Malik floored it as Knox quickly told him which direction to take.

In a matter of fifteen minutes, the agents had made it across town and were sitting in the parking lot of a strange one story building for a place of worship. Behind the building was the hulk of empty structures on the construction site for the future Muslim school. The parking lot was still somewhat full; attendees of the mosque were just leaving out the front doors to go back to their cars to go home after their evening prayer. Knox noticed right away that there was no observable sense of panic in the exiting Muslims' faces. Malik parked the car, and the agents immediately got out and met up with the lieutenant standing outside the front door, standing next to his patrol vehicle.

"What took you guys so long? I thought you feds were supposed to be hot stuff?" the lieutenant asked jokingly. Then he motioned inside and changed to a more serious tone, "Captain Reynolds is inside. He rode with me. He's filling the imam in on what's going on."

Beth was just about to tell the lieutenant that the agents would take over from here, but Knox walked in front of her and offered a hand. "Thanks, Lieutenant. We'll go and get the story. Thanks for bringing the captain." The tall brawny lieutenant smiled and nodded his head, but then gawked at Agent White's rear end as she walked by and followed Knox.

Malik cleared his throat as he caught up and chuckled, "Sorry man, but that seat's taken." He punched the lieutenant in the shoulder and followed his teammates into the mosque.

When the agents entered, they saw who they assumed to be Captain Reynolds slowly walking to the door with a Muslim Imam, Imam Masadi al-Hara.

The agents overheard the imam finishing conversation with the captain as they approached the door.

"Captain Reynolds, I appreciate your concern for my welfare," the exiled Iranian was saying, "But, I assure you, as long as I am at the mosque I am safe. Look around...do my brothers and nephews look like the kind of family to let harm come to me?"

The agents and the captain glanced around at the pillars along the walls; he had a good point. There were six good, strong looking and opposing Muslim figures standing along the side and back walls of the mosque. Captain Reynolds, a short and stocky black man, looked up and saw Agent Knox, and motioned him over to the imam.

"Agent Knox, I presume – Captain Bo Reynolds. This is the Imam Masadi al-Hara. Imam – these are the federal agents trying to capture the Jesus Assassin."

The imam looked at Agent Knox, and then at Malik and nodded, "Welcome...I am pleased to meet you Agents. But as I was just telling the captain, I am fine and well-protected. There has been no assassin here at our mosque today; otherwise, I would have called you and your men a long time ago," finished the imam with his Iranian accent.

"If it's all the same to you, Imam, we'd at least like to drive behind you on your ride home...to make sure you aren't followed," Knox offered in return. The imam stood there in what appeared to be deep thought for a moment, and finally replied, "Very well, Agents. You may reinforce my safety as I drive home tonight. But I am afraid you will have to wait another half hour or so – I have some cleaning up to do around the mosque."

The agents nodded in understanding, and began heading out the door. Before Knox headed back outside, he told Al-Hara, "Imam, thank you for listening. We just want to take all precautions, sir."

As he stepped outside, the captain caught up with him shortly after saying his farewells to the imam. "Thank you, Agents, for offering to do that. We have been a little short-staffed tonight, and I honestly couldn't even get a K-9 unit over here to try to do any tracking. The west side of the city is marbles right now...and we've had random shootings on the south end about half the night."

Knox pumped the captain's hand, and then finally offered the typical FBI response that Beth had wanted to say earlier: "Thank you for your help, Captain, but we can take it from here." The captain smiled as he shook Malik and Agent White's hands, and then headed over to the lieutenant's car and climbed in. The agents watched as he made a waving motion forward to the lieutenant who was already waiting in the patrol car. The police officers sped off out of the parking lot, and the feds remained behind to ensure the safety of Imam al-Hara.

****

    The assassin lay there underneath the blanket, scrunched down in the back seat of the large sedan. He had been waiting there since late afternoon, once he realized which car belonged to the imam, and he had recognized the imam by the turban he wore on his head that nobody else seemed to wear. Brady had the hypodermic needle primed and ready once he realized it was dark outside. The imam had not been back to his car since he had arrived again in the afternoon; Brady thought that was fortunate. Even though he had entered from the rear passenger's side door, he had broken the door handle off on the passenger's side…and he really didn't need the imam to see that little piece of handiwork. Unfortunately for Brady, he had not been privy to any of the events that had transpired regarding the discovery that he was in the area. He had no idea that federal agents had tracked him down, or that his Jeep had been discovered in the woods nearby. He had chosen to just enter his state of waiting calm; the one that he was trained to enter as a SEAL sniper. That's why he wasn't startled or surprised by the sudden opening of the driver's side car door, or the shaking of the front seat as the imam climbed in and plopped down into his seat for his long drive home. Oddly enough, Brady was there to assure that the drive would not be very long at all.

Imam al-Hara had climbed in, got comfortable in his seat, and cranked the engine. Once the motor was up and running, he put the car in reverse and arced the car out of the parking space, and began aiming his big Buick Sedan towards the exit of the parking lot up closer to the mosque itself. As he slowly made his way through the parking lot, he was suddenly grabbed from behind. He felt a sharp pain for a brief moment at the base of his skull, opened his mouth and eyes, just about to scream, and lost all control of the vehicle. Brady quickly extracted the syringe, and briefly looked out the windshield. He ducked down in the back seat and braced himself at the last second, as the car went careening out of control, directly towards a street lamp.

****

Agent Knox was in the driver's seat again, and he cranked the car up as he and his partners cautiously watched the imam steer his vehicle towards the upper exit to the parking lot. It was dark outside, and the imam's rear window was tinted – so the agents couldn't see inside the car from their SUV.

As they began to slowly follow the imam's vehicle, Malik spoke up, "Hey – what's he doing?" Just as Malik spoke, the agents were dumfounded as the imam's car suddenly took a strange left turn and smashed straight into a street lamp.

As Knox slammed on the brakes, Malik and Beth were out of the car. Agent Knox quickly put the parking brake on and got out the driver's side as fast as he could. The other two agents were already off and running after a shadowy figure, who was garbed in black from head to toe. The hooded man ran like an oversized wide receiver, pumping his arms and making up tons of ground. Beth couldn't quite keep up, but Malik looked like he was even faster than the assassin.

All three agents knew who they were after, and shouted at different intervals as they ran, "Stop – FBI! Brady – stop right there! Robert Brady – you're under arrest!" seemed to come from all three investigators at one point or another. Knox finally caught up to Beth, and everyone realized their target had run straight for the construction site.

Malik was hot on the heels of Brady, and he quickly turned the corner of the mosque and saw him run into a three story building; an unfinished structure of immense proportion, with only walls of wood and sheet rock up, supporting the building hallways and giving the interior its general shape, but nothing more. As he ran through the doorway into the dark, he saw the assassin's shadow pass up a flight of steps. Malik adjusted quickly and followed. He flew up the stairs, and ran down a corridor that was dimly lit by utility lights hanging along the walls. He was upon another doorway and didn't have time to slow down before realizing it was dark immediately upon entry. As soon as he ran across the threshold, he was suddenly hit by an arm bar and taken to the floor hard. There was just enough light for him to see a foot come crashing down towards his chest; Malik threw up his forearms in a tight bend and caught the boot. He twisted furiously and spun his body around so that he was up on his feet, ready to take on his assailant. Brady quickly backed away from him in the dark; moonlight shining on parts of his black outfit. Malik's training in Israeli martial arts, or Krav Maga, had prepared him for fighting most people. But he could tell right away that this man Brady was going to be a handful. He was almost identical in size to Agent Knox, and outweighed Malik by about fifty pounds. But the assassin was backing further into the room. Malik then realized, he was giving himself more room to fight because of his large size. The further back he went into that particular room, the higher the ceilings and wider the walls. They squared off and began circling. Part of one side of the wall was open to the air; no wall at all. The other side had incomplete windows; no glass to break – just large holes that lead to the ground three stories below.

Malik then feinted to grab for Brady's arm, but then struck him with a sharp elbow across the side of his head. Brady's quickness allowed him to avoid the brunt of the blow, and caused a small cut to open on the side of his face from the fast graze across his forehead. Brady came back with a solid kick to Malik's hip, and made him cringe to his side for a short moment. That gave Brady the chance he needed to throw Malik off the floor and into the construction site below...but he refrained. Agents Beth White and John Knox ran into the room, and charged towards Brady, forcing him back to the corner of the room.

Beth spoke up with her pistol drawn, "Robert...just stop running. If you come along quietly, and cooperate, we can maybe find a judge who will give you some leniency."

Brady smirked. "Leniency? You think I want leniency? Lady – I don't know who you are, nor do I care, but I don't have anything to lose."

Knox spoke up, "We know, Brady. We saw the video...and the journal." Those words caused Brady to pause.

Then Beth added, "We know about your family, Robert. We know about all of them; your parents, too." Brady paused a little longer. Beth continued, "I've lost someone, too. My brother – my best friend in the world – was killed in the line of duty by an evil man. I wanted revenge, too. That's why I became an agent."

Then Brady slowly edged his way around the room to one of the windows. "Then you know why I can't just give up. Not yet – the mission isn't complete."

Just when Knox was about to lunge and attempt to tackle Brady, he and Beth both saw a small, bright red light appear on Brady's chest from the side of the building with no wall. Knox suddenly saw the world in slow motion, as if he were one of those super heroes who could slow down time. Only he had no control over the situation. Just before the sharp report of a sniper rifle hit their ears, Beth had leapt over to Brady and pushed him out of the way. As time ebbed by ever so slowly, Knox was jumping over immediately after to catch his lady as she fell. He could see the time lapse motion of a wound opening up on her side, and blood immediately soaking through her blouse on both sides of the small seam between the ballistic pads of her vest. Knox's weight seemed to be carried back to the wall as he caught his partner, and he slowly sank down with his back against the wall; Beth's body and head falling as his lap also approached the ground. The world seemed to be moving slowly a moment longer for the word to squeeze out of Knox's throat, "NOOOOOOO!"

Brady had made it to a window sill and poised himself to jump from it to whatever was below. As he was perched with most of his body ready to jump off, he turned back towards Agent Knox.

"I'm sorry."

And he was gone. Malik was just dusting himself off as he stood up; he had also seen the whole thing, but had been hunched over in miserable pain from Brady's intense side-kick to his thigh and ribs. He looked at Knox, as Knox pulled out his cell phone and hit 9-1-1. Just before he spoke into the phone to the 9-1-1 operator, he shouted to Malik. "Get him, Malik. I don't care what you have to do…get him! He's the only one that can lead us back to the bastard that did this!" Malik jumped through the window as fast as Brady had, and disappeared into the darkness.

****

John Knox sat there against the wall, tears already welling up in his eyes. Time had gone back to normal for Knox, and he cradled and supported Beth's head and neck in his lap. He realized she was moaning faintly, and quickly spoke up to encourage her.

"Hang in there, Honey. You're going to be just fine." Knox was only telling her this to keep her going a little longer – so he could have some selfish last seconds with her before she left this world.

Agent Knox had seen death come in many forms, and he immediately knew from the amount of blood that had already soaked through onto his clothes from hers that it was too late. When everything was still in slow motion for him, he had called 9-1-1 and hurriedly told the dispatcher to send an ambulance as fast as she could. He remembered the awful sensation of not being able to get the words out fast enough as his partner lay there dying in his arms. He knew these next few minutes would be the last minutes of Beth's life, and he didn't want her to be afraid.

Beth suddenly spoke in reply, "Babe…I know it's bad. You don't have to sugar coat anything with me. I can feel how bad it is. But it's okay."

She gasped for enough air to keep talking as Knox argued, "No Honey – an ambulance is on its way. I promise they are coming as fast as they can, and we'll get you patched up. I just need you to hang in there." She reached up and slowly traced a tear line on her lover's face with her finger.

"I want to tell you something. I want to tell you why everything is going to be okay." She swallowed some of the extra air she had inhaled as she had been gasping for air in her state of shock. Then Beth continued, "Last night, before I slept, I read some more of my Bible. I got to the part in the third chapter of John…and I kept reading it. I thought about you, and I thought about my parents. I thought about so many people out there that I know would make God think this world is worth saving. And then I prayed, John. I prayed that God knew I believe. I mean I really believe with all my heart that Jesus is a real Person. He was the perfect sacrifice for you…for me…for Malik."

John dried another tear from his eye and spoke back, "Honey that is awesome. I am so glad for you. But the ambulance is almost here. I hear the sirens now." He wasn't lying; even Beth could hear the faint sounds in the distance of the approaching EMS truck.

Beth spoke again with a certain tone of finality in her voice. "John – before I go…there's something I want you to do."-"Anything, sweetie. You name it," Knox briefly interrupted.

"Please tell Malik. Tell him the story he needs to hear. Tell him about us; about me and my journey. Most importantly, tell him about Jesus. And add him to OUR list of the people that are worth saving. Know that I love you, John." Her voice faltered with those last few words, and she reached up to touch his face one last time. "Thank you…thank you for everything." She finished her last words on this Earth slow and distinctly, as if she really wanted Agent Knox to remember her thankfulness more than anything else – and then she was gone.

Knox sat there sobbing for what seemed several minutes. He never got to tell her he loved her one more time. Knox sat there and cried as he waited for the EMT's. EMS workers arrived shortly thereafter, placed Beth in an open spot on the floor, and began going through the motions with Beth's lifeless body - but Knox knew it was too late. He stood at the edge of the dim, unfinished room and stared out into the darkness wondering how Malik's progress was going. He knew he should probably check on his partner, but most of his true sense of reason had left him. At work, Beth had been his reasonable half for the last two years. For the moment, all the reason he could muster was gone.

Greensboro, North Carolina
Roof of Mosque / Muslim School Construction Site

The Arbiter quickly found the shell casing of the 30-06 round, and cursed himself for not pulling the trigger a millisecond sooner after seeing the red dot from his laser site. He hated unpractical kills, and his target had just gotten away. He made a quick scan as he finished gathering his gun parts and folded away his portable sniper rifle. He threw his bag over his back as he found the shortest way down from the rooftop. He jumped off an overhang and landed on a dirt pile. He shuffled down the side of the dirt pile and ran for the construction site. The Arbiter had to find Brady before he got a chance to find another vehicle and hit the road again. He cut a quick left as he came close to the building whose window both the assassin and the Interpol man had jumped out. There was a large hill of dirt that built up to a level just under the height of the window. The Arbiter followed the downward slope of the dirt with his eyes and decided to head in the direction of the bottom of the huge hill. When he got there he shined a flashlight down at the dirt, and could see two tracks of large footprints with long strides headed to a large lumberyard right there on the construction site. The Arbiter was not going to let the Interpol Inspector catch his man, and he didn't care what he had to do to get to Brady.

****

Brady flew out the window and landed almost immediately on a large hill of dirt, and hit the ground running. Although it was dark, the full moon gave off enough light to keep him from running into anything. Man - what he wouldn't give for his night vision shades, but they were back in the Jeep Commander. He stopped for a brief moment and thought maybe he would head that way, but then he heard the thud of the dark-skinned investigator's feet after he had jumped out the same window, and he quickly bolted to the left and into a small lumberyard. He could hear the footsteps of the pursuing agent, so he ran and ducked behind a large pile of two-by-fours.

Malik had come around the corner of other woodpiles in the nick of time to see the movement. He suddenly slowed down and approached the large pile of wood cautiously. When Brady jumped up to spring the trap, this time Malik was ready. He blocked a heavy blow with his forearm and he counterpunched to the side of the neck. Brady returned a block and countered towards Malik's face. Malik would counter, and then the assassin would counter. It was like a mad dance of knees and elbows – an MMA fight between two skilled men of contrasting minds. Yet their minds almost seemed linked as each fighter almost knew what the other man was going to do next. However, Malik was faster – and it was wearing on Brady. The tide was soon turned as Malik began landing more blows than Brady desired, and Brady was looking for a quick getaway from this pesky opponent.

As they scrambled around their manmade arena, with metal pipes and wooden boards and piles of concrete; all sorts of things that can hurt someone – the air began to fill with dust and both fighters coughed. Brady held his breath for an instant as Malik choked on some dirt, and that was when he struck. Brady brought up a knee as he grabbed the back of Malik's neck and pulled his head towards his knee. Malik's two arms shot across to block instinctively, but not fast enough to prevent the shock of the blow. His body arced backwards from the force of the knee thrust, and he thought he would get hammered again, when something struck Brady from behind. Malik stepped back a few steps, still shocked by the blow of Brady's knee. He watched as two hooded figures sized each other up in the moonlight. It took about five seconds for it to sink in Malik's head that the new arrival was the man who shot Beth. But when it registered, Malik's shout froze the two dark clothed men in their fighting stances.

"You shot Agent White!"

It was almost like the Arbiter could read the Inspector's mind as he drew his sidearm to kill the Arbiter. The Arbiter quickly side-stepped the muzzle of Malik's gun, and quickly disarmed him by reaching up and twisting the gun quickly downward and out of his hands. The gun fell harmlessly to the ground, and the Arbiter punched Malik squarely in the chest. If it had been a punch from Brady, it would have sent him back flying…but the Arbiter was the same size as Malik. The blow sent him back a few steps, but his fury and anger brought him back forward to Agent White's shooter. He came on with a flurry of elbows and low shin kicks. The Arbiter almost had trouble keeping up, as a few sharp, painful but less powerful strikes broke through and were sure to bruise later.

Meanwhile, Brady had taken advantage of the investigator's interference. He wanted no part in this encounter with the agent for the Activity sent to kill him. He knew the man was just holding back against the law man because Malik was not on his hit-list. He used the distraction to make a clean break for the direction of his Jeep. He quickly ducked around some piles of gravel and cement blocks, and then hurdled a temporary fence made of black plastic and stakes in the ground. He saw the tree line and made a beeline for it.

Malik thought he was getting the better of the man who had tried to ruin their whole case and take out Brady from afar, wounding Beth in the process. However, Brady had been right. The Arbiter had been holding back, and he quickly lashed out with countermoves that put Malik on his heels. Malik had never tangled with such accuracy in strikes and blocks before. He suddenly had no answer for the thrusts of fingers and forearms from different positions, and found himself getting beat. He thought he was about to deliver a huge counterpunch when all the sudden he found his arm locked down in a hold while the hooded man crouched low to the ground. Malik yelled out with a scream as his forearm was snapped in two, and then hung loosely at his side as the Arbiter stood him up and shoved him away. As Malik stumbled back, the Arbiter looked over next to Malik and saw a strange lever-activated device containing a large amount of lumber, but held in place by a large sheet of metal connected to the lever at the bottom. While Malik was still shrieking in pain from the broken arm, the Arbiter jumped to the lever and kicked it with his leg. The sheet of metal holding the lumber slid out of place, and the large pile of two-by-fours went sliding down on top of Malik. With nothing to interfere, he ran in the direction he last saw Brady running. As he approached the woods, he could see blue lights flashing through the trees. The police had found Brady's getaway car. The Arbiter knew that meant Brady would have to find another way to travel.

He still ran towards the illuminated section of the woods. He would stay far enough out of the line of sight of cops and FBI to scan the area for any signs of Brady. He found what he was looking for…a couple of broken branches and a small shadowy path across the road. He knew that was the trail Brady took, because that's where he would have gone if he discovered the cops had his car under tight wraps. He waited until the coast was clear on his side of the small highway, and when he thought no police were looking and no cars were coming, he bolted across the road and into the dark path. He saw that the path cut a swath to another short road that went right up to a sewage treatment plant. This was where the Arbiter knew Brady would find his next ride out of town.

He saw the gate to the plant; he figured this must be some secondary sewage treatment facility; the security amounted to a padlock on a gate; and that padlock was hanging there loosely through the hole in the latch. Yep – the Arbiter was in the right place. He ran over to the gate and looked around. He didn't see any video cameras; he guessed nobody really wants to break into a sewage treatment facility. He crept around a large round sewer tank, and on the other side were several work vans. Before coming all the way around the tank out into the open, he could see Brady climbing up into one of the big white Chevy vans. He heard the motor turn over, and then he watched Brady maneuver his way in reverse, and then shift into Drive and go back around the other side of the tank up the road to the gate. The Arbiter saw another empty van. He was hoping he hadn't forgotten how to hotwire a vehicle. Since Brady was driving in the other direction, the Arbiter ran over to the next Chevy van in line. The door was unlocked, but the inconvenient owners didn't happen to leave any keys. The Arbiter reached under the steering wheel and ripped out a small panel covering some wiring and a miniature console. Brady ripped apart a couple of the wires, and then rubbed the ends together. The engine of the Chevy van roared to life, and the Arbiter was in business. He slowly took his newly acquired vehicle down the same path that Brady had taken. He stopped just as he saw Brady ahead, pulling out through the gate of the plant. The Arbiter watched him drive away slowly, comfortable with the fact that he hadn't been made by Brady yet. He ended up going out the same gate, and followed Brady from a safe distance down the road. He would catch up to him sooner or later. Although he had a pistol to eliminate Brady, his game was one of stealth, just as Brady's had been. The Arbiter decided to follow Brady. He would watch him, wait for the least expected moment, and then strike. He no longer needed the help of the agents. The Jesus Assassin was his loose end to tie.

****

Agent Knox's head shot up at the sound of a shriek in the darkness. He glanced back at the EMT's as they finished their futile work on Beth. He gathered some resolve; there was nothing more he could do for his girlfriend. He closed his eyes and said a quick prayer, and he looked at the window. He took a running start, and hoisted himself up and through. He landed shortly on some kind of hill, and ran in the direction he had heard the loud, painful cry. He rounded several piles of different construction materials, and headed towards large stacks of wooden planks. He almost hit his head on a plank sticking out from one of the piles, and ducked under at the last second. He turned the next corner, and found his Muslim friend, lying under a large pile of two-by-fours. Knox quickly started removing the pieces of wood, and saw the obvious signs of broken bones. Both of his lower legs looked twisted at a weird angle, and his right arm was severely distorted in shape. He knew better than to move Malik, but didn't know whether he was dead or alive. He quickly knelt down next to his neck and placed two fingers below Malik's jawbone. There was a strong pulse. That was a good sign. He checked the area for any signs of the assassin – or worse – Beth's killer; and he ran back to get the EMT's. They had one more body to check; at least this one could still be helped.

Greensboro, North Carolina
Greensboro Central Hospital

Knox was sitting there reading the newspaper at the foot of Malik's hospital bed. He read anything but the stories on crime or the FBI, the Jesus Assassin, or anything that pertained to violence. Instead he flipped back and forth between the Real Estate ads and the Sports Section. He always hated this time of year in sports…baseball, baseball, and more baseball. He flipped back to a page of three story brick homes in the Greensboro Proper area, close to downtown. He was starting to contemplate moving back down south when Malik started to stir.

It had been four days since their encounter with the Jesus Assassin, and Malik had been in and out of consciousness. He hadn't quite had enough will power to speak until this moment.

"Did you happen to get the license plate of the truck that hit me?" he mumbled.

Knox laughed and put the paper down. "Hey, friend. How are you feeling? I got you some orange juice if you like."

Malik gathered a little strength and started to sit up. Agent Knox got up to assist his friend; he got some extra pillows from the chair nearby and stuffed them behind his teammate's back. Malik looked around the room, and asked Knox, "Where's

Beth…she's not"-Knox held up a hand, and put the orange juice in Malik's reach.

"Malik…Beth didn't make it. I'm sorry – you've been in and out, but I had to tell you." He gave Malik a moment, and the two law men sat there quietly. Malik had a good, soft cry. After a few sniffs, and sips of orange juice, he looked up at Knox.

"Knox – I'm sorry…it's my fault. If I had just taken Brady down sooner, it wouldn't have happened."

"You just stop right there, Malik. Nobody is taking the blame for this…nobody except whoever fired that sniper rifle!" Malik looked back down. "Yeah – I heard the shot, too. Any evidence to the shooter?"

Knox shook his head. "Nope…some new agents have been assigned our case; for obvious reasons. They couldn't find any casings from anywhere on the construction site, or the roof of the mosque. But I have a hunch it's whoever sent us to Brady's cabin. We were used, my friend."

Malik nodded. They both figured out there was some kind of government conspiracy here. Knox had told Beth and Malik that he thought that Brady was still working for the CIA in some fashion, and just used his resources to carry out his crimes against Muslims. If that were the case, it stood to reason that the US powers-that-be decided they did not need to be linked to the responsibility of so many dead imams.

After another awkward moment of silence, Malik asked Knox, "When's the funeral?" Knox replied simply, "Day after tomorrow."

"You think you can get me out of this place by then? At least for the funeral?" Malik asked his newly trustworthy friend.

Knox smiled and patted Malik's bed. "I'll sure as heck try." Malik looked into his friend's eyes and softly said, "John – I know how much she meant to you. She talked to me a little bit about you, you know. She loved you so much. I've seen women in love before – that chick was ready to marry you."

Knox chuckled, even though a tear came down his cheek. "Well, she was fond of you, too friend. As a matter of fact, she told me – before she was gone – to take care of you."

Malik reflected on these words, and replied, "You do realize – you and Beth were my only real friends over here; at least the only ones that I have had contact with in the last ten years or so." Malik leaned his head back over his pillows and smiled. He thought back to a moment when he and Beth were in a hotel room suite, laughing and joking after Knox had turned in early. "She was pretty special, wasn't she?"

Knox smiled and nodded, "That she was, Malik. That she was." As they sat there a while longer, Knox's wheels started turning in his head. He thought about the man that pulled the trigger; that took Beth from him and his friend Malik. He thought about how they had been baited to hunt the assassin, only to draw him out for this mysterious sniper to mistakenly kill their beloved Agent White. He thought about Malik, and how he would have to go back home to Belgium after this. He thought about Interpol, and the questions Malik might have to answer. He thought about Beth's last wish; how she wanted Malik to share in the joy and comfort that she had so recently found – the same joy that raised a temperamental John Knox into adulthood. Then he had a wild thought. "Hey Malik…once you're all healed up, and you've flown home to talk to your chief…I have an idea." Malik raised an eye brow, confused at the clever look in Knox's eyes. "How'd you like to join the FBI?"

Hatteras Island, North Carolina
Town of Buxton

Against the doctor's better judgment, Agent Knox was informed that provided certain medical protocols were adhered to, Malik could be flown to the funeral on the Outer Banks of North Carolina. On the way out to the Outer Banks, Knox took care of the essential medical needs of Malik, such as changes of wound dressing, or making sure he was well fed (At least he could feed himself with his one good hand).

The funeral service was at the same location as Beth's burial; a quaint cemetery outside a small Methodist Church in the middle of a small unincorporated community called Buxton. There were several family members gathered under a tent. There were also several federal agents from the Detroit Field Office in Michigan. SAC Jones McCoy had made special arrangements with Agent White's parents. He knew that the area where Beth's parents lived was off the radar of national media attention, and he also knew that Agent White deserved whatever the FBI could afford to give to honor her bravery and sacrifice.

Although Beth had grown up Catholic, her parents had become Protestants in their old age. Beth was just so tied up in her work ever since she lost her brother, she just didn't always make the time and effort to travel to the Outer Banks of North Carolina – where her parents had decided to settle down.

Several people stood, or sat, up front with Beth's casket. Her parents were closest to the casket, along with several friends of the family who had known both Beth and her brother. Then there was McCoy, her boss for several years, who had hand-picked her for his office as a rookie, and watched her mature and blossom, and find her true but opposite equal in John Knox. Then there was Agent John Knox, standing next to a heavily bandaged and well-casted Inspector Malik Sharif. There was a small, intelligent pastor, who said some warm words as he addressed the crowd in attendance. There was a bag piper, who played the traditional music heard at most law enforcement funerals. Then there was the folding of a flag. After the flag was folded, it was given over to the SAC, Special Agent in Charge McCoy. Knox stood behind Malik's wheelchair with the utmost respect to honor this somber moment...the SAC walked up to Beth's parents. He knelt down in front of Mr. and Mrs. White. "Mr. and Mrs. White...it is with great respect and honor that the FBI give you this flag in honor of Beth's great service to her country – with great fidelity, bravery, and integrity. Thank you for sharing her with us." McCoy handed the small, tightly folded up bundle of American Flag over to Beth's father. The bag pipes started up, and the salt air and wind carried the mix of high and low notes across the small town of Buxton – past the little bait shops, past the pier, past the little beach houses nearby. Beth White had gone on to be with the Lord, and Knox knew in his heart of hearts that she was in a better place than this.

Greenville, South Carolina
The Islamic Mosque of the Upstate

Robert Brady had accomplished 11 mission objectives. Several weeks went by, and he had let his trail grow cold. He knew the FBI was frustrated; they had come so close to catching him in Greensboro. He attributed everything to God's timing. Although he regretted the shooting of the federal agent that happened as the Activity had tried to take him out, he felt like it was simply God's will that he succeed in escaping the grips of the US government.

After a few weeks on the run down the convenient Interstate 85, Brady had taken the opportunity to learn the lay of the land in Charlotte, North Carolina. He had discovered a large mosque not far from the professional football stadium located in the heart of the city. He took his time learning the habits and rituals of the different worshippers and leaders that attended the mosque. In the weeks since he had left the sewage treatment plant in Greensboro in a Chevy van, he had acquired a new Jeep. Of course it was stolen…he had conveniently jumped in at a gas station when an innocent young college girl had abandoned her Jeep Wrangler to run in and pick out some junk food and energy drinks for her little road trip to see a friend. The bright young lady had left her engine running and everything, and the Jesus

Assassin was a resourceful – and observant – individual. When she casually walked back to her Jeep and looked back up from her cell phone, she was in awe that her Jeep had just vanished. It took her nearly two minutes in a conversation on her phone with her friend to realize that perhaps her Jeep had been stolen.

Brady treasured the moments he had taken in Charlotte to stalk the head imam of the mosque, and follow him back to his home. He had watched the imam check his mail and proceed up the steps to his porch. He had watched the imam lock his doors and had seen the lights go out at his front door. The assassin reminisced the joy of breaking into the home, quietly making his way through motion sensors; he knew where the infrared beams would aim in the room and where they wouldn't. He took the cautious path to the imam's bedroom. He had simply walked over to the side of the bed and killed him in the same manner as his second target; no resistance – no sound. He had committed the perfect silent kill…the way his government had taught him to do. When he left back out the front door in the dead of night, he had the sudden sensation that he was being watched. He had looked around for any sign of a vehicle, or hiding place that the Activity may have hidden their hit-man. Although he saw no one at the time, he had quickly ventured back to his Jeep, and swiftly drove off down the road. Little did he know that the Arbiter had followed soon after, and was still on his trail.

Brady sat in the stolen jeep now, staring across the four lane highway at the mosque. It was a short warehouse-shaped building, but with a green tin roof topped with a strange gold dome and crescent moon. He had been studying this imam's habits for the past two days, and he had discovered that the overweight bearded man was quite the insomniac. He would come to the mosque at odd hours of the night, go inside, and come back out an hour or so later. He had watched the imam walk into the mosque approximately forty minutes before, and he had not come out. Brady was not going to be as stealthy on this killing. He decided that since this was his last target, and there was no security, and the holy man about to exit the building would not expect a shadowy figure to charge at him in the dark of night - he would meet the sinful blasphemer head on. Little did he know that in the upper shadows of the parking lot next door, there was a set of eyes of yet another hooded figure, watching him ever so carefully. It had become almost a game for the Arbiter, following Brady's every move, driving behind him at the perfect distance; stepping out on foot and stalking his prey, but not quite ready to pursue the assassin directly. It was a thrill to the Arbiter to know that his skills were superb; he was able to sneak up undetected on the best in the business. The un-said word throughout the quiet circles of the Activity was that the activist was the best there was at the stealth game. The Arbiter was out to prove otherwise, and serve the Activity at the same time. That was, after all, why they paid him the big bucks.

The front door of the mosque opened up, shedding a little bit of light from the interior of the building. The large imam turned around to lock the door. He slowly turned the key and turned it halfway back, trying his best not to break yet another key by turning it too hard and getting the other part stuck in the lock. This was the third lock he had changed. After pulling the key out successfully, he checked the door to make sure it was secure, and then turned to walk to his vehicle. As he was walking to his vehicle, he casually looked up at his car, and there was a dark, hooded shadow standing in front of his door. The imam foolishly spoke up, "Can I help you, sir?"

Suddenly the black figure ran at full speed towards the imam. The large fat man didn't quite know where to turn, and shook one way and then the other in his robes. Before he knew what to do, the man in black leapt up at him; his full weight knocking the imam backwards, the assassin landing on top of him and knocking the wind out of him. As the imam struggled to breathe again, the Jesus Assassin took his syringe and planted the needle into the man's neck. Just as he was drawing his last breath because of the fast-acting, never-failing venom of a black mamba…some headlights cut on in the parking lot adjacent to the mosque. As the lights came on, the last thing the imam ever saw was a brilliant green reflection from his assassin's eyes.

The engine of the car with the headlights revved, and the assassin couldn't believe the irony of it all, as he noticed that the mosque's property line at the end of the parking lot was shared with a local Baptist church. Death was calling for him now with each rev of the engine across the way, daring him to make a run for his car. The assassin reached into his pocket and grabbed his last gold cross. He felt the sharp edges in his pocket, and realized he had done it – he had finished his mission. Stealth was no longer required. What happened to him didn't really matter to him now, though he wouldn't go down without a fight. He withdrew the cross, kissed it, and tossed it onto the dead imam. Without further warning, he withdrew his pistol that he always had in his thigh holster. He fired several shots and made a run for his car at the same time. The Arbiter was ready for this maneuver, and quickly became a moving target as the assassin emptied his magazine. Bullet holes appeared multiple times around head-level in the windshield. The Arbiter cut donuts as he ducked down in his seat. Brady reached his vehicle parked across the four lane road, and fired it up. His tires squealed as he peeled out of the parking lot, and the Arbiter was following close behind.

The Jeep Wrangler was a pretty fast vehicle, for such an off-road machine. The Arbiter followed at break-neck speed in the same Chevy van that he had stolen from the sewage treatment plant back in Greensboro. He was gaining on the assassin, and Brady noticed that the closer they got to downtown Greenville, the more traffic picked up. They were approaching an intersection with a traffic light; there was a large insurance company building on the left, and a small shopping center on the right. The light switched from yellow to red, and Brady blew through the intersection. By the time the Arbiter made the same light, horns blared as he had to swerve quickly to the right, and back to the left, to avoid the cars cutting across and then an oncoming car in the opposite lane. As they were getting closer to the city, they passed a large private Christian university on their left. Brady couldn't believe he didn't pick up on the presence of the hit-man. He knew the guy was good; the man chasing him had already proven that back in North Carolina and Virginia. But why show himself now? There was no way the man pursuing him now just happened to catch up to him today. This man had been spying on him; stalking him; toying with him. He needed to get away from this man, and come up with a plan. But it was too late; the chase was on, and the Arbiter was obviously not going to give up until he dealt with Brady personally.

The two vehicles came roaring into a left turn, tires screeching as they passed a small Italian restaurant and then a rock climbing rec center. Brady suddenly slammed on the brakes of the Jeep, and left the motor running as he jumped out of the vehicle and ran towards a cemetery. The Arbiter followed, parking the van with reckless abandon, almost running into the back of the Jeep. He ran after Brady, and they cut up through a large graveyard in the heart of the downtown area.

After ducking around gravestones, cutting through gardens, and hurdling benches, he came out of the entrance to the cemetery at the top of a hill that entered into Main Street. He stopped to catch his breath, and the Arbiter was gaining on him after getting the assassin back in his sight. Brady made a left down Main Street, passing an expensive hotel and a little pizzeria that was still open for business. As Brady ran by, he knocked a box of pizza out of the hands of a large security officer who had just gotten off work at midnight.

The officer, Officer Steele, shouted back at the fleeing assailant, "You gonna buy me another one?" Right about then another dark hooded man shot by, and Steele just scratched his head and tried to scrounge up what could be salvaged of the messed up pizza.

Brady almost got hit by a bicycle rickshaw as he glanced back over his shoulder to look at the

Arbiter gaining on him. He turned back around just in time to step up on the back wheel and jump back into a run, passing several bars and restaurants on his left. As he crossed another intersection, two police officers watched with apathy as two men in dark hoods chased each other past them and further down the road. One officer glanced at his partner, and they both shrugged and went back to monitoring the crowd at the bar where they were picking up extra duty. Perhaps if they'd paid closer attention, they would have noticed the guns in the holsters on their right legs.

Brady veered a sharp left at a water fountain with a strange looking sculpture, and ran down several steps into a beautiful downtown park. He paused to guess a direction to go, and saw a large suspension bridge that crossed a river. He ran towards the bridge. He decided that was where he would make his stand; he was just about at the end of his aerobic threshold anyway. The Arbiter jumped down about six steps at a time. He saw Brady run towards suspension cables, and realized it was a bridge. Then he saw Brady stop in the middle of the bridge, standing directly in the center, almost taunting him – but probably just getting his wind back. The Arbiter didn't believe in wasting energy, so he slowed to a walk. As the Arbiter got to the beginning of the bridge, Brady took his gun out of his holster and held it out for the Arbiter to see. He motioned as if to tell him to put his down, and he would do the same. The Arbiter was intrigued; this was indeed a worthy foe. He took out his pistol and placed it on the entrance to the bridge. He then purposefully walked towards the Jesus Assassin.

As the Arbiter came close enough to hear, Brady spoke up, "Just who are you? I have never had anyone who could keep up with me like you. I at least deserve to know who you are, since I already know who sent you."

The Arbiter snickered. "Ha – I guess I can give you that much. You are Robert Brady, right? My employers sent me to kill you."

"Robert Brady's dead; been dead a year now. I am just the leftovers, after the Muslims took my reason for living – so you're just wasting your time."

"Nevertheless, I am here to kill you. But since you asked, I am known as many things…a fixer; a hit-man; a problem solver. But your former boss simply refers to me as the Arbiter."

Brady looked puzzled, and scoffed, "Hmmm…never heard of you. Well, regardless, I think it's time we finished this. That's a sick little game you played. I know you've known where I was all along. You had to follow me from Greensboro; there's no other way you could have found me."

The Arbiter pulled his hood back. Brady realized right away that he was of Middle Eastern descent.

The Arbiter raised one eye brow and replied, "You've got some nerve, speaking of sick little games. You do realize they call you the Jesus Assassin, right? I personally don't have a stake in any religion. Although I come from a family of Lebanese Christians, I don't claim any one particular deity. But you have been killing people just because they differ from you in beliefs. That – and the unmistakable motive of revenge."

Brady held up his finger and pointed at the Arbiter, "You don't have a clue why I've been doing it! It's not even about what I believe. It's because of the utter evil I have seen carried out by those that believe in Islam. You people can have your Hindus…your Buddhists…your pagans. But Islam is the only religion in the world that is known throughout for its barbarous treatment of those that oppose their way of thinking."

The Arbiter had been slowly creeping closer to the man in the black hood. He thought about launching his attack without warning, when the man drew back his hood as well. Brady flashed his green eyes at the Arbiter and had one more thing to say.

"Tell me…if you had your family taken from you; everyone you ever cared for and would do anything for – what would you have done differently?"

The Arbiter paused as if he would answer…then he launched a high kick at the assassin's head. Brady ducked and weaved at the same time, attempting to knock the Arbiter off balance by slapping away his leg. The Arbiter countered with a kick from the other leg, catching Brady off guard and hooking him with his foot in the back of the head. Brady reacted instinctively by rolling sideways, coming up into a crouch and bull-rushing the Arbiter. The Arbiter used his lightning fast reflexes to deliver a flurry of strikes to Brady as he came in, using his momentum to make the blows even more painful as they were delivered in fist-pounding agony. Brady came up stunned; he had never faced a more deadly adversary. Brady was used to being the Alpha male. This was a whole new sensation from which he had to find an escape. He dove forward into another roll across the bridge to his weapon. The Arbiter did the same towards his own. The two assassins moved simultaneously, as if choreographing the entire scene for a movie. They both scooped up their pistols, turned, and fired. Brady's shot went wide left as the Arbiter ducked to his right while he shot. The Arbiter's shot was true…Brady's gun fell from his hands as the gunshot wound in his head insured his demise. As the smoke rolled out of both guns, the Arbiter finally answered the assassin.

"Nothing…I would do nothing differently."

The Arbiter walked over to the now lifeless body of Robert Brady. He began removing Brady's clothes, putting them into a pile as if he'd done this kind of thing before. Once completely stripped down, the mysterious man known as the Arbiter laboriously hefted the large naked body to a standing position at the cables of the bridge. With another great effort, he used his lower body to force the assassin's body up and over the top cable. He winced as the body crashed into the shallow water and the rocks below. The Arbiter picked up the clothes of the assassin, and made a casual walk to the steps that lead out of the park. He stopped at a trashcan, stuffed the clothes, weapons, and miscellaneous items down in the container, and went on his merry way. It was one o-clock in the morning, and the Jesus Assassin was no more.

****

Jack was a bouncer. He was just getting off his shift, and had finished saying his good byes to the bartenders and bar backs at Chicora Alley. He had parked his car on the other side of the river, and he was making his way back as he crossed the walking bridge in the middle of park. As he was walking, something pale in color caught his eye off to the side of the bridge. He stopped and took a closer look over the top cable railing. His eyes got really big as he said a four letter word to himself. He immediately took out his phone and dialed up Greenville City's dispatch center. He had several friends in law enforcement. He didn't feel like this situation warranted 9-1-1, so he dialed the direct line to Dispatch; he happened to know their number by heart.

"Greenville City Dispatch...do you have an emergency?"

Jack replied, "Not an emergency, but there is a dead body lying face-down underneath the walking bridge at the park." He gladly gave his name and number, and even waited for the coroner and cops to show up. The county coroner thanked Jack for his report, and sent him on his way. The area at the bottom of the bridge was cordoned off with the usual gaudy yellow CAUTION tape, and the crime scene was processed. Later a shell casing would be found untraceable, along with the untraceable slug that was somewhere in the middle of Brady's head.

Two hours later, a security officer by the name of Josh manned the gate at the local hospital close to Downtown. As the coroner showed the clip board to the officer, describing the contents of the coroner's van, Josh raised the gate and waved in the vehicle containing the body of Robert C. Brady. A delivery truck had pulled up behind the coroner, so another security officer by the name of Brad made a special trip down to sign off on the correct paperwork for a certain dead body under the name of John Doe.

Nobody would ever know the true identity of the body that came in to that hospital morgue in Greenville, South Carolina that morning. Nobody would ever know that so ended the tale of the Jesus Assassin. No – Robert Brady hadn't died on that bridge in Greenville. Robert Brady had already died a little over a year before – when a crazed jihadist took the lives of his wife and daughter…a daughter who'd had the most beautiful, brilliant green eyes.

EPILOGUE

Detroit, Michigan
FBI Field Office

Jones McCoy stood behind his desk, sipping his cup of coffee - with two agents sitting in the chairs that always took up the space on the other side of his large oak desk. Agent John Knox occupied the chair on the left, and a not-quite-ready-for-the-field Agent Malik Sharif sat in the chair on the right.

McCoy started, "Well, it's official. I had to pull a few strings, but the folks in D.C. informed me today that I can officially make you two boys partners. So, Malik...welcome to the Bureau." He held out his right hand for Malik to shake as he balanced his coffee in his left;

Malik stood up and pumped McCoy's hand vigorously. "Sir, I won't let you down. Neither will my partner over there." Malik shot a quick wink over to his new partner.

Knox just smiled and laughed. "Thanks, McCoy, for pulling that off. We owe you a big case for that one," Knox offered. SAC Jones McCoy responded. "It was the least I could do. You guys worked hard on that case. By gosh – you almost had the assassin in North Carolina."

There was a moment of silence before Malik said, "So SAC...whatever became of the case? We haven't heard. Of course we know why we had to be taken off the case, but we haven't heard anything." McCoy shook his head, "That's because there isn't anything. Anything relating or pertaining to Robert Brady is virtually non-existent. Any mention of the Jesus Assassin has disappeared from the media. This goes far beyond us, boys – and there isn't a thing we can do about it."

Knox looked at Malik, then back at McCoy. "Oh there's one thing we can do about it. That night in North Carolina, we lost a good agent. That agent wasn't taken by the Jesus Assassin, but by someone else. That same someone else just about killed my new partner right there. I swear right here and now – that as long as I am alive, I will catch the man who killed Beth," Knox finished.

Malik spoke up, "You can count me in, too, partner."

McCoy put down his cup of coffee. "Well, I don't know how you're going to do that...but somehow, I believe you'll get it done. In the meantime, I forgot to mention one thing." The two new partners looked at each other curiously, then back at McCoy. "There was one stipulation regarding Malik's lateral transfer from Interpol to us."

Knox grinned and said, "Oh great...what is it this time. There's always something those big wigs want down in Washington."

McCoy cleared his throat, "Um Malik, my lad...you have to go to Quantico." Malik simply replied, "Say what?"

McCoy just nodded, "That's right son...you're going to the FBI Academy."

Knox just had to laugh, all the while keeping Beth's last wishes in mind.

Riker's Island, New York
Riker's Federal Penitentiary

The Russian mobster, Nicolai Roschevensky, had all sorts of connections – the kind of connections that gave him his own personal cell without a cellmate. It was for this reason that he slept so soundly. What Nicolai didn't know, and had no way of knowing, was that during the day, when all the prisoners were out in the yard, someone had found a slightly different way into his cell. Certain arrangements had been made. Someone – namely, the Activity – wanted Nicolai dead. The man slept on the top bunk. This had been noted by the Activity's other sources within the prison, and the Arbiter had been made aware. So as Nicolai slept so soundly up top, and snored so loudly...the mattress on the bottom bunk began to slide away. A hooded figure emerged slowly from underneath the mattress. As he stood up, he took a brief glance through the bars of the cell and saw no need for panic. He withdrew a small blade from a small sheath attached to his wrist. As he stood up and slowly approached the snoring Russian, Roschevensky snorted violently, almost making the hit-man poke him in the nose. Then, with surgical precision, the Arbiter cut the man's throat.

He pulled gently on the back of the toilet in the cell, and it gradually slid away from the wall. There was a hole on the other side that the Arbiter had been given permission to make by certain powers-that-be. As he weaseled his way into the small hole, he pulled the toilet back to the wall behind him. The Arbiter had tied up the first loose end with the Russian Mafia. He had several more members of the family to go – and if anyone thought they would stop him, they were terribly …mistaken.

48113566R00192

Made in the USA
Charleston, SC
25 October 2015